Crusader

Canada

BOOK TWO IN THE DANNY SHAW / MANFRED BREHME TRILOGY

CRUSADER

JACK MURRAY

LUME BOOKS

LUME BOOKS

Published in 2022 by Lume Books

ISBN 978-1-83901-443-7

Typeset using Atomik ePublisher from Easypress Technologies

www.lumebooks.co.uk

Part One

Arrival (July–Sept 1941)

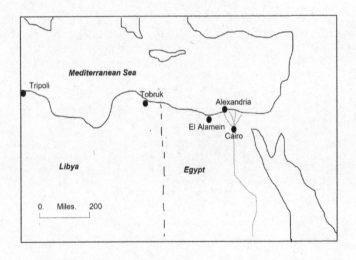

Part One

Arrival (July–Sept 1941)

Chapter One

Tripoli, Libya, July 1941

Manfred woke up. He wanted to sit up, but his body refused to obey this simple instruction. It lay in rigid protest, stiff like an old man. His arms and legs felt like they were encased in plaster casts such was the deadening weight anchoring them to the bed. Then he began to shake; gently at first, then more violently. His teeth chattered and he wondered if he was dreaming because one thing was clear – it was hot. I must have a fever, he thought. His mind was more lucid now, fully awake.

It was dark. For a few moments he didn't know where he was. Then his eyes began to adjust to the lack of light. Around him he could see lots of beds. With an effort of will, he sat himself upright in bed. Correction. The mattress on the floor. Mattress? Manfred smiled grimly to himself. The clacking sound of someone snoring loudly made him turn his head. This song of fatigue had many singers. His ears had finally woken up. All around him he heard the soaring notes of men sleeping. Other senses were casting off their slumber. The room stank of unwashed men gradually turning sour in the heat.

3

He lay back in his bed and stared at the ceiling. It was beginning to come back to him. Tears stung his eyes. He was crying, softly and silently for his friends, but mostly for himself. So, this was it. He was at war now. It was official. Two letters, at least, had probably already been written. What would they say? Would they talk of the bravery of these children of the Fatherland? Or would they tell the truth? One had died drowning in fear because he'd never learned to swim. The other had killed himself, believing, rightly, he'd been abandoned, left alone in the sea to his fate.

Manfred turned in the bed. He could see that Gerhardt was lying on the next mattress. For a moment he thought about waking him. Then he thought better of it. Let him sleep.

He lay back on his bed and stared at the ceiling. His watch had been ruined in the water, so he had no idea what time it was. Briefly, he considered trying to sleep again but that would only risk the dream returning. He felt separated from his old life, and it was too dark to find his way back now.

An hour passed. Manfred shifted position every few minutes. A stabbing pain was developing in his back. His eyes traced the cracks in the ceiling. They were like the delta of a large river.

Eventually he gave way to a dreamless sleep. It seemed to last seconds. He was woken, along with the rest of the men, by the barking of a sergeant stalking through the room. Manfred groaned, then realised he had been a little louder than intended. He saw Gerhardt looking at him strangely. Manfred looked back at him questioningly. Gerhardt's face softened a little, and then he smiled.

'How are you feeling?'

Suddenly, the events of yesterday returned to Manfred making his face burn red. He felt his chest tightening, but not for the memory of Lothar. Instead, it was for himself and his reaction to seeing his friend kill himself. The shame of his anguished cry and inconsolable sobbing overwhelmed him.

Gerhardt had witnessed all of it.

He could not shake the vision of Lothar bobbing on the water with the rest of the debris from the ship. The vision of his friend's final moments would remain with him forever: the tears in his eyes, the distress caused by his abandonment, and then the awful moment when he turned the gun on himself. He'd seen Lothar's face contort with anguish before being transformed into a bloody mess. The binoculars had made it seem as if he was only a few metres away, close enough to have helped. Yet he could not help. He could only bear witness to the sickening ruthlessness of war. Manfred's chest constricted again. Then the anger came.

Of course, he'd screamed. Who wouldn't have? He remembered the binoculars falling from his hands, crashing against the deck. He remembered the sailors dragging him below. There was some sympathy. Some. Gerhardt had seemed surprised by the intensity as well as the rapidity of his friend's hysterical reaction.

They'd taken him to a cabin to separate him from the rest of the men. Manfred remembered the lieutenant shaking his head to the crewman. Keep him away, he'd said. He remembered the irritation in his voice. Gerhardt was ordered to try to calm him down. It had taken some time. Then Manfred remembered the ship's doctor had given him an injection.

It was all coming back to him now and he felt acutely the sense that he was being watched, judged, even. He looked around. None of the other men now getting dressed seemed to know or care who he was. Only Gerhardt had seen his disgrace. He realised Gerhardt had asked him a question. He could see the concern on his face, or was it doubt?

Manfred nodded to his friend and said, 'Don't worry. I'm fine now.'

Gerhardt nodded and did not say anything else. Manfred was grateful for this. He didn't want to explain himself at that moment. He certainly did not want to share his feelings about what he'd felt. All he wanted was to forget, to erase the image of Lothar's head dissolving before his eyes; he wanted to forget the scream, his scream, the looks on the faces of the officers, the look in the eyes of Gerhardt. His anger was growing. Anger at himself. Anger even towards Gerhardt for bearing witness to his shame. Then, for a moment, his rage turned towards Lothar. His friend.

His dead friend.

The sergeant was making his way back along the narrow strip between the beds yelling at the young men. Manfred hurriedly dressed. Even in this he felt embarrassed. Fear drove him to dress. He was afraid of being picked out and made an example of. A quick glance at Gerhardt reassured him that he was not alone in this.

The sergeant passed them, and the two friends grinned as he went by. All at once the rage died. He was with Gerhardt again. His co-conspirator. This was a relief. Then Manfred felt someone come alongside them.

'How are you, Manfred?' asked Christian Reus, a young soldier they'd met at officer training. With Christian you could never be sure if he was genuinely interested or probing for an opportunity to have fun at your expense. He called the Fuhrer 'the corporal'.

'Fine,' replied Manfred, hoping to strike the right line between honesty, politeness and sufficient reserve to close any further inquiry on this subject.

Christian nodded. Out of the corner of his eye Christian saw Gerhardt shake his head and understood immediately that any discussion on what happened was forbidden.

'It's hot,' said Christian, glancing out towards the window. The sky was cerulean blue.

Yes, it was hot, and it was barely six thirty in the morning. Manfred could feel the closeness of the air and a dampness on his forehead. The sergeant was literally bellowing at everyone to leave the room for parade. The boys passed him, getting showered in spittle as they did so. Had they not been so tired and hot it would have been funny.

Had they not been going to war.

They filed mutely out of the room. Manfred sensed Gerhardt and Christian falling in either side of him like two bodyguards and he felt a flash of irritation. He was neither a coward nor an invalid. He would not be treated as such. Yet, his mind was already scattering seeds of doubt on this certainty. He would have to prove himself, not just to his friends but to himself.

There was rage in the heat of the sun. Manfred staggered as he hit an invisible wall outside the makeshift barracks. He and Gerhardt followed Christian and the rest of the new arrivals into a large square. Gerhardt's heart sank at the prospect of parade ground exercises. Oddly, Manfred welcomed this. It represented a return to normality. For the moment he wanted to dissolve into the army, its routines, its arcane ceremony, its respectful conformity. Only within the whole did he feel he could escape his humiliation; only within battle could he find redemption.

'Why can't they fight somewhere less hot?' whispered Gerhardt as they went through each drill.

'Can you imagine what it'll be like inside a tank?' replied Manfred under his breath.

'Trying not to,' admitted Gerhardt.

They fell quiet as the gaze of the sergeant major settled on them.

7

Perspiration rained down each of their faces. It was scant consolation to know everyone was suffering in the same way. Then again, wasn't that the point? Shared discomfort, pain and exhaustion were the raw materials from which character was built. The strength it provided had a tensile quality. As individuals and as a group they would be stretched in unimaginable ways. They could not break.

Tripoli was hot and foreign in ways that went beyond the imagination. Nothing the boys had read or heard could have prepared them for the mixture of sights, sounds and smells they encountered on their first venture out of the barracks.

All around the market was an astonishing mixture of local dark-skinned traders, and blond-white German soldiers. The noise was as loud and varied as the colours were vivid. If ever a people liked shouting more than your average middle-aged Junker in a beer festival, it was these strange beings, thought Manfred.

The day had passed peacefully. Parade, breakfast, a lecture and then a chance to walk through the city. Neither Gerhardt nor Christian had mentioned his breakdown. Manfred knew this was a kindness, but they would not forget, either. The sin of weakness would be cleansed on the day he came face to face with the enemy. Only then could Manfred redeem himself not only in their eyes but in his own.

The smells had initially sickened Manfred. He was used to the clean, crisp air of Germany. Here, the air was almost palpable. The smell of sewage mixed with something else, food certainly, human waste probably, but also something more intoxicating. Soon, they became used to its different moods. Sometimes teasing, sometimes unapproachable, always beguiling.

The women fascinated them also. Dark-eyed, beautiful, alluring, available and untouchable in equal measure. Some were covered from head to foot in black. Others seemed to appreciate something that was self-evident to Manfred. It was hot. Hotter than Manfred could ever remember. How could anyone live in such a climate? Yet live here he would. For how long, he knew not. More reason to get the job done quickly.

He felt a dig in his ribs and turned to find Gerhardt nodding in the direction of one particularly beautiful young girl. Long dark hair gleamed in the sunlight. She moved with a grace that would have made a Bolshoi ballerina seem like an inebriated elephant.

Both boys grinned. A lot of the other young men had come back to the compound boasting of their exploits. Further inquiry often confirmed what everyone knew; they'd paid for their entertainment.

With the fearlessness of youth, the arrogance of his race and the certainty in his good looks, Gerhardt plunged forward into the attack. The young girl was around the same age as the boys. She seemed to be working at a fruit stall, although neither boy could recognise the strange objects piled like apples on the wooden cart.

Gerhardt lifted a piece of fruit. He looked at the girl and smiled. He raised his eyebrows. The girl looked nervously at him and then glanced to a large man who appeared out of nowhere.

The man was as malevolent as the girl was innocent. A scar ran from the tip of his eye along his cheek down towards his earlobe. His arms were as thick as Manfred's legs. Behind him, Gerhardt heard Manfred erupt into laughter. He reddened as the man glared at him.

'How much?' asked Gerhardt, holding what he later established to be a guava. The man had no German but seemed to guess the nature of the inquiry. He pointed to a sign. Gerhardt bought two. He handed the money over and picked another from the stall. He threw the fruit in Manfred's direction. Head-bound, it cut through the air like a fleshy, green bullet. Manfred plucked it casually out of the air one-handed and bit into it. The two boys skulked away from the stall stifling the sort of guilty schoolboy grins that could only be provoked by the intoxicating inaccessibility of female beauty.

'Now you see why they go to the whores, my friend,' commented Manfred knowingly. 'So, the big question is: was that her father, her brother or her husband?'

'There are parts of Germany where he might be all three, country boy,' replied Gerhardt.

The two collapsed laughing. Around them, traders looked at them in amusement. They were used to seeing grim-faced soldiers. The two boys seemed altogether less alien. Finally, Gerhardt had recovered enough to speak.

'I bet he could skin you alive before you'd time to draw your gun.'

Manfred nodded in agreement. He took another mouthful of the guava, then said between mouthfuls, 'My God, after him the Tommies will be a walkover.'

Gerhardt laughed because he could. He knew he would feel differently in the future. But here, now, in the marketplace with his friend, they were safe. The enemy was far away. The enemy was on the run from the mighty Afrika Korps. Rommel was their leader.

And they would win.

Chapter Two

The three-ton truck trundled bumpily along the road towards the British camp at El Alamein, a small coastal town about one hundred and fifty miles north-west of Cairo. Sweat tickled the forehead of every man on the truck. Arthur Perry mopped his brow with the sleeve of his uniform. Glancing down at his sleeve he saw it was heavily soiled. He looked around him at the others, none of whom seemed to be any better off. A mutinous silence had fallen on the group as their discomfort rose along with the temperature gauge. There was no hiding place for the group from the African sun.

'Why not stick a handkerchief on your head, Arthur, like you do in Margate,' suggested a young man further up the truck.

'I know what I'll stick on you,' replied Arthur to Danny, who just grinned back at him.

'You'd have to catch me first, old man.'

'Bloody hell, watch out Adolf; Shaw's here, and he knows where the reverse gear is. Anyway, what makes you think the sun ever shines in bloody Margate?'

11

The rest of the truck laughed, grateful to have something that would take their minds off the three things that were most occupying them at that moment: the heat, the flies, and the fact that they were heading towards combat against Rommel's Afrika Korps.

Just the thought of that name made Danny feel nervous. The Afrika Korps had spent the previous few months inflicting defeat upon defeat on the Allies. Tobruk was under siege; the Germans were now inside Egypt. Both Alexandria and Cairo could sense the dark shadow looming.

The truck hit a bump on the road causing a wave of complaints to the driver. If he heard them then he certainly didn't care. He seemed a morose kind in Danny's view. In fact, it was Danny's observation that many of the soldiers he was meeting were sullen. They seemed sapped of energy and fight. At first, he blamed the heat, but other darker thoughts were now surfacing. He stopped himself thinking about the sense of defeat these soldiers radiated. Instead, whenever such thoughts entered his mind, he broke them in a manner that was as British as it was effective.

'Are we at the beach yet?' asked Danny. There was no answer, just some smiles from the other soldiers on the truck.

'That'll be no then.'

A few of the men chuckled and rolled their eyes.

'Hey, Arthur, do we need to make a stop yet? Your prostate will be giving you the hump soon.'

Arthur threw his beret in the direction of Danny. The young man caught it and made to throw it out of the truck.

'You'll join it in a minute,' laughed Arthur before making a one-handed catch when Danny lofted it back. This brought a ripple of mock applause from the other soldiers in the truck. Like Danny, they were all young men. Danny and Arthur had got to know a

12

few of them in Alexandria, where they had been stationed for the last few weeks.

'I could have played cricket for Surrey,' said Arthur acknowledging the applause.

'Why didn't you?' asked one of the men.

'I was rubbish,' replied Arthur. The questioner received a friendly clip on the back of his head from Danny. He'd heard it all before. They always fell for it.

'You just keep setting them up, son,' added Arthur with a smoker's cackle.

'Hey, driver,' shouted Jim Hamilton in his heavy Midlands accent, 'I need to siphon the python.'

'You mean worm, don't you, Jim?' said Arthur.

'Cross your legs,' came the shout from the front of the truck.

'I mean it,' said Hamilton. He did too.

The smiles round the truck managed the improbable feat of being both sympathetic and highly entertained by their comrade's problem.

'Bit of a pre-dick-a-ment, Jim, isn't it?' said Arthur. Hamilton laughed while pointing out it was not funny.

They continued along the road, each bump adding to Hamilton's distress and everyone else's entertainment. Finally, Hamilton could take no more. He stood up and walked to the rear of the truck. Looking down at two of the recruits seated at the end, he said, 'Grab a hold of my legs.'

The rest of the truck enjoyed the short and anatomically challenging response from the two boys who told him what he could do with this idea.

'It's up to you but I have to go. Better I'm stable than falling around the place. You'll get caught in the crossfire long before we reach the Jerry.'

Reluctantly the two men took a hold of Hamilton, who proceeded to irrigate the desert.

'There'll be palm trees when we come back here next,' commented Arthur, fascinated by Hamilton's epic surge.

In fact, epic barely covered the duration of Hamilton's relief effort.

'When did you last go anyway?' asked Danny.

'Christmas,' replied Hamilton.

Arthur, in fact the whole truck, were awestruck by Hamilton's performance.

'You been storing it in a jerrican?' inquired Arthur.

To the sound of enthusiastic applause, and without any collateral damage through friendly fire, Hamilton returned to his seat much lighter of mood as well as bladder.

'I think I need to go now,' said Arthur.

The two boys at the back of the truck indicated to him, in terms as explicit as they were succinct, that he'd be on his own in this endeavour.

The first sight of the camp based at El Alamein was impressive. So much so that it silenced for a few minutes the men on the three-ton truck. Stretching for a couple of miles were hundreds of M3 and Crusader tanks, lorries, half-tracks, and jeeps. Amongst the motor vehicles were tents of varying sizes, all a khaki colour. It was difficult to know how many soldiers were in the camp, but it could have been a few thousand or more. Danny glanced at Arthur and raised his eyebrows.

This was it. They were at war.

A couple of planes buzzed in the skies over the camp. Danny caught his breath before recognising the distinctive shape of the Hurricane. The two planes landed somewhere in the distance at the far end of the camp.

Arthur was the first to find his voice as he gazed at the enormous assembly of men, machines and tents. It was a canvas and metal city in the middle of nothingness.

'Bloody hell.'

This seemed to sum up the feelings of the other men on the truck. They were silent for a few moments and then Arthur added, 'I don't see the swimming pool they promised in the poster.'

The truck erupted into laughter as they pulled into the camp. A few of the soldiers glanced up in irritation at the new arrivals. Some shook their heads. Danny noticed one soldier restraining another from marching over to the truck, which had halted in a large square with several tents on the perimeter.

'We should go easy a bit, Arthur. They look a bit down.'

Arthur nodded.

'They look whipped,' said Ray Hill, another of the young men Danny and Arthur had befriended in Alexandria. They did, too. The faces of the men in the camp seemed unvaryingly battle-shocked. Their movements were slow, as if they were wading through quicksand.

Danny was stunned by the appearance and demeanour of the men in the camp. To a man, they seemed underfed. Many went without shirts. Others wore shirts, unbuttoned. A vacuum seemed to exist where spirit, discipline and morale should have been present. If this was what Rommel was fighting against, thought Danny, no wonder he's winning.

Observing the arrival of the fleet of trucks was a colonel. He was a man in his early forties. Beside him stood a slightly younger man, a captain, smoking a cheroot. He looked at the new arrivals and shook his head dismissively.

'More lambs to the slaughter.'

The colonel glanced at the captain and felt his anger rise. Rather than rebuke the captain, he said, 'See that Sergeant Reed sorts the men out.'

'He's on his way,' said the captain before remembering to add, 'sir.'

The colonel was a distinguished looking man wearing a shirt and shorts. Greying hair peaked out from under his cap. The man beside him was tall, elegantly dressed, seemingly immune from the intense African heat. Fair-haired, with a slim moustache and clear blue eyes, he would have been a movie producer's dream of how a British army officer should be.

Lieutenant Colonel Lister would have begged to differ.

The two officers watched Reed march towards the trucks. He began to direct the new arrivals to form ranks. Lister looked on with approval. Now this was a soldier, he thought. He glanced again at the tall captain. There was nothing he could do. He was stuck with him.

Danny jumped down from the truck and turned to Arthur with a big grin on his face.

'Do you want some help?'

Arthur's two-word response suggested not, raising another chuckle from the group. Danny regretted the wisecrack, not because he was worried about offending Arthur; he realised too late that their light-hearted manner was drawing unwelcome attention from the men in the camp. Danny motioned to the others to stop laughing.

But it was already too late.

A nearby soldier sped over towards them. His eyes were hostile and accusing. Danny could see trouble brewing and put his hands up in apology. By doing so he became the focal point of the soldier's rage.

'What's so bloody funny?' snarled the soldier.

'Nothing, chum,' said Danny. 'Sorry, it's been a long trip.'

One of his mates shouted, 'Leave it, Harry!' But the soldier was beyond listening. He was as tall as Danny, wiry like so many of the soldiers they'd seen on the way in and shirtless. The outline of the soldier's ribs glistened in the early afternoon sun.

He aimed a swing at Danny who, he had decided, was to blame for the laughter. This was probably true, but nonetheless unfair. Danny easily ducked the punch. The momentum of the soldier called Harry, carried him towards Danny. Moments later Danny flipped him into the air, and he landed on the ground with a thud. Danny stood over him and offered to help him up.

A bunch of soldiers, aware of the ruckus, stopped what they were doing. Harry snarled and was on his feet in an instant. There was a mad gleam in his eye. Danny knew this was not going to end immediately yet he fancied his chances. The man before him was older, with combat experience, but Danny was taller and more muscled. The two men, eyes fixed on one another, circled slowly.

'Disgraceful,' said the captain. He was about to move forward when he felt the stick of Lister stop him. He looked aghast at the lieutenant colonel. 'You can't seriously countenance this?'

Lister noted, once again, the absence of 'sir' from the captain. He studied the captain for a moment. Finally, he removed a pipe from his mouth and turned towards the two opponents.

'Let them blow off steam. It might do people around here some good to see what fighting looks like.'

The captain turned and glared at his superior officer. Lister looked back to his captain, a half-smile on his face. For a moment the captain seemed primed to say something but then thought better of it. Further back, Sergeant Reed had caught the eye of Colonel Lister. The merest shake of the head told Reed to let things play out. He nodded back to Lister.

Harry made his move on Danny. Despite anticipating this, Danny was immediately conscious that Harry was no mug. Seconds later he almost proved it by throwing Danny to the ground. Danny only just managed to stay on his feet. Before Harry could press home his advantage, Danny swept in low and nearly deposited his opponent once more on the ground. However, this left him open to counterattack. Seconds later Harry swung his leg underneath Danny while he was still unbalanced by his initial attack. Danny hit the floor but bounced up again immediately, cursing himself for being too complacent. Too many easy victories in the past had left him unprepared against someone of genuine ability. The triumphant grin on his opponent's face angered Danny. Blood surged through his veins; he wanted to put an end to the fight.

The two men circled one another, snapping occasional arms out in search of a hold. With each passing second, the anger dissipated as his respect for the man in front of him grew. Danny noted that Harry no longer had his fists clenched. This suggested to Danny that he too was no longer burning to hurt him. Perhaps there was recognition that they'd both gone too far. But the crowd was urging them on. There were one or two wolf whistles too, a prelude to mockery and lewd comments, if Danny knew these men. Reluctantly he prepared to launch himself at his opponent.

They clashed again. This time Danny was ready for any move Harry tried. Similarly, Harry was wise to Danny's youthful power allied to technique. A minute of grappling for advantage resulted in neither man gaining an edge. Harry was breathing hard. Danny felt sure that if he kept the pressure on, he'd soon gain the advantage.

At this point Reed saw Lister nod. Lister had seen the contest was likely to end soon. It was time to end what had been an evenly matched contest. Lister did not want to see a soldier who had already seen action over the summer suffer another defeat. The sergeant stepped forward and the two combatants relaxed their pose. Each had a rueful grin on his face. More than anything, Danny felt relief. He'd wanted the fight to end and this felt fair, honours even.

'Sorry, mate, the name's Harry Cornwell,' said Harry holding out his hand.

'No need, I'm Danny. Danny Shaw,' replied Danny, gripping the outstretched hand.

'You can handle yourself, Dan,' commented Harry as he brushed sand off his body.

Danny laughed. 'You too, Harry. No one's done that to me since I was a kid.'

'You're still a kid, Shaw,' growled Sergeant Reed at Danny. 'Get your gear and fall in line.'

This was clearly not a request and Danny suspected that patience was not the sergeant's best quality. He jumped to it immediately and fell in alongside Arthur.

From the side of his mouth Arthur said, 'Well done, kid. Another ten minutes you'd have 'ad 'im.'

'No talking in line. Attention,' barked Sergeant Reed. Behind him the two officers had arrived to meet the new men. They walked along the line of the new arrivals.

Finally, they moved back to stand alongside Reed. The sergeant ordered the men to stand at ease. The group moved as one. Reed nodded.

'Welcome to El Alamein,' said the lieutenant colonel. 'My name is Lister. As you can see, I am your commanding officer. I won't lie to you, we've had it pretty rough. The men here have been in combat almost non-stop for months. We're up against a determined enemy. The German soldier certainly presents a greater challenge than many

19

of the Italians we have faced. But they are men also. They are beatable. You will help us defeat them. And make no mistake, defeat them we shall.'

Lister finished his speech and ordered Reed to disperse the men. Danny and Arthur fell out and followed the others to their stations.

An hour later the men who had arrived in the convoy with Danny reassembled in the centre of the garrison. Danny sat down with Arthur and Corporal Phil Lawrence in a semi-circle along with a hundred or so of the new arrivals. They were all part of the tank regiment. Some would be in tanks; others, like Hamilton, would form part of the echelon that supplied them with fuel, food, water and ammunition.

A lieutenant stood in front of the new arrivals. The lieutenant was older than Danny but not much. The sun had reddened his skin, but there was no mistaking him for anything other than a British officer. The impression was confirmed when he began to speak.

'Don't think he's been to the Dog and Duck lately,' whispered Arthur.

'Shh,' said Danny, grinning, as they listened to the lieutenant. He was standing in front of a map showing Egypt and the eastern region of Libya, Cyrenaica.

'Gentlemen, welcome to your new home. If we do our job well, hopefully it won't be a long stay. Sadly, we've some unwelcome guests that need to be ejected.'

There was a ripple of laughter.

'My name is Lieutenant Turner. I'm with the Royal Tank Regiment. The map behind me shows you where we are.' Turner used a stick to indicate a spot in the map.

'You may have noticed we're in the desert. What we lack in water and amusement is more than compensated for by the number of flies.

20

The good news is that there are not so many of them in the middle of the desert. The bad news is that's where we'll meet Jerry. So, if the flies don't get you...'

The lieutenant left the rest of the line unsaid, but the men smiled and nodded their understanding. It was clear the young lieutenant was popular and had a good way with soldiers. Lieutenant Colonel Lister was standing at the side looking on. He liked Turner and the easy authority he exuded. He glanced at the captain beside him and wished these leadership qualities were shared by all of his officers.

'The western desert is not full of sand and dunes. Forget Beau Geste or Laurel and Hardy. It's an arid combination of sand and rock. Did I mention the heat? This is not summer in Blackpool, believe me. As much as the days are hot, the nights can be bitterly cold.'

Turner's stick wandered along the Mediterranean coast from El Alamein westward to Libya. He indicated a line running down from the Mediterranean near the border between Egypt and Cyrenaica. 'This is the Halfaya Pass. Running south is an escarpment facing Egypt which is around six hundred feet high. The pass is the route that takes us from here to the enemy. Not surprisingly, Jerry is keen that we don't come through. Hence, its other name, Hellfire Pass.'

Danny had heard mention of the Hellfire Pass. Now he could see why it would have been so named. He felt a prickle on his skin that was nothing to do with the flies or the heat.

'You can go first through there, Danny-boy,' whispered Arthur.

'Age before beauty, old man,' replied Danny.

'On the border, the Italians have made a wire fence. Not quite sure what it was meant to do. It'll hardly stop a tank. The minefields will, though. To get there from here, we have a coastal track. I won't call it a road. To our south we have the Qattara Depression. This is a salt plain which is impassable. It runs from Alamein down the escarpment

21

to a great sand sea. I think this is what we think of when we hear the word desert. Light vehicles can drive over it but not heavy armour. This means Jerry will not be able to come around our flank without stretching his supply lines to an impossible degree. No, this is the only way he can get to us, and us to him. It's a narrow strip as you can see, and it leads up to the coast.'

'Glad we're in a tank going through that,' whispered Phil Lawrence. Danny and Arthur couldn't agree more.

'Once we're past all this, up here is our goal.' Turner's stick tapped on Tobruk which lay on the coast of Libya, three hundred miles to the west of Alamein.

'Our boys are there and they're getting quite a pounding. Jerry has them surrounded and, as we found out over the last few months, they're desperate to take Tobruk. If they take it, they'll have another port to bring in men and equipment. They'll not have to worry about us attacking them from behind their lines. As you may gather, Tobruk is of tremendous strategic importance to both sides. If we can end the siege, we'll have a foothold in Cyrenaica from which we can strike westward towards Benghazi, here,' said Turner pointing to a coastal city to the west of Tobruk, 'and then to Tripoli. With the fall of Tripoli, Libya will be ours. Any questions?'

Arthur nudged Danny in the ribs.

'Go on, son, now's your chance.'

Danny whispered back, in no uncertain terms, that this was not the case.

Arthur put his hand up. Danny glanced askance at his friend.

'Yes,' said Turner, 'that man over there.' In fact, Turner seemed rather surprised by this. His request for questions was always met with a stony silence.

22

Arthur, grinning broadly, said, 'My mate Danny here has a question. He's a bit shy.'

The group erupted into laughter as it was plain from the look on Danny's face that the last thing on his mind was to ask a question.

'Go on, son,' urged Arthur. 'Stand up.'

By now Turner was grinning broadly as was Lieutenant Colonel Lister. Turner was now in on the joke.

'Up you get, young man.'

Danny rose reluctantly to his feet, managing to give Arthur a kick on the way up.

'Ow,' exclaimed Arthur, 'no need for that, Danny-boy.'

The semi-circle of men seemed to close in on Danny as he realised all eyes were upon him now. He took a deep breath and decided 'in for a penny'.

'What's your name?' asked Turner.

'Shaw, sir.'

'Carry on, Shaw,' said Turner, trying to supress his grin.

'First of all, sir, thank you for a very clear presentation on the geography of the country and our objective. My friend Private Perry here, that's Arthur Perry everyone, is a bit slow so I'll explain it to him again later.'

A roar of laughter greeted this, none louder than Arthur.

'So, my question is…' Danny paused while he thought furiously of something to ask. 'My question is how much of the success of Rommel is down to him or to better equipment?'

Danny heard Arthur exhale loudly. It was probably the only sound in the group. If you could have heard a pin drop it would probably have been from the grenade Danny had just lobbed. Turner raised his eyebrows and glanced at Lister. The exchange of glances caused Danny's heart to sink. Had he gone too far? Danny risked a glance in the direction of Lister. There was a smile on the lieutenant-colonel's face. Beside him stood the same captain from earlier. His face was thunder. A few of the other officers seemed amused by the cheek of the newcomer.

'Perhaps I should answer this question,' said Lister, taking over. He walked towards the group and stood beside Turner. 'It's a very good question, I might add, from Shaw. It's one, I suspect, that you men have asked yourselves more than once. We should be careful about turning Rommel into some indestructible force. He's a man just like us. He will be prone to mistakes like all of us. We just need to put him under the kind of pressure he's put us under. When that happens, we shall see what he's made of.'

Danny was still on his feet with his eyes on Lister. However, he could see the other officers nodding in agreement.

'In terms of their armour, there's no question of the destructive potential of the eighty-eights. And yes, the Panzer Mark III is formidable. But we have more Crusaders now and we have control of the air. And we have something else on our side which the Nazis do not. We are right. They are not. The German soldier is fighting for oppression. We are fighting for freedom. This is a critical difference. Always remember that. If you do, then you'll realise, when it matters, that we're more than a match for him.'

Danny sat down again and gave Arthur a triumphant nod. His friend affected not to see this, but the sides of his mouth twitched.

Unsurprisingly there were no more questions, and the meeting broke up. Danny, Arthur and Phil trooped back to their vehicles in the company of Ray Hill and Jim Hamilton. By now, out of earshot of the officers, they berated Danny in horrified amusement.

'Bloody hell, Danny, I didn't mean that you should question the way the war's been run,' said Arthur.

24

'I couldn't think of anything else,' whispered Danny, grinning ruefully to his friends.

'Bloody idiot,' concluded Arthur.

Lister watched them go. Without waiting for the colonel, the captain spun around and walked away. The colonel stared at the back of the departing officer in shock. For a moment he thought to call him back and give him a piece of his mind about respecting superior officers. But that would have been too much like a martinet, too much like the man who'd just left him. The officer disappeared into a large tent marked 'Officers' Mess'.

Lister motioned for Sergeant Reed to join him. Reed was tough, competent, and respected; everything that the captain was not. Turner walked alongside Reed towards the colonel. The latter represented the best of English public schools while the captain, on the other hand, exemplified the very worst combination of conceit, arrogance and questionable judgement. Any further thoughts he had on the subject were interrupted by Reed.

'Sir,' said Reed saluting. 'The men are with Corporals Heath and Cornwell.'

'Good, find out who that boy was. He was the one that had the scuffle earlier, wasn't he? He handled himself well, I thought.'

'Yes, sir,' said Reed, a half-smile on his face.

The sergeant had thought so, too.

Chapter Three

El Alamein, Egypt, August 1941

Late afternoon revealed no let-up in the heat. Danny and his mates were, by now, in full grumble mode, albeit under their breath as they sat and ate what was to become a very familiar diet of stewed bully beef, biscuits and tea.

'Bloody hell,' said Arthur, 'I don't know what's worse, the heat, the flies or this frigging food.'

'Food's not that bad,' said Jim Hamilton, polishing off the last of the bully beef.

The rest turned to the Brummie like he'd just confessed to regular, consensual and mutually enjoyable congress with sheep.

'What?' asked Hamilton defensively.

'I wouldn't leave any dirty underpants out when he's around,' said Arthur.

'He might eat them,' added Danny. This led to an assault with Hamilton's beret, which Danny, helpless with laughter, could not defend himself against.

'I've an idea,' said Arthur. 'Kill two birds with one stone, so to speak. We leave this damn food out for the flies; that'll kill 'em off and then ...'

'You'll starve?' added Danny.

Arthur's face fell.

'Good point, although eating that stuff might do for me anyway.'

A corporal came over to the group.

'Finished yet?' he asked, without any introduction.

'Waiting for dessert, service here's a shambles,' said Arthur, taking a risk thought Danny.

The corporal grinned. 'Cook's not much better, either. Right, on your feet. I'll take you to your new home.'

Danny felt a flutter of anticipation, or perhaps it was excitement. Or nerves. One way or another, he was about to join the war for real. He would meet the men he would share a tank with. He wondered what they would be like. What would they make of him? One of the joys of youth is vanity. Not in any sense that you are better than anyone else. More often than not, it's the opposite.

The vanity of youth is not about the idolisation of self so much as the belief that those around you are in any way interested in you. Part of growing is realising no one is interested in you. Maturity is when you cease to care.

One by one, Danny's friends went to join their new team. With a nod, Danny said farewell to Arthur. Danny's tank was the last in the row. He saw the large sand-coloured Crusader silhouetted against the cloudless evening sky. The purple-grey hue was suffused with lines of orange. Heat radiated off the surface still making the horizon blur.

As he approached the vehicle, he heard the chatter of some men on the other side. While he hoped that they would be men that, at least, would be likeable, he realised it would be even better if they were men he could count on. He had no doubts about himself on that score.

A freezing night gave way to a morning that grew hotter by the minute, as if some supernatural hand had switched on a pilot light. Danny was the first up, or so he thought. He noticed one mattress was already empty.

An unshaven man with flecks of grey in his stubble squinted up at Danny from under his makeshift pillow.

'Make yourself useful, lad.'

This was Cecil Craig. He didn't like being called Cecil. An Ulsterman in his early thirties, he could as easily have passed for fifty. Craig had been around since the start of the North African campaign. Sergeant Reed's first instruction to Danny, when he introduced the Ulsterman, was to ignore anything he said. Danny took this to be an odd form of compliment to his new comrade-in-arms. Craig was the driver as well as the mechanic.

Charlie Felton, the wireless operator, was only a little older than Danny. A country boy like Danny, this meant he was at the receiving end of constant ribbing about his intellect and the nature of the relationship with his sister. He took this in good part, but Danny suspected that he did not have much time for his chief tormentor, Joe Holmes. In truth, Danny did not take much to the burly gunner either. He was as unwelcoming as Craig but without the undercurrent of dry humour that characterised the Ulsterman. Danny looked down at the prone figure still snoring on the ground and recalled the gunner's first words to him the afternoon before.

'Took your time getting here, son. You miss civvy street?'

Danny wasn't sure if this was a comment on his lateness at signing up to join the army or the fact that the new arrivals had missed Operation Battleaxe, the summer's failed campaign to relieve Tobruk. Danny ignored the remark then and resolved to ignore any jibe. These men had been through so much; some resentment was inevitable, and scepticism was certain until you had proven yourself.

Danny stooped down and started to brew up some tea. As the new boy he was expected to perform some of the more menial tasks. He took over from Felton, who was happy to be relieved of these duties if the broad grin on his face was anything to go by.

Sergeant Reed approached the colonel. A brief salute from both men. Just as Reed was about to report, the captain appeared from behind the tent flap. Reed saluted again. The captain lifted his stick to his forehead but was already looking up in the sky.

'Sir, the men are ready for drill.'

'Very well,' drawled the captain, ignoring the fact that Reed had been speaking to Lister. A brief look passed between Reed and Lister. The colonel's blue eyes crinkled just enough to calm the anger in Reed.

Lister walked forward accompanied by a number of the other senior officers. Walking alongside him was the second in command Major Warren and two other majors, Laing and Miller.

The captain uttered an oath as a legion of flies descended on his face. How he hated this country. The sooner his transfer came through the better, he thought. He risked a glance at the two men beside him. Lister and Reed were thick as thieves. Neither respected him. He knew that much. Probably with good reason. But what did he care? After six months, he was still standing here while King, McDonald and the other captain whose name he could never remember were lying dead somewhere in the middle of the God-forsaken wilderness.

More fools them.

Sensing he was not wanted, the captain moved away and left Lister and the other majors to do the inspection. Reed walked with Lister towards the new arrivals. The colonel puffed on his pipe, waiting for the captain to move out of earshot.

'A little early, sir,' said Reed nodding towards the pipe. Lister rolled his eyes.

'Therapy,' replied Lister. He did not smile but there was enough of a look in his eye for Reed to enjoy the joke. Lister relayed the orders for the day.

'Ready when you are, sergeant.'

Reed began to bark out orders for their rifle drill. This was followed by a brief inspection by Lister and Warren. Danny and his friends were standing in the back row so avoided further contact. Danny felt relieved; he was worried that he'd already blotted his copybook not once but twice. The inspection over, Reed accompanied Lister back to the other officers.

'Have you had your breakfast yet?' asked Lister.

'No, sir.'

'Hurry along then, Reed. By the by, what did you do with the young chap?'

'Shaw?'

'Yes, that's the one.'

Reed, a veteran of nearly two years of the desert campaign, looked unusually sheepish at this point.

'Ah,' said Lister, smiling. 'Good choice.'

'Let's see, sir.'

It was going to be a new experience being with people who were not friends. The tank rumbled along the rocky desert path. Danny sat in the hull beside Charlie Felton trying to understand how the wireless worked. Under any circumstances this would have been straightforward, but bumping along the road, the heat was melting Danny's skin, the sun-softened metal was hot to the touch and the two men almost had to coordinate their breathing rhythm to ensure there was enough room for them.

Still, Danny was excited, undeniably scared yet oddly desirous to have his first encounter with the enemy. Meeting his tank mates had solidified a feeling that had grown within him since his arrival. Aside from Sergeant Reed and the tetchy Ulsterman Craig, he couldn't help but feel they were beaten. The mood was sour, particularly that of Joe Holmes. Even the otherwise friendly Charlie Felton seemed resigned to defeat.

'I thought it would be easier than this; got that wrong,' admitted Felton as they drove along. 'Their Mark IIIs are better than our Crusaders, no question.' He looked around him then lowered his voice so that only Danny could hear. 'Better led, too, for my money.'

'What's wrong with Lister? Seems alright to me,' said Danny.

'He is but he's new. He only arrived a week or two before you. He's a tank man though. So is the sergeant,' said Felton. His eyes flicked upwards towards Reed. The sergeant was riding on top in the turret. 'I don't think the higher ups have much clue. A few months ago, we could have been having beer in Tripoli. Now, we're fighting for our lives to defend Cairo.'

'Rommel?' asked Danny.

Felton nodded. The young wireless operator introduced Danny to the interior in more detail.

'V12 engine. Fast but unreliable and the fan drive wears out so cooling breaks down all the time. Means it's hot as hell in here usually. Still, we're as fast and mobile as we need to be, and that's what matters when you have a Panzer throwing metal at you. Our two-pound gun is smaller than theirs. This means we have to get close to their tanks if we're going to hurt 'em. Good thing is it's difficult to hit a tank on the move, never mind one moving quickly, so it's a trade-off.'

'How fast on sand?' asked Danny.

'Fifteen miles per hour. Doesn't sound much but try hitting something travelling that quickly unless we're head on. Also, it's quite low, so it's a smaller target. You'll be loading. Holmes is the gunner and Craig's the driver. He's down here,' said Felton pointing to the driver's compartment. 'Usual layout. Clutch on left, pedal in centre and accelerator on the right. You've driven one of these before?'

'Yes. The A9 and A13.'

Felton shook his head.

'This is better. Still not as good as what Jerry has, though. To the left is the instrument panel. The driver can look through there and this side window. Holmes is here with the gun. Telescopic sight there. He traverses the turret. It goes quite quick.'

'You'll be loading,' continued Felton. 'That's what I was doing until you came. You have your own periscope and a bullet-proof visor. The commander sits up there. In our case that's Sergeant Reed. You come in through the roof of the turret. Levers are at the side, here. They open. Get used to them. You never know when you'll need to bail out. Once a tank starts to brew you get the hell out.'

'Have you brewed up yet?'

Felton nodded.

'Yes, my first one did. We were lucky. We all got out, but you don't want to hang around. I've seen what some of the poor blokes look like who don't.'

Felton was silent for a moment as the memory returned of sights no one should ever see or experience. Danny looked away and pretended to look at the instrument panel. He could hear the quickening of Felton's breathing. A minute later Felton could continue.

'The engine is behind the turret. Have you done the mechanic's course?'

Danny nodded. 'Yes. I'm also a smithy, so I can turn my hand to repairs if need be when we're at the camp.'

'Leave that to the recovery teams. We can only do maintenance. You can help me with that, though. Bloody pain,' said Felton before adding with a grin, 'Right, I think that's the tour over. That'll be five bob, please.'

'Can I take it out for a spin?' asked Danny.

'Don't see why not,' said Felton, grinning.

Danny had ridden inside a tank many times before. He was used to being bounced around. It was surprising just how hard and rocky the desert surface was. This was not the soft sand he'd been expecting but something even less welcoming and unyielding. It felt alien and threatening. In England, the most dangerous thing he'd encountered was an angry heifer protecting her calves; not to be underestimated, remembered Danny.

'What brought you here then?' asked Danny as they headed out of the leaguer with Felton demonstrating the controls.

Felton glanced at Danny. He seemed a little ill at ease and Danny felt remorseful at asking. Felton, after a few seconds, decided to say more.

'I ran away from home when I was sixteen. Hated my dad. He was a bad 'un. I didn't like the way he treated Mum and me. Found work on a farm in the next county. They put me up. Stayed there a few years then this all started. I signed up. Just before I left, I went back to the house to see my mum.'

'Was your dad still there?'

'Aye, he was. Looked a bit spooked when he saw me in my uniform. I told him if he ever hurt Mam again, I'd kill him. He wasn't so brave then. I hear from Mam. She says things are all right. I'll go back and check first chance I get. Bastard.'

They returned to the leaguer in the early afternoon. A quick lunch was followed by a series of maintenance checks on the vehicle. This, as Danny was to discover, was as essential as it was relentless. The tank was their protection, their carer, their home in the desert. Its functioning was essential for the safety of the unit.

Each crew member had a role in ensuring everything from the engine to the tracks was in good working order. Danny realised that his acceptance into the group was born when they heard he'd been a 'smithy'. His familiarity with the tensile qualities of metal meant that he could help replace damaged tracks and the already damaged armour.

The next few weeks in the camp allowed this acceptance to develop but, by now, Danny wanted respect to be forged in the heat of battle.

Life in the camp took on a strange dream-like quality. The war seemed to be somewhere else or, at least, someone else's problem. The sands drifting lazily in any light breeze seemed like a metaphor to Danny of their time in the camp. Unquestionably, the war was turning out to be a little easier than Danny had anticipated. While his life was relatively untroubled by war it was no more comfortable.

The flies and the sand made life miserable for all. Water was rationed to less than a gallon per man per day. Away from the camp, in the desert, it was limited to half a gallon. Through an elaborate system of filtering the daily ration sufficed for drinking, for washing, shaving and washing clothes. Private rationing combined with crew pooling ensured cooking utensils and plates could be washed. It was a different world from the NAAFi, never mind the comforts he'd enjoyed in Little Gloston.

Sport was an important bulwark against the enervating effects of the heat. It maintained morale and discipline. Colonel Lister made it clear that everyone had to participate. As a result, football and cricket matches became a break from the regular chore of patrols, drill, vehicle maintenance and military exercises.

Danny joined one of the teams as a goalkeeper. In Little Gloston there'd been little opportunity to play football. He could ride horses, wrestle, and run from angry farmers but anything involving a ball was beyond his frame of reference. Owing to his height, it was felt he might make a good keeper.

Arthur, despite his age and less-than-athletic figure, volunteered to play outfield.

'You know, the Hammers came to look at me play once. I'd have played for them, too,' said Arthur to his team.

'What happened?' asked one soldier.

'I was rubbish,' replied Arthur, before bowing to the other soldiers, who broke out laughing.

'Every. Bloody. Time,' complained Danny, shaking his head. Danny marched forward and put Arthur into a gentle headlock before adding to the group of soldiers, 'Is it too much to ask that we don't give him the opportunity?'

Danny released him while Arthur beamed triumphantly at having ensnared another victim to his stock joke. They lined up in readiness for the start of the match. The referee blew the whistle for the kick-off. Despite the banter about his football ability, it was apparent to Danny that Arthur could play a bit. His first strike on goal went fizzing past Danny's outstretched hand.

Joe Holmes turned and snarled at Danny, 'You're supposed to stop those, yokel.'

Danny ignored the jibe and pointed out, 'Can't stop what I can't see.' Just then he was distracted by Arthur's boisterous celebration. He grinned at his friend which was a big mistake. Seconds later Holmes came striding over towards him, rage in his eyes. He jabbed a finger at Danny and snarled, 'I don't see what's so bloody funny.'

'How about your pathetic attempt at defending, Holmes? Try tackling him you dolt. It's not like he's a small target.'

'Leave it out,' shouted Arthur from the halfway line. However, he was still in too much of a celebratory mood from scoring a goal to care about any insults.

Afternoons such as this ensured the pain of defeat receded. As Colonel Lister had suspected, sport, the arrival of new tanks, men and supplies slowly did its job of rebuilding a regiment battered by failure and mourning the loss of comrades. The slow process began of integrating men as inexperienced in soldiering as they were unready to face a test such as the Afrika Korps. Fate had forced these disparate men together. Fighting would forge something akin to love.

Chapter Four

Halfaya Pass, Egyptian/Libyan border, August 1941

'If I hear that song one more time,' complained Manfred, 'I'll throw the damn radio in the air and take a machine gun to it.'

Karl Overath looked at the young man, laughed, and turned the volume of the radio up. Beside him Horst Kastner began singing a more ribald version of the song playing Lili Marlene. Even Manfred smiled as the song descended into an increasingly sordid conclusion. Kastner's fine base baritone made a startlingly absurd contrast to the degeneracy of the subject matter. Laughing was a business fraught with risk where they were. He covered his mouth quickly lest one of the many flies decide to set up residence there.

The two senior men in the tank had been in the desert for over six months. They knew the ropes. There was a hard-bitten menace to them but also the casual self-assurance that Manfred craved. If anything was going to keep him alive, Manfred was sure it would be them.

People like Sergeant Overath and Corporal Kastner were the heart of the Afrika Korps. Between them they had nearly twenty years of experience in the army. The two men had come out on the first wave of Germans accompanying Rommel. Survivors of a dozen or more encounters with the enemy, Manfred had made it an article of faith to listen and learn from them.

Overath was taller than Manfred with a face burned brown by the intense African sun. It made his blue eyes seem cold. The truth was very different. Like Corporal Kastner, Overath was warm in person, professional in conduct and effective in combat. The claustrophobic closeness of tank warfare required men that were more akin to brothers than comrades.

Over the course of the year, they had seen men come and go from their tank, some transferred to other commands; a few, very few in fact, were killed. The two men were accustomed to new arrivals and recognised the importance of integrating them quickly so that they worked not just as a unit but as a single organism.

For the week that Manfred had been in the camp, he'd barely seen Gerhardt. He'd lived, eaten, worked and slept with his crew mates. From around six in the morning until late into the night, the other crew members drilled in the tank, familiarised themselves with everything to do with its maintenance. By nightfall, Manfred would collapse exhausted onto his mattress, welcoming sleep like an opium addict his next smoke.

His arrival at Gambut coincided with a pause in the day-to-day fighting. The Afrika Korps had driven a wedge between the 9th Australian division at Tobruk and the rest of the Allies and yet the besieged garrison was still holding out against attack after attack. The port of Tobruk was proving a massive thorn in the side of the Axis. Manfred knew he would soon be part of the next wave of assaults on the port. The knot in his stomach was growing even though they had yet to pass Halfaya, on the border with Egypt.

***

'I'm bored,' said Kastner. He looked up at the relentless sun and shielded his eyes.

'Would you prefer to be out there?' asked Overath, pointing across the empty valley towards the enemy position before adding, 'Wetting your pants.'

'Good point. Give me a cigarette,' ordered the corporal to his sergeant. Manfred smiled and shook his head. He liked his two companions in the tank. There were few airs between them. They'd seen too much. Manfred knew better than to question them on what they'd done. Instead, he listened closely whenever either chose to speak about their experience. These were rare occasions and usually only when they were instructing the new recruit. The two other members of the crew were relatively new. They had arrived three months earlier, just when the Allies had tried to relieve Tobruk.

The other two boys were a year or two older than Manfred. One was not very talkative, the other too much so. Initially, Manfred was drawn more to Overath and Kastner. He had more to learn from them. More than this, both men radiated self-assurance. This confidence was not based on mindless bravado. Their capabilities, their professional competence had already found expression in the harshest of climates against a resolute enemy. Manfred recognised, as he worked alongside these men, how little he really knew about war.

Overath's position as commander meant his position was in the turret of the tank. He took orders via his headphones from the head of the troop, Lieutenant Basler. The rest of the crew stayed below. Andreas Fischer was the driver. As tall as Manfred, he seemed to fill the small interior space in other ways. He liked the sound of his opinions and he expressed them often. His enjoyment of these beliefs was in marked contrast to that of his unfortunate listeners.

Jens Kohler was as taciturn as Fischer was a blowhard. He was wiry and tireless. While Manfred did not especially take to him, he sensed that he was not a man to lose his head under pressure. His greatest value to the team was his ability as a mechanic. The Panzer Mark III was reliable, but it still required a good deal of maintenance. Kohler enjoyed the company of the engine more than human company. Neither Overath nor Kastner seemed minded to change his nature.

Kastner operated the gun. Direct tank on tank conflict was rare, yet Kastner would have had some experience of it. Manfred was desperate to know more but he sensed in the big Austrian a reluctance not only to discuss this but, somewhere behind his eyes, a sadness. Sometimes he would see a look pass between the two men. It wasn't doubt. They were here to do a job. One that needed to be finished quickly. But there was something there that Manfred knew he would soon experience himself.

Kastner was clearly a man who merited his own command. Manfred suspected this was only a matter of time. He had leadership qualities in abundance. These would be needed as the war in the desert progressed and men were lost. Manfred wondered how Overath would cope when that time came.

If he survived long enough.

Fischer was from Bavaria. He was never going to be mistaken for anything other than an Aryan. Movie star looks combined with an arrogance that bordered on caricature; his own sense of destiny weighed heavily on the shoulders of his tank comrades. Manfred had never felt entirely comfortable around such people. His own nature, while not particularly shy, was more reserved. Or perhaps he felt, as he often did with Erich, a sense of resentment towards such confidence.

It was clear neither Overath nor Kastner liked Fischer particularly. But, equally, they trusted him. Young men such as Fischer had a look in their eyes which was nothing to do with patriotic fervour and everything to do with ambition.

Fischer saw himself as command material. The promotion he craved required more than self-confidence or the usual combination of bravery and competence; it needed something else. A survival instinct. Overath and Kastner had all of these qualities, and in Fischer they recognised a similar spirit. Perhaps in Manfred, too. But Manfred saw they were each amused by Fischer's preening ego. They tolerated him because, in their early firefights, he'd shown something to them which was nothing to do with fearlessness, or cold-blooded killer instincts.

Quite simply, he could be relied upon.

This was the only type of acceptance Manfred sought now. To be recognised by such men as one of them. His status as *Fahnenjunker* meant nothing when sat with men who had engaged the enemy. Fischer was also a *Fahnenjunker,* and had graduated from the same academy as Manfred, four months earlier. In fact, they had just missed one another.

Manfred was expected to perform a number of roles during this period. To begin with he was trained up as the wireless operator. His job was to coordinate what was happening with the other tanks in the unit. By the time they did eventually engage the enemy, it was likely he would be a loader. This position occupied the turret with Overath and Kastner.

More than anything now, he wanted the opportunity to test himself in combat. The stigma of his reaction to Lothar's death burned deep. His death played out in the recurring dream. Only through battle would he find the atonement he sought, not from other men, but from himself.

For now, he was the new boy, and he was made to feel it. Overath and Kastner, in particular, directed a steady tirade of insults in his direction. The humour rarely rose above crude and Manfred never took offence. He recognised it as a conditioning of sorts as well as a sign of their acceptance.

'Don't move,' whispered Overath one morning.

'What do you mean?' breathed Manfred.

Overath pointed to something small and black sitting on Manfred's makeshift pillow. Out of the corner of his eye, Manfred saw the malevolent black shape; its segmented curved tail tipped with a venomous stinger was pointing, poised and ready to strike at Manfred. A pair of grasping pincers were an inch from his nose. Manfred froze, white with fear.

'One sting from that,' whispered Overath solemnly. He motioned with his hand across his neck. The meaning all too clear.

'Kill it,' urged Manfred between gritted teeth.

'Shhh,' replied Overath, finger to lips and slowly crouching over him.

By now, Kastner and Fischer were looking on. Concern etched over all their faces. For a minute they all sat around Manfred in silence. This became too much for Manfred.

'What's happening?' he whispered.

'It's sleeping, I think,' whispered Fischer, afraid to wake the demon from its slumber.

Kohler began coughing at this point while the others shushed him. He ducked his head away while his coughing fit continued.

'Can't you use a stick to swat it away?' asked Manfred, now thoroughly confused at the inactivity of the others.

'Too risky,' said Kastner. 'They're too quick. It could sting you before Fischer has swiped it away.'

42

'Me?' said Fischer, somewhat put out. 'I'm damned if I'm doing it. You do it.'

Kastner pointed to the insignia indicating his rank.

A stick was produced from nowhere and handed to Fischer. Overath looked meaningfully at the young driver and put an arm on his shoulder. Fischer nodded and looked seriously at Manfred. By now Manfred was frantic but equally desirous not to show this. Through gritted teeth he snarled, 'Get a move on.'

Fischer slowly moved to the rear of the scorpion, gently lowered his stick onto the pillow. Then with a jerk he flipped the scorpion onto Manfred's face and screamed.

Manfred screamed also and bolted up, beating his face and chest to get rid of the fearsome beast that was about to kill him.

The fearsome, and very dead beast.

It had expired a day or two previously. This critical fact was unknown to Manfred. In fact, the scorpion had changed hands many times having been used in a series of practical jokes around the camp. Victims were sworn to silence. This had been Manfred's turn.

Manfred stared down at the deceased arachnid. Finally, he looked up, grinned sheepishly at his comrades who were in varying states of hysteria and uttered one word.

'Bastards.'

Lieutenant Basler walked through the row of tanks and called the men to make ready. Overath spied the lieutenant making his way along the thin strip separating the two rows of twenty-five tanks. He glanced at Kastner who had also noticed Basler's arrival.

'Holiday's over, boys,' said the sergeant, throwing a cigarette to the ground. The others needed no other instruction. They were on their feet and standing to attention as Basler passed them. It was clear that both Overath and Kastner were keen not to get on the wrong side of the SS lieutenant. Manfred wondered why he was not in his own separate regiment. Various hypotheses had been proposed, the most popular of which was that he was there to keep an eye on the men and inform senior officers of any dissension in the ranks. The reality was that the rest of the detachment had been killed a few months previously. He'd neglected to ask to be transferred back to Germany.

With a click of his fingers and a jerk of his thumb, Manfred and the crew immediately climbed onto the vehicle or entered via the hatch. Manfred crawled down the body of the tank to the bow where the wireless was situated. His position was front and right. He had plenty of room, and it was not uncomfortable, at least on short journeys.

His only concern, unvoiced, was the lack of an escape hatch. Both he and Fischer were particularly at risk. They were situated to the front and exposed to any shells that were fired within close range. The lack of a quick escape hatch was an additional point of vulnerability. At least the armour at the front was thirty millimetres thick. This was more than enough to stop bullets from any range and shells from at least a kilometre or more away. Manfred avoided thinking about what happened in closer combat. If the men operating the anti-tank guns did their job, the Allied tanks would not get so close. Even when they managed to get closer, the Mark III and Mark IV guns outranged them.

Despite their proximity in the cramped interior, the two boys did not communicate much during exercises beyond relaying information or instructions. Manfred was surprised by this initially. His initial overtures towards friendship were unreciprocated. He gave up by the second day. There would be no comradely friendship in the manner of Overath and Kastner. Manfred was fine with this even if it was disappointing.

Overath and Kastner sat in the cupola of the tank. Overath, as commander, took up his position in the hatch at the top of the turret. The position was relatively exposed, but it gave him a three-hundred-and-sixty-degree view of his surroundings. Kastner, as gunner, sat forward and below Overath.

The two men, unlike Manfred and Fischer, kept up an ongoing conversation throughout any manoeuvres, none of which was complimentary to the other tanks, their driving, or their combat effectiveness. Manfred enjoyed the show immensely, but Fischer and Kohler had long since grown tired of it.

The patrol drove out along the edge of the escarpment that was Halfaya Pass. The pass ran from near the Mediterranean Sea down through Egypt. Situated close to the Libyan border, the pass represented a natural block to any attempt by the Allies to thrust forward into Libya. The only way of taking the pass was through direct assault or outflanking it. The former risked a high cost to life; the latter meant that supply lines would be stretched, and a wedge could be driven between any attacking forces.

The strategic importance of the pass was recognised by both sides. For the moment it lay in the hands of the Afrika Korps. The landscape was hilly, rocky and barren. No greater contrast could be found to the beautiful green valleys of Germany from where Manfred had come. This was alien. The heat, the flies, the people all seemed to hail from a different world.

Manfred understood the importance of gaining victory in the desert. It would open the road to the badly needed oil reserves in the Middle East. Every soldier in the Afrika Korps realised that without oil the war engine would slowly grind to a halt. All the more reason for their exasperation with Hitler's decision to invade Russia the previous month. At a stroke he had depleted their forces and armour.

It showed clearly where Hitler's priorities lay, and it was certainly not North Africa. None of the men in the crew appeared to have much time for the Fuhrer, although open mockery was frowned upon by Overath, fearful of repercussions from others in the camp, particularly from Lieutenant Basler.

Another day passed patrolling the perimeter of the camp.

At dusk they climbed out of the vehicle and jumped to the ground, exhausted and hungry. Their fatigue was made worse by the knowledge that they still had a couple of hours work to do checking the tank over to ensure its travel-worthiness for the next day when they'd continue doing nothing that seemed remotely connected to winning a war.

When at last they had completed the required checks, Manfred went to cook for them. Kastner reached wearily for the wireless set and turned it on. After twiddling with frequencies for a minute, Kohler came across Marlene Dietrich singing, 'Lili Marlene'. In English. Grins erupted around the wireless.

'Not that again. Has anyone got a gun?' asked Manfred.

Overath and Kastner roared with laughter and began to sing along in German. Even Fischer smiled.

And so ended a day that would repeat itself for three long, stulti-fying months in the desert, as the Allied and the Axis forces seemed to agree, in an odd breakthrough for humanity, that it was simply just too hot to fight.

'Do you remember that cup final?' asked Gerhardt.

'You were lucky,' replied Manfred sourly.

Oddly, Gerhardt didn't disagree on this. Despite his ultra-compet-itive nature, he was, at least, honest about things that mattered. And football mattered. Even in the kickabouts here, both Manfred and Gerhardt stood out although the standard was quite high.

'Do you know that after that match,' continued Gerhardt, 'a man came over to me. He said he was from Schalke.'

'Schalke? Bloody hell.'

'I know. He said there was a war coming but I could get out of it if I joined them.'

Manfred looked at Gerhardt in surprise. There was a trace of jealousy, too. They'd both played in this match. Why hadn't Schalke invited him to play for them? Probably because Gerhardt was a better player. He hated to admit this, but it was true.

'What did you say?'

'Where do I sign? What do you think I said, you idiot?' said Gerhardt with a grin.

The two boys collapsed laughing in the cold night air. When they'd finished, Manfred asked the next, obvious question.

'But, my friend, I can't help but notice you're here. What happened?'

Gerhardt looked a little crestfallen at this point.

'I saw my friends signing up. It was too much for me. So, I wrote to Herr Himmler, not you know who, and told him that I would join the army. He was very good. I got a letter from him a week later which asked me to contact him when I got back from the war. He also wanted to know the name of that blond-haired clodhopper on the other side.'

'Bastard,' said Manfred, laughing and throwing some punches towards his friend's arm. Gerhardt was guffawing too much to care.

They separated and went to their tanks. Manfred sat down and extracted a letter from a bag. It was from his father. The letter was two months old. He started to read it again. It made him feel happy to see his father's voice on paper. His father wrote good letters. Long, gossipy, and surprisingly frivolous as if he understood the soldiers need to read something, anything, when so far from home. There was little about his mother. That told its own story. The country's confidence that they could win the war seemed to be on the wane. Like with the last one, the suspicion was growing that this would be a long, drawn-out affair.

Kohler sat down beside him.

'Good news?'

Manfred laughed but there was a trace of bitterness there too.

'My father says everything and very little at the same time. The Fuhrer tells us we're winning the war.'

'So we must be, then.'

Chapter Five

Little Gloston, England, August 1941

Stan Shaw's arm ached like hell. From his elbow to his shoulder, he felt a stabbing pain from every strike of hammer on metal. Trails of sweat sneaked down his smoke-blackened face. What was he to do? He kept hammering in defiance of the pain, in defiance of the heat of the forge, in defiance of the slow erosion of a way of life he had never questioned. The barn echoed to the sound of his hammer. He looked up, half expecting to see his boys. To see young Ben Desmond. Perhaps even Lord Robert.

Mopping his brow, he set his hammer down and went to the water pump. The cold hit him like a blast after the heat of the forge. He looked overhead and wondered where summer was hiding. For a few minutes he pumped water into the sink and then drenched himself. The freezing water restored life to muscles that were groaning from the relentless pounding of his trade. Satisfied that he was clean, he made his way towards the cottage located beside the forge.

The pathway was but a few yards, but it moved him from a smoky-grey atmosphere into a world of delicate pastel-hued flowers and birds chattering in trees. Hard to believe they were at war. Hard to believe the boys who used to play, wrestle and work around him were gone. The thought made him catch his breath. The war to end all wars; the war he'd fought; the war in which he'd seen lifelong friends killed had only been a prelude to something potentially much worse.

The front door led directly into the kitchen. This was to enter more than a room; it was an escape from the worry that hung heavy in the air around him. The warmth of the kitchen was both physical and emotional for Stan. Beside the Aga cooker he'd lovingly restored years previously was his wife, Kate. There had been no other women in his life. There had been no need. A lifetime together except for the eighteen months when he was at war. The aroma in the kitchen was as welcoming for him as the smile on Kate's face.

'Something new?' asked Stan.

Her eyes narrowed and she went to hit him with the wooden spoon. This was his standard question to anything she cooked. He caught her arm which, in truth, was swung towards him with less-than-venomous velocity. Seconds later she was in an embrace which she made little effort to disengage from.

Kate was unsure how long they were standing thus before they heard a gentle rapping on the open door. Stan broke off from holding Kate and was somewhat shocked to see the tall figure of Lord Henry Cavendish standing in the doorway. Standing beside him was his daughter. Her face managed the improbable feat of being both shocked and amused in equal measure.

'Lord Cavendish. Lady Sarah.'

'Hello, Mr Shaw,' said Henry. 'Sorry to interrupt,' he added smiling. 'Rather glad we didn't arrive a few minutes later, truth be told.'

By now Sarah was coughing and laughing at the same time. Henry glanced down at her and said grimly, 'You're not supposed to find that funny young lady.'

Sarah Cavendish reddened immediately but the smile was impossible to contain. Stan and Kate looked at the young woman and apologised.

'Please don't,' she replied. 'I'm glad to see that it's not just Mum and Dad who are like this.'

This brought an arch of Henry's eyebrow that suggested his daughter's views should be more circumspect, ideally unspoken. The Shaws invited their guests into the cottage.

'I'm just doing a round of the village. I wanted to hear news of our boys.'

Our boys thought Stan. More than just our boys, he realised. They belonged to the village. To a way of life.

He looked at Henry. He'd watched him grow up, from being a quiet, rather distant boy, into a surly, very distant teenager before becoming a gentleman that his father and grandfather would have been desperately proud of. Young people: there was no telling, really, which way they would go.

His daughter was the image of their mother, Jane. Tall, slender with fiery red hair and sea-green eyes. Like Henry, her youthful arrogance had made her distant and difficult to know. Over the last year Stan had noticed the natural warmth from her mother's side begin to emerge as she herself became a young woman.

'How is the young lord?' asked Kate. For a moment she'd almost called him Robert, such was her familiarity with the young man.

'At school, desperate to be eighteen so he can join up.'

Henry shot Stan a glance. He saw the face of the older man darken.

'What of Tom and Danny? Any news?'

'Sit down, you'll have some tea?' asked Kate.

The group sat down around the table that dominated the middle of the kitchen, like almost every other cottage in the village.

'Both are in North Africa now, I think. Neither say very much,' acknowledged Stan. 'But it's not difficult to read between the lines. Tom, if you remember, was on Crete before he got evacuated. He's been fighting the Boche in North Africa, too.'

Henry half smiled at the term used by Stan. It had been common during the Great War; it seemed less so now. This was a different time. Young people wanted to do things their way. They seemed to speak a different language these days. He glanced at his daughter who was becoming both unrecognisable and yet someone he knew well. The narrative of her growth so matched her mother's. He caught his breath sometimes, fearful for a future that seemed so uncertain.

'He doesn't say much about what they've done or where they are. I think he's in Tobruk. His regiment went there over the summer.'

Henry nodded but it was not good news. Tobruk was surrounded by the Germans and the summer's operation to relieve the siege had failed. There was little he could say that was positive on the subject which would not betray his worry. He moved the subject on.

'What of the men he's with? I gather there are a lot of Australians there.'

'Yes. No finer fighting men, sir. He talks a lot about them and the men he's with. They're a good bunch apparently. Not many bad apples. Mind you, they've been through a lot already. You find out a lot about a man in these situations.'

'I imagine it's a comfort to you to know he's with men he trusts,' said Henry.

'It's everything, sir,' replied Stan.

'From what I know of Tom, they're lucky to have him.'

The evident sincerity of Lord Cavendish's words moved Kate Shaw and she fought hard to stop tears appearing in her eyes. Even the flinty features of Stan Shaw softened slightly. To hear such things about your son from a man whose opinion you value meant a lot at that moment.

'And Danny? How's he finding it?'

Kate noticed that Sarah raised her head slightly. Thus far she'd said little beyond their greeting. She had been content to look down at the table. For a moment Sarah and Kate exchanged looks before Sarah turned to Stan.

'Bit hot, I gather,' chipped in Kate. 'Too many flies.'

They laughed at this. Outside it was gun-grey overhead and summer was still sleeping.

'He says that he's not seen action yet. They spend all their time on patrols and maintenance. He can't say anything, but I suspect that means they'll be making a big push to relieve Tobruk,' said Stan, tapping his pipe on the table and striking a match.

'They certainly need to,' replied Henry, nodding. 'Does he know Tom may be there?'

'We don't know for certain, but he'll know which regiments are there, I imagine,' replied Kate. There was fear in her voice.

'And the people he's with?' asked Henry, deftly moving the conversation onto more optimistic territory.

Kate glanced at Sarah again. Her eyes were back on the table. Her hands locked together in a knuckles-white grip.

'Mixed bunch from what I gather. Some of them he's known since the camp at Thursley. Some of the others are a bit less friendly. They don't accept newcomers easily.'

'I suppose it's understandable,' said Henry.

'I wrote as much to him, sir. Some of these blokes have lost their chums. They just want to get back at the Boche. Seeing newcomers arrive, none of them have a notion what they're about to face. It's unsettling and you're resentful. You want to get back at them but you're also afraid.'

At this point Stan felt a gentle nudge in his ribs from Kate. He realised he was becoming more impassioned than he'd intended. He smiled sheepishly. Henry shook his head and smiled also.

'I think I know enough of your son to say he'll win them round. He has many admirable qualities. They both have. Any family would be proud of them.'

Kate beamed with pride. She couldn't have agreed with this assessment more. Stan nodded to Henry in gratitude.

'Oh, sir, you'll be interested in one other piece of news from Danny. Not one you'll be surprised by, I'll warrant.'

'Oh, what's that?' asked Henry, genuinely curious.

'There's a captain there who Danny thinks you might know. I gather he's not thought of too highly by the men.'

'Really who?'

Stan told him.

Henry sat back in his chair and whistled. This was not good news. He said, almost to himself, 'I'd wondered where he would end up.'

Sarah looked confused. 'Who did you say?'

Her father turned to her. He seemed troubled by the news. Finally, he smiled to her and said, 'Captain Edmund Aston. Do you remember him?'

Chapter Six

Cairo, Egypt, September 1941

Captain Edmund Aston rose from the bed and dressed. He looked down at the woman lying asleep and his lips curled into a smile. It was all so easy. Always had been. While the cat's away, he murmured softly to himself. The woman began to stir. Finally, she opened her eyes and looked up at Aston.

He was searching for his shirt when he turned around to face her. Such good looks, but she could not ignore the cruelty of the smile. Or was it contempt? She could hardly blame Aston because what it said about her was certainly no better. While she entertained this man in her house, a good man was at the front.

Good, but oh so dull.

Deadly, deadly dull. He'd kept her in a certain style. In return she'd given him two sons, both at Harrow. If not a dutiful wife, she'd certainly been a supportive one. At least one of his promotions had been earned through her thankfully unappreciated and uncommon creativity in managing his career. This resulted in him spending too much time away from home. Who could blame her if she sought company? This was not so often as to raise suspicion, but just enough to keep her feeling young and beautiful.

Edmund Aston was the latest in a line of suitors who thought they were using her. Of course, she accepted, they were using her. This could work both ways. He was magnificent. A magnificent cad. A bounder. Whatever you wanted to call him, it was probably true and worse. But, my word, she thought, he was beautiful. A Greek god but certainly no angel. Nothing so boring. He knew secrets about her that would have induced a coronary in her husband.

'Must you go?' she asked, hoping the answer would be yes.

'Yes, must dash,' replied Aston curtly. 'I have a polo match at the Gezira. Are you coming?'

The answer to that question was a resounding no, thought the woman. You're an amazing lover but I'm tired of you. Just leave now.

'Do you mind if I don't, darling? I don't want people to talk.'

'Do you really care what people think, Sandra?'

Clearly you don't, you bastard, thought Sandra.

'As a matter of fact, Edmund, I do. It's up to you whether you want to continue this…' She paused for a moment to find the right word. Affair seemed inappropriate as it implied at least some degree of feeling on the part of both sides. She settled for something more accurate. '… liaison. But, if we're to continue, it's best that Freddie doesn't get wind of things, don't you think?'

'I suspect you're right, old girl. Mum's the word,' said Aston flashing a smile towards the bed.

Yes, thought Sandra again. He's magnificent. A magnificent bastard. She didn't bother looking at him as he left the room.

Aston walked along the narrow street thronged with turbans, tarbooshes, khaki caps and black berets. The half million population of Cairo had been supplemented with tens of thousands of British troops. The smells fascinated Aston. He'd grown up with the smell of manure, having lived in the countryside, and spent a considerable amount of time on horseback. The odour of incense was an exotic addition which helped offset the less welcome smell of exhaust fumes.

Much to his surprise, he loved Cairo. Quite apart from the fact it meant he was away from the desert and the war, the colours, smells and the teeming humanity was unquestionably as intoxicating as it was different from the rarefied world from which he had come. He missed England terribly but, oddly, not when he was in Cairo. It seemed that the parts of England he adored most had moved there with him. If only he could obtain the transfer he desperately sought; then life at war would prove to be a pleasantly diverting experience.

A leisurely stroll followed by an equally leisurely breakfast meant it was much later that morning when he arrived at his destination. The sign outside read, The Gezira Sporting Club. Aston glanced up at the sandstone and redbrick façade. An Egyptian flag fluttered in the light breeze alongside the Union Jack. With only the barest hint of acknowledgement to the Egyptian doorman, Aston entered the sporting club and made his way to the bar. He always felt that his performance gained a little when he'd had a snifter or three prematch.

He met up with a number of fellow officers from his own team and the opposition.

'Great minds think alike, I see,' said Aston upon arrival.

'Cutting it a bit close old chap,' said one lieutenant whose name he could never quite remember. In the club, rank was forgotten along with the reason they were all there in the first place. Discussion on the war was frowned upon, particularly as things had been going rather badly.

'Putting a filly through her paces,' replied Aston, a smile flickering on the side of his mouth.

This brought a roar from the assembled audience, and he sensed them drawing closer to hear more.

He took a sip from his gin and continued, 'No longer a filly, if truth be told.' Seeing the group edge nearer to him, Aston warmed to his theme. 'Knew her way round the track, to be fair.' The laughter built as he finished off his drink and nodded to the barman for another.

'How did she respond to the whip?' asked one like-minded fellow officer.

'Needed it in the home stretch to take us through to the finish line, old boy.'

One officer at the bar turned away in anger. Lieutenant Turner listened in dismay as the officers bayed and guffawed at Aston. He turned back just in time to catch Aston's eye. A sneer appeared on Aston's lips.

'You ready to take a beating, Turner, old chap?'

'We'll see, Aston,' replied Turner, rising from his seat. A smile appeared on Turner's lips as he passed Aston. In fact, he was seething inside and desperate to get on the pitch and defeat a man he considered a scoundrel and possibly worse.

'Don't get his back up, Aston,' shouted one officer as they all banged their tables in anticipation of the upcoming match and the clear rivalry between the two men.

Aston made a face to his fellow team members as Turner walked past. This brought chortles from the men. They all began to rise. It was time to change and take to the field. The baying had ceased, replaced by a murmur of excited chatter.

They followed Turner out of the bar. Aston felt a hand clap him on the shoulder. This kind of familiarity irritated him immensely, but it was bad show to display anything but good fellowship. He looked at the brigadier and forced a smile.

'I get the feeling Turner doesn't like you, old fellow.'

'One too many defeats, methinks,' replied Aston.

'I would have thought you tank boys would be thick as,' pointed out the brigadier.

'I'm cavalry and always will be,' replied Aston. A few of the other men overheard Aston and cheered their approval. The brigadier decided nothing good was likely to come from a chat. He withdrew with a heavy heart. An atmosphere like this in the bar was certain to be carried onto the pitch.

When they reached the changing room, an Egyptian man dressed in a suit smiled as the officers streamed through. He caught the attention of the brigadier.

'Sir, the umpires are waiting outside. The match is due to begin now.'

'Tell them they can bloody well wait all day as far as we're concerned. We'll be out when we're out,' interjected Aston before the brigadier could reply.

'Here, here,' said one of the officers. The brigadier merely raised his eyebrows and shrugged his shoulders to the downcast Egyptian. He glanced at Aston as he walked past him and shook his head.

Aston led his team out towards the backline where the Egyptian grooms were looking after the ponies. He was the team captain by virtue of having the highest handicap. The only other player on the pitch with a handicap approaching his was Turner. The other three players had lower handicaps which matched in aggregate that of the opposing team.

Overhead the sky was blue and cloudless. A slight breeze blew in Aston's face. Aside from the heat, it could have been in England.

Then he looked at the stable hand and the motley selection of ponies. Perhaps not. He climbed on his horse with barely a nod at the groom who had been holding him for the previous half an hour, melting in the heat, while they waited for the players to emerge.

The noise of a plane overhead caused a stir amongst the ponies. Aston didn't bother looking up. He patted the neck of his horse and said, 'Easy boy.'

The groom handed him a mallet and Aston trotted forward making some cursory warm-ups by swinging the polo stick round and round. He arrived at the halfway line and lined up in front of Turner.

'Been waiting long?' asked Aston innocently. A half-smile following this question.

Turner ignored him but could not avoid hearing baying laughter from Aston's colleagues. He gripped his mallet tightly and tried to calm himself through his breathing. Moments later the umpire in the striped shirt threw the ball into the middle. It barely hit the green turf before it was lost in a melee of clashing sticks, flailing arms and a hailstorm of hooves.

Moments later Edmund Aston was charging forward, his arm windmilling to hit the ball. He was clear of the chasing pack. One more swing would see the ball through the posts. He drew his arm back, and his arm began its downward descent, a mallet hooked into his. The crack of the sticks seemed deafening. Seconds later he had overrun the ball and a mad scramble began to recover it.

Aston glared angrily at Turner, who had denied him a clear scoring opportunity. Turner grinned and then took off in pursuit of the ball. With an oath, Aston kicked after the group who were disappearing up the pitch. He came to a sharp halt when he saw one of his teammates bumping Turner from the line of the ball.

'That's it, Basil, well done,' shouted Aston. A few moments later the ball whistled past him, and he gave chase. This time he made no mistake, carefully flicking the ball forward and sending it calmly between the posts.

Cheers went up from the watching crowd, most of whom were entirely neutral and intent on getting completely drunk. The game restarted to the sound of two planes overhead.

By the fourth and final chukka, the match was all square but the temperature on the field was rising dramatically. The bad blood between Aston and Turner spilled over and infected the other team members. Several incidents shocked, or entertained, the crowd depending on the level of drink consumed. The brigadier watched grimly as officers from the British army seemed more intent on inflicting injury on their opposite numbers than the Afrika Korps.

He didn't have to look too far to see where the blame lay. Once more Edmund Aston crossed the line of the ball which, in theory, incurred a penalty. His blatant disregard for both the rules of the game and its etiquette had gone mostly unpunished by the Egyptian umpire. Had it been any other player, the brigadier would have been shocked. But not from Aston.

An unthinkable idea rose in the brigadier's mind. Unthinkable, yet where Aston was concerned it was a possibility that could not be ignored. Had he bribed the officials to turn a blind eye to his team's infractions?

The brigadier had known Aston for eighteen months or more. He was a regular patron of the Gezira when on leave and an outstanding polo player. But he knew there was another side to the captain. Rumours of his indecent activities had spread. The brigadier was no prude. He knew soldiers. They liked a drink. They liked the company of women. A trip to Sisters Street was one thing but Aston's knavery

61

included carousing with the wives of men who were out in the desert. Was Aston the sort of man to bribe an official? Sadly, thought the brigadier, his lordship was entirely capable of such wickedness.

As this thought was crossing his mind, the brigadier saw Turner and Aston hurling obscenities in each other's direction. All around the brigadier, the crowd was lapping it up. The stream of violations by Aston seemed to provoke admiration rather than approbation. His dismay at the crowd's reaction turned to anger when he heard one officer, already half-sozzled by gin, proclaim, 'If we'd Edmund running the show, we'd have kicked Rommel's arse out of Tripoli long ago.'

This was met with a round of 'here, here' from men that did not know better. The British army's reward for this combination of arrogance and stupidity was to give them command. Little wonder Rommel had steamrollered his way to Egypt, just like he had through France.

The brigadier turned away from the match and limped downstairs. His polo playing days had ended a year ago after his first encounter with the Italian Folgore regiment. Unlike many Italians, this regiment had never surrendered. The resulting fight had been bitterly contested and had given the British an inkling, soon confirmed by the arrival of Rommel, that victory in the North African theatre was not a foregone conclusion.

As he descended the stairs, he heard another roar of amusement. Yes, thought Brown, a quiet word with the two gentlemen concerned was needed. There could be no lingering bad feeling when they all returned to the garrison at El Alamein.

Turner strode into the changing room followed by his team. He thought about heading to his team's side of the changing room, but the raucous sound of hilarity coming from the other side of the lockers drew him like a moth towards the flame. He heard Aston joking *sotto voce* with his teammates and a few other officers who'd come down to offer their congratulations. He guessed the subject of their hilarity. Turner was fighting a losing battle against self-control.

Aston looked up as Turner approached him. He could see the burning rage in the lieutenant's eyes. He put a cheroot to his lips and smiled at his defeated opponent.

'Glad to see you've come to offer your congratulations, Turner.'

'Congratulations,' spat Turner. 'Don't give me that, Aston. What you did out there was nothing short of a—'

Turner stopped short as he saw ten pairs of eyes on him. He realised that to go further would move their dispute into dangerous territory. His face was red from the sun, the anger white hot within him. A slow smile spread across the face of Aston. He was goading him into an indiscretion that would cost him his career. The man knew no depths. Turner's rage had reached the point of explosion.

'You were saying, old chap?' replied Aston, coolly. His eyes never left Turner's. He was enjoying things immensely.

Silence descended. The ticking of the clock on the wall echoed around the changing room. Then one of Turner's team came over and gently took the arm of the lieutenant. Turner glared at Aston and then his acolytes, each in turn. He made no attempt to disguise the contempt he felt for all of them.

The tug on his arm became more insistent. Finally, he nodded to Aston and turned around. His departure was accompanied by stifled smirks. Lieutenant Crickmay, the man who had come to take him away said, 'You were close to something you would have regretted.'

'I'd love two minutes with that man, alone.'

'You'd have to join a long queue, I suspect.'

The two men went to the other side of the changing room to join the rest of the team. They were all exhausted from their efforts on the field.

'Sorry, men,' said Turner. 'I let you all down.'

'No you didn't Jeff,' said one of the team. 'You can't play against that. I don't know what match the umpire was looking at.'

'Absolute disgrace,' said another.

'You should lodge a formal complaint. From what I could see, Aston's play was outrageous,' said Crickmay, 'and I, for one, would like to know more about what that umpire was up to. I wouldn't be surprised if…'

Turner shot Crickmay a look, then smiled.

'It sounds like you'll say something I might regret, Arthur. But, for what it's worth, I'm thinking exactly the same.'

Crickmay grinned ruefully. The other men smiled also. The moment passed. It was some consolation, albeit scant, that Aston's behaviour could not go unnoticed by top brass, a point made forcibly by Crickmay afterwards. His disregard for fair play and civilised conduct on the field, agreed Turner, signalled an absence of character that would certainly be revealed in more critical situations. He felt for all of the men under Aston's direct command. He was one of them.

The men changed in a grim silence broken only by the sound of footsteps approaching. A sergeant saluted them. Turner's heart sank. He had suspected the matter was not going to finish when the match ended. The look on the face of the sergeant confirmed this.

'Lieutenant Turner, sir. The brigadier wishes to see you immediately, sir.'

Turner nodded and quickly knotted his tie. Then he followed the sergeant around to the other side of the changing room. At least, he realised, it wasn't going to be just him.

Their arrival was greeted with hoots of hilarity from Aston's team and friends. Aston scowled in the direction of Turner.

'Do you want some books to put down the back of your trousers?' said one wag, to the noisy glee of the others.

'Give it a break, St John,' replied Aston grimly. His eyes never left Turner's. Animosity poured from them like lava. The two men followed the sergeant out of the changing room and up a few flights of stairs to an office. The sergeant knocked, then held the door open for the two men who entered. The door closed behind them.

A grin broke out on the face of the sergeant. He stood to attention in front of the door, as close as possible, so that he could hear every word spoken.

Aston took one look at the face of the brigadier as he entered. Any hope that this would be a mild rap on the knuckles from an ordinarily mild-mannered officer was quickly dispelled. The brigadier's face was like thunder. In fact, Aston had never seen him look so angry. He immediately stood to attention and saluted. It had been a long time since he had acted this way in front of him.

Aston's belated action caused a further wave of contempt in the angry officer. At this moment he realised, in a moment of epiphany, that the brigadier was no one's fool, especially not for any half-arsed nobleman masquerading in officer's clothes. He glared at Aston and then at Turner. He felt some sympathy towards Turner. The on-field provocation had been almost unendurable.

Almost. The brigadier's opening sally set the tone.

'That is the worst display of behaviour I have seen on any sporting field in my life.'

'Even if you hadn't been officers in His Majesty's Armed Forces, it would have been the worst display of' – he paused for a moment;

the word 'cheating' hung in the air like a malodourous stench, but this would have raised the temperature to dangerously high levels, even for him – 'gamesmanship, Aston. A naked, blatant and frankly, disgraceful disregard for the spirit of this game.'

Aston blanched and was about to reply when one look from the enraged officer silenced him. This was not the right time. His mind swirled furiously with thoughts on how to turn the situation to his advantage. He wanted nothing more than to stick a twelve-inch boot into the softest part of Turner, not that the goody-two-shoes probably had much use for that part of his anatomy.

'And you, Turner, acting like a petulant child. Complaining at anything and everything happening on the field.'

There was no mistaking the rage in Turner's eyes. The sense of injustice. Yes, he had been provoked but the manner he had dealt with the baiting by Aston had not been becoming of his position in the army. Turner almost had to bite his tongue to avoid confirming the brigadier's assessment of his behaviour.

He stared up at both men as if daring them to say something. Neither did so. This was a relief. It meant they had understood the seriousness of the situation and, hopefully, how much their conduct had let their regiment down.

'I have cancelled both your remaining leave. In your case, Aston, that was two days. You had three, I believe, Turner. I will also send a brief report to Lieutenant Colonel Lister. He can deal with you as he sees fit. Dismissed.'

The brigadier rose from his desk after the two men departed. He went to the window and looked out onto the grounds of the club. What should have been a fun occasion, one where everyone could let off steam, had descended into something ugly. The behaviour of Aston, in particular, went against everything he believed in. That

66

Turner had been caught up in the crossfire was partially his own fault but what man could have stood by and accepted such a violent disregard for rules? His report to Lister would, at least, reflect where the weight of blame lay. He doubted it would be news to the colonel.

Aston and Turner glared at one another outside the office. Aston could see the hatred in Turner's eyes and realised that had this been anywhere else, Turner would have been on him at that moment. Aston was seething too.

He'd intended using this period in Cairo to press his suit to return to a non-frontline posting. This had been shot down in flames. And all because of this jumped-up lieutenant who couldn't take a bit of argy-bargy on a polo field. Instead, Turner's acting like a cry baby had merely drawn attention to the more robust approach to winning by Aston. He felt like screaming at the whimpering excrescence before him.

It's not going to end here, thought Aston. He'd bide his time and extract a full settlement for the inconvenience Turner had caused him. In the meantime, he'd have to get Lister back on side before trying his luck again with Cairo, perhaps in autumn.

The two men's steps echoed along the corridor. Neither spoke. Hatred had wound its tendrils around them. Now they were connected like blood brothers where revenge was a promise and death the reward.

Chapter Seven

Cairo, Egypt, September 1941

Arthur stared at the beer Danny had placed in front of him. The dew glistened on the cold glass. Anticipation and desire met in an almost sordid longing in Arthur's eyes. Although thirsty, Danny had not taken a sip yet. He sat staring at his friend, fascinated by the quasi-religious experience Arthur was undergoing. Slowly, Arthur wrapped his fingers around the glass and lifted. Danny raised his glass also and they clinked.

Arthur poured the liquid down his throat greedily, clearing half the glass on his first sip. He let the glass fall heavily onto the table but was careful not to spill a drop.

'Well?' asked Danny.

'Tastes like camel piss. Right now, I don't care.'

Danny watched in awe as Arthur necked the rest of the drink despite his unenthusiastic opinion of its flavour. Then Arthur threw some coins onto the table.

'Go on, get us another.'

'It's your turn,' said Danny.

Arthur pointed to the barmaid. She was around thirty and French. 'She'll serve you long before she looks at me. That's an order, Private Shaw.'

'Yes, Private Perry,' saluted Danny.

Danny finished off his beer and stood up. He surveyed the bar. It was crowded, full of servicemen, all British as far as he could see. The only local people in the bar were women. Danny didn't see any Egyptian men. Among the British, there weren't many officers. This type of bar was for the men in the ranks. A smoke haze made Danny's eyes water momentarily. The noise was deafening. Danny could hear a radio playing music from a Forces station. Dance band music played, and a few brave souls attempted to dance. The rest were here to drink.

Danny and Arthur were not here to drink. At least not just to drink. Another couple of beers and both were ready to take their leave from the bar. The beers were meant to be a reminder, but the taste was nothing they recognised let alone enjoyed. They moved through the crowd and the noise to the exit and then out into the afternoon.

The autumn air was harsh and charged with something more than an electrical current. They walked past heaving cafés where music played, soldiers swayed and mixed with locals in a friendly then not so friendly dance of cultures. Unseen and unuttered was the feeling that they were not welcome here. Danny sensed it before the third beer desensitised him.

The two men stood at the seafront and let the flush of wind bathe them. The flies were here, of course, but not so many and not so aggressive. More aggressive were the beggars. Danny resisted initially but sometimes the sight of a mother with a baby strapped to her back found a way through his guard.

'Where to now?' asked Danny.

Arthur affected a plummy voice. 'I thought we'd have a snifter down at the Fleet Club with Binky, Bunty and …'

Danny's laughter drowned out the final name which concluded his coarse rhyme. As they walked, they spied traders on the street. They picked up some local garb and tried it on in the street. They both looked ridiculous if the reaction of the local populace was anything to go by. They joined in the general merriment.

Their enjoyment was unforced, and full of the life they felt. They knew that soon, and for a long time, the chance to enjoy the cold, soft blueness of the water would no longer be possible. It would be replaced by the harsh glare of the sun, and the sandpaper sensation of dirty clothes on their skin.

'Are you going to Sisters Street?' asked Arthur later as they walked away from the market. His eyebrow was arched and there was a sly smile on his face. 'You might meet the love of your life.'

'We can go along for a drink. I'm not sure I want to survive the might of the Afrika Korps only to pop my clogs because of the clap.'

'It won't kill you,' pointed out Arthur.

They walked on through the streets and arrived at a crowded street. Danny read the sign in a comedy French accent.

'Rue des Soeurs. Shall we?'

'Just keep the girls off me, Danny-boy. They can't resist a man with obvious experience.'

Danny made a great show of studying his friend, head to foot.

'I'll do my best but there may be too many of them.'

They started off at a café. There was coffee and cakes. There were also some young women who came over and joined them unbidden at the table.

70

'Hello, ladies,' said Arthur with a wide grin. 'Now what might your names be?'

The first woman was a striking mixture of Moorish and French. Very pretty with dark brown hair, she sat down and put an arm lazily around Danny.

'I'm Lulu, this is Celine,' said the woman in heavily French-accented English. The other woman was older and did not seem to speak English. The only gentlemanly thing to do was to buy them a drink. Soon a bottle of wine was brought over to the table. Danny and Arthur were happy just to hear the sound of a woman's voice and they let Lulu talk.

'I came over before the war. I'm from Marseilles. I was with my fiancé. He wanted to get away from the Germans. So, we came here. The war followed us.'

'Where is he now? asked Danny. He saw Arthur's eyebrows shoot up and a faint smile appear on his lips. He found out why a moment later.

'He's behind the bar.'

Danny glanced up at a large man serving a coffee to another soldier. He ignored Arthur who was chuckling away to himself. The ladies had acquired a taste for the wine and were content to drink away at the expense of their company. When the bottle was finished, Arthur, by dint of a slight movement of his head, indicated it was time to move on.

It was early evening now. The street was alive with men weeks away from death.

'Bloody hell, there's more soldiers here than at the front,' commented Arthur.

Danny nodded but did not seem happy.

'I wonder how many of them have been out there.'

'What is it Colonel Lister calls 'em?'

'Chairborne base-wallahs.'

'Sounds about right.'

All around them they heard the piercing shrieks of Sodom behind the walls of bars and bedrooms along the street. From one bar they heard a radio playing. Danny recognised the voice of Al Bowlly.

'Let's try here.'

The two men walked towards the bar. As they did so a large Chrysler motorcar pulled up outside. Out stepped a lieutenant from their regiment. He noted the uniforms and insignia of Danny and Arthur. He grinned broadly and said, 'I hope you're not the military police.' He was joined, moments later, by another lieutenant.

'Colonel Lister asked us to keep an eye on you both, sir,' returned Danny.

'Quite right, too. I can't be trusted. Nor can Delson here,' said Lieutenant Crickmay. 'What if we buy you both a drink in return for your silence?'

'It may require a couple of drinks,' responded Arthur quick as a flash.

'Cheap at half the price, or is it double? I can never remember.'

Lieutenant Crickmay led them into the bar. He and Delson were slightly older than Danny but not much so. Crickmay was a popular member of the regiment. Slightly shorter than Danny, he was obviously smart and not just intellectually. His dapper appearance would have made him a figure of fun, mockery even, had he not been so highly regarded by the officers as well as the men. His moustache was as clipped as his accent and his clothes were well cut and made Danny feel as if he were wearing a sack. Danny decided there and then that when all this was over, he would, never again wear anything that was not well cut and stylish. He drew the line at cravats, though.

'Where are you bound for?' asked Crickmay, one eyebrow arched.

Arthur smiled. 'I'm a happily married man, sir, but there's nothing to stop young Shaw, here, giving the ladies of Cairo a treat.'

'Be careful what you get in return, old boy.'

Danny smiled and said, 'I think I'll take care of my dad here; see that he gets back in one piece. Where are you gentlemen heading?'

'We'll head on to the Sporting Club and console Mr Turner. He lost a big match on the polo field earlier. Doesn't like losing, especially if it's to Edmund.'

Danny and Arthur looked quizzically at Crickmay.

'Sorry, Captain Aston,' explained Crickmay while attracting the attention of a rather large barman to ask for their glasses to be refilled. This required no explanation, and none was offered.

Much to the surprise of both Danny and Arthur, Crickmay and Delson stayed with them for a chat. After a companiable hour spent together, Crickmay and Delson took off in the Chrysler leaving Danny and Arthur to consider their options.

'Nice chaps,' said Arthur. He nodded to the barman for more beers. 'I suppose we're all in the same boat.'

Danny smiled but was not sure if he agreed. It was different for men like Crickmay and Delson. While neither were from the upper classes, their background afforded them different opportunities. It would have been inconceivable for Danny and Arthur to sally on up to the Sporting Club and join the polo set, much as Danny would have loved to. He'd been riding horses since he was a boy. He'd even stolen rides on the horses of Cavendish Hall when they'd been left out in the fields. Old man Edmunds had nearly caught him on a couple of occasions. In fact, he'd even given him a clip round the ear a few months later at the Christmas carol concert. Danny smiled at the memory.

He thought of Bill Edmunds for a moment. He was the groundsman for Cavendish Hall. The father of Jane Cavendish. The grandfather of Sarah Cavendish. Another world, yet Jane Edmunds had made the transition from groundsman's daughter to lady of the manor. It was different for women. She was a beauty. Any man in his right mind would have given up everything to be with such a person. Would the opposite apply? Could he ever hope to be with someone like Sarah?

He thought again of Crickmay. He'd been an architecture student. Now he was lieutenant, dressed like a lord and driving around Cairo night spots in a Chrysler car. Out in the desert he was a highly regarded tank man. He'd become one of them through his own merit. Anything was possible, realised Danny.

Only death was certain.

They took a train journey back to El Alamein the next day. The mid-afternoon sun made the carriage hot, crowded and stuffy. Sitting opposite them was Lieutenant Turner. He recognised Danny and Arthur.

'Do you both have the same squadron leader?' asked Turner.

'No, sir. Major Miller is my squadron leader, sir,' replied Danny. 'Captain Aston is my platoon leader.'

'Captain Longworth for me, sir,' replied Arthur.

'Miller is a good man.'

Danny noted the shadow that had passed over Turner's features at the mention of Captain Aston. There was also the notable absence of anything good to say about the man.

'Have you spoken much with Captain Aston, Shaw?'

'No, sir, keeps himself to himself. Funnily enough I've met his brother. Older brother that is. He married the cousin of Lord Cavendish. He's the lord of the manor, so to speak, of where I come from.'

It was clear Turner had little time for Aston, so they moved on to other subjects. It was not appropriate to talk about any upcoming

74

operations, so they confined themselves to more technical chat about their vehicles.

The three-hour journey passed quickly, perhaps too quickly. This would be the last leave they would receive for many months, assuming they made it through. They arrived at the station in El Alamein. The cries of porters, beggars and sergeant-majors were the welcoming chorus for those returning from leave.

They marched from the station to the camp. Bathed in sweat and fighting the ever-present flies they joined their unsympathetic comrades at the leaguer.

'Just in time for a brew,' cackled Craig to Danny.

'Thanks,' said Danny.

'No,' said Craig, 'just in time to make me and the rest of us a brew. Go on, holiday's over. One other thing.'

'What's that?' asked Danny.

I don't want any sand in my tea, the last time ...'

The sentence went unfinished as the cackling Ulsterman was enveloped in a stranglehold by Danny and wrestled to the ground. For the moment, the war was on leave. In its place was hilarity, comradeship and a desire not to think too far ahead.

Part Two

Prelude (Sept–Nov 1941)

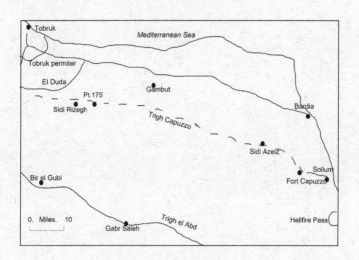

Chapter Eight

Ladenburg (nr. Heidelberg), Germany, September 1941

Peter Brehme sat trance-like in his office listening to the clock. It was the only sound in the house. Leni, the housemaid, had gone home. He was alone. A sheet of paper lay on the desk. On top of it sat a fountain pen. He stared down at the paper and thought of what to write. A tear fell onto the paper. Slowly the paper absorbed the droplet into itself, spreading into a small halo.

A wave of anger rose in him, and he smashed his fist on the table. He despised weakness and its evil co-conspirators: sentiment and pity. Yet here he sat, alone, feeling these emotions. His mind was thick with thoughts of Manfred and what he wanted to tell him. As if his boy hadn't enough to deal with.

Brehme felt the walls close in around him. He could hardly breathe with the pain he felt, and it surprised him. Was he not free? Free from what? In the next room was a coffin. Renata Brehme lay there. His wife of thirty years was dead. The tears fell freely now. The disease that had claimed her mind over the last couple of years had finally claimed the rest of her now.

Freedom felt like a cage from which escape was impossible. Moments later he was on his feet and heading towards the front door. He forgot to put a coat on yet barely noticed the chill of the night air. His mind spun around so much he hardly knew where he was walking. Passers-by acknowledged him but he marched on, oblivious to their salutations.

The Platz was mostly empty. A few soldiers on leave, perhaps, and some older couples walking their dog. Around him he saw shops boarded up. The names on the shops, Jewish names, told a story that Brehme did not want to think about. Instead, he shut his mind to the obscene truth occurring all over the country. He could do nothing to stop it. Gone were people he had once considered friends. He hoped they'd made it to Britain, but he knew, deep down, many had not. The whispers of their fate were growing louder. He tried to close his mind to the sound of their cries for help and hated himself for doing so. The anger was with him again. Why should he take upon himself the sins of others? He, and everyone around him were suffering in their own way. He marched on, eyes straight ahead towards a house from which all joy, love and humanity had been excised and replaced by misery.

Leaves fell like tears over the grave of Renata Brehme. Aside from Peter Brehme and the minister, only Manfred's friend Erich and his family were in attendance, along with the town mayor, Stefan Lerner, his wife, Marita, and the ever-faithful Leni. Renata had lost all ties with the people of the town in the last few years. She'd changed so much in that time.

Brehme nodded in gratitude to them as they stood graveside and watched the coffin lowered into the ground. Rain drizzled gently onto Brehme's hat and dripped slowly down. He was dressed in civilian clothing rather than his uniform. There were enough damn uniforms about the place. Martinets the lot of them.

Lerner stepped forward after the minister had finished the brief service of interment. He looked sympathetically at his old friend and shook hands. There was nothing that could be said, but he said it anyway.

'I'm sorry, my friend. It was too soon, yet not soon enough. It's a terrible illness.'

Brehme nodded mutely. He attempted a smile, but it died on his lips.

'If you need anything, Peter, you know that Marita and I are here.'

'I know, Stefan. Thank you for coming.'

Gerd Sammer stepped forward as the Lerners departed. By no means would Brehme have thought of the Sammer family as friends. However, the boy was a friend of Manfred. He shook hands with Gerd Sammer. Then Sammer's wife, Angela, kissed him on both cheeks. The usual sentiments were exchanged and forgotten seconds later. Erich Sammer stepped forward. Like Manfred, he was a young man, serving his country, serving the Reich. A young man to be proud of, thought Brehme bitterly. He looked at Erich and hoped the dislike on his face was not obvious. He was here; that was something. Brehme accepted that he should show some gratitude. In truth, he was appalled. The black uniform the boy had worn specially to the funeral, the false sentiment, the hypocrisy of sympathy.

'Thank you for coming, Erich. Manfred will appreciate that you thought of us.'

'Of course, sir. Please accept my condolences for your loss.'

Brehme nodded. Erich was still shaking his hand. It occurred to Brehme that the hateful child was probably expecting him to say something else.

'You are well?' asked Brehme after a few moments.

'Very well, sir, I'm going to be married this time next year.'

This time next year? You may not be alive then son, thought Brehme. Then he realised that this was both unkind and unlikely. The boy had managed to avoid getting his hands dirty so far. Brehme didn't doubt he'd find a way of shirking the rest of the war. Oddly, Brehme admired him for this. As unspeakable as he and the rest of the family were, at least he'd had the sense to figure out a way to avoid the fighting. Had he, Brehme, not done the same twenty-five years earlier?

'Congratulations, Erich. Who is the lucky girl?'

'Anja Mayer, sir.'

The name meant little to Brehme beyond the suspicion that she was the daughter of the Nazi oaf who'd probably talked Manfred into volunteering. You'll make a perfect pair thought Brehme. He heard Erich say something about telling Manfred the good news, but he'd stopped listening.

The Sammer family departed, leaving only Brehme, Leni and the minister. Then, citing the coldness of the morning, the minister left, followed soon by the tearful Leni. Brehme stood and watched the grave digger fill in the hole. A wooden cross sat at the head of the grave. Renata Brehme, born July 23rd, 1893. Died September 7th, 1941.

He wasn't sure how long he stayed. Half an hour, an hour, it mattered not. Slowly Brehme trooped back to the house. Leni was there and had prepared a feast of food for anyone who might have returned from the burial. Brehme looked down at the banquet on the table. His stomach was empty, yet he felt no hunger. There was so much food. They both stood and looked at the table to the sound of a ticking clock. Leni's face reddened as she caught Brehme's eye.

'I'm not sure I shall be able to eat all of this, Leni. Why don't you take some of it back for your family?'

Leni nodded and watched Brehme leave the dining room. She heard the sound of his office door closing, echoing around the empty stillness of the house. Brehme made no attempt to hide his sobbing. Leni stood transfixed by the sound. It was like an animal in pain. She felt tears begin to sting her eyes but not from any sense of sympathy for Brehme. It was fear, an overwhelming sense of foreboding at seeing a man she had always revered for his strength so lost now. What would become of him she wondered? What would become of them all?

Brehme sat at his desk. He stared down at the blank sheet of paper. It had to be done. He dipped the pen into the inkwell and began to write in slow deliberate strokes. The letter would not be long this time. When it came to these matters, he believed in being direct. His upbringing, his profession, his approach to fatherhood had been built on simple, compelling ideas of right and wrong, good and bad. The space between his emotions and his capacity to articulate them was too great, even on paper.

He scratched out a letter, blotted it then held it up to read. With a sigh he realised it communicated little to his son of what he was feeling. The facts were there, unvarnished by sentiment, shorn of emotion. Perhaps this was for the best. Manfred was a bright boy. He knew his mother was ill. He would see it for what it was: a sad, perhaps tragically early end to a life that had already served a purpose.

The words began to blur. He could no longer see them clearly. Meaning was lost except in the tears that fell. He wiped his eyes and realised that death was all around. It was happening now in Germany: the bombing, the disappearance of the Jews. It was happening in North Africa, England.

Renata Brehme's death was but one more sad event in a world where loss was inevitable, hope extinguished and sorrow unrelenting.

Brehme didn't expect people to care. Even Manfred, separated as he was by distance, would not feel the same sense of grief. The regret, the pain, the sense of guilt would be Brehme's alone.

He folded the letter and slipped it into an envelope. A few minutes later he was outside the house and walking into town to make the post. He felt the wind turn the rain in towards his face. Silently, he made his way along the street, ignoring the people ignoring him.

Chapter Nine

Bir Thiba, Egypt, 18th September 1941

At 0730, the squadron broke leaguer. Thirty-eight tanks set off west in the direction of Thalatia. Danny asked where exactly Thalatia was. It met with an amused response from Reed. The sergeant pointed to the tanks in front and on their left.

'Who do you see out front?'

'That's Captain Longworth's A Squadron, sarge,' replied Danny, his heart sinking as he suspected everyone in the tank was listening to the exchange.

'Very good, Shaw,' replied Reed. Even the strained rumble of the engine, the sound of sand and rock crumbling under the tracks seemed to quieten for a moment as they waited for Reed to respond.

'Well go and ask him where Thalatia is because I don't bloody know.' Reed handed the microphone to Danny.

The crew erupted into laughter, none louder than Danny. A quick glance round the tank confirmed no one had heard of their destination. It was just another name. Many of these names would develop an entirely new and deeper significance in the future. For now the geography of Danny's new home was still an ongoing discovery.

'Hey, Craig, have you ever been to Their Labia?' asked Danny.

Craig shot Danny a look but there was a broad grin on his face.

'Many times, son. More than I can remember. I didn't stay long mind you. Flying visit so to speak.'

The tank rocked to more than just the bumps on the track.

'I'm sure the place will be delighted to have you back.'

'I'm always welcome,' said Craig with a wink. 'As a matter of fact, it's called Thalatia dummy. Not many know this, but it was home to several Pharaohs; Ramses lived there.'

'Ramses?' asked Danny, affecting a public-school accent. 'Is he of the Hertfordshire Boggy Bottom Ramses?'

'No, you're thinking of Tutankhamun's cousin,' replied Craig.

'What was his name again?' asked Danny, stroking his chin in thought.

'Neville.'

'That's right. He played right back for Bury before the war.'

'Have you two finished?' asked Reed although there was a smile on his face as he said it. Craig rolled his eyes and Holmes smirked at the ticking off.

Danny returned his gaze to the periscope and looked around him. It was quite a sight. The whole squadron was on the move. They were in an arrowhead formation. Danny's tank was part of the B Squadron led by Major Miller. They were on the right of the trident with Captain Longworth's A Squadron at the point and C Squadron, led by Major Laing, to the left. The tanks were twenty-five yards apart and travelling at twelve miles per hour. Visibility was good as the hard surface stopped much sand flying up. Danny could see that all of the tanks were hatches open with all of the individual commanders visible.

'There's something about the way army life strips you of your dignity,' said Arthur. 'You lose a sense of yourself. There are no individuals. Just a collective. I no longer exist. I'm just part of one big, impersonal machine.'

'Really? What makes you say that?' asked Danny.

Arthur zipped up his flies. Moments later, Danny zipped up his flies, too. There were around thirty men, standing in a line facing away from the tanks, likewise engaged in a similarly natural function.

'Just a feeling, son. Just a feeling.'

They strolled back in the direction of the vehicles.

Overhead the sky was cerulean blue. A few clouds lolled around lazily looking for shade. It was not a day for hard graft. Danny was transfixed by the sky. It seemed so vast, so blue, so clear.

'Difficult to credit it's September.'

Sweat was trickling down his forehead and heat bounced off the hard sand making it seem like they were standing by an open oven. Danny followed the single cloud, observing its slowly silent progress into the distance. A dark spot appeared to the left of the cloud. It was barely visible, but it was a break in the blue.

'What's that?' asked Danny but the shouts were already coming from the leaguered tanks forty yards away.

'Bloody hell,' said Arthur and grabbed Danny's arm. The two men began to run.

'Not so fast, Danny-boy,' shouted Arthur.

'What?' shouted Danny, who was a few yards ahead of Arthur.

'I need cover,' laughed Arthur.

Danny's suitably pithy response was lost in the sounds of shouting in the leaguer. Hundreds of eyes were now glued to the western sky as the speck grew larger. The sound and the shape of the plane became apparent. It was a Junker Ju 88. A fighter-bomber. Fast and mobile, it was a constant threat in the North African campaign.

Panic rising, Danny realised he wouldn't reach the tanks before the Ju 88 made its first pass. The sound of the aircraft's engines was no longer a buzz. It was a roar. The plane was now diving over the tank squadron. Men scrambled for cover. Others clambered onto the turrets to man the machine guns. Machine guns began to chatter overhead. The Ju 88's guns sent a stream of rounds that tore the air asunder.

Danny hit the ground and felt the ground rock as Arthur dived down beside him with his hands over his head.

'Can't even take a quiet leak these days,' complained the Londoner.

The machine guns mounted on the tanks only had a two second window to hit the target. The Ju 88 passed overhead and into the distance. Danny rose, pulling Arthur up with him. All around him, other men who had been relieving themselves did likewise and were soon running towards the relative safety of the tanks.

They reached the tanks just as the Ju 88 was banking. The squadron held its collective breath. Then, with a sense of relief, they saw the aircraft heading away. The German pilot was no more up for a fight than they were. What was the point? He couldn't stop the convoy and he was risking his life and, more importantly as far as his commanders were concerned, the aircraft, in a futile gesture.

What he had done was empty a part of his magazine. He'd be able to brag about it to his fellow pilots back at the airfield. Tanks were spotted. Tanks were engaged. Yes, I will have another tot of brandy, Heinrich. Thanks, old chap.

Danny arrived back at his tank as Major Miller came past with Captain Aston.

'Anybody hurt?' asked the captain in a manner that suggested that not only did he not care but it was probably your own damn fault. Even Miller looked at him with a degree of surprise.

Reed glanced at Danny before confirming there were no casualties. The two officers continued to the next group of men. Moments later Holmes spoke.

'Right, I'm off.'

He started heading in the direction of the open-air latrine.

'Feeling a bit nervous, then, Holmesy,' shouted Craig.

Holmes did not reply. His riposte was confined to a hand gesture that suggested Craig should focus his attention closer to home.

An hour later Captain Aston swung by. He was smoking a cheroot. Like many of the officers, he was wearing corduroy trousers, suede boots and a colourful paisley cravat. Standard uniform requirements in the desert were a little more relaxed than Danny had expected. Aston seemed to take a particular pride in flouting what little regulation was imposed in desert dress.

Reed immediately stood to attention, but Danny sensed a wariness in him also.

'At ease,' drawled Aston, still holding the cheroot in his mouth. Finally, he removed it and flicked some ash away before replacing it.

'You'll no doubt be as delighted as I am to hear that we have to do some patrols in the area. The 7th Hussars are due to make contact tomorrow. We have to make sure that Jerry hasn't got any nasty surprises lying in wait.'

'When do we leave, sir?' asked Reed.

'Are you filled up?'

'Yes, sir.'

'We leave in ten minutes.'

Thanks for the warning, thought Danny. The look on Reed's face was stony rage. The sergeant didn't have to say anything. The crew were clearing up and had packed away their cooking utensils. Three minutes later, they were inside the tank with Craig and Felton cranking their twenty-tonne home into action.

The engine started just as Reed heard over his radio the order from Miller.

'Drivers advance.'

Twenty-four hours later, B Squadron linked with the 7th Hussars and led them to the leaguer occupied by 6th RTR. Danny watched as Lieutenant Colonel Lister came out to greet his counterpart from the Hussars, Lieutenant Colonel Byass. They and the other senior officers immediately made for Lister's tent to escape the violence of the afternoon sun unleavened by any breeze.

The arrival of the Hussars also brought some welcome news in the form of mail from the outside world. They were brought round by one of the more colourful characters in the regiment, Lieutenant Crickmay. The last time Danny had seen him was in Cairo. Like Captain Aston, his dress sense was as singular as his desire not to have war intrude on him enjoying life. The crews grouped round Crickmay.

'You're in luck. The Hussars managed to catch the mail plane, so we have a few weeks for you to catch up on, except you Holmes. You're even less popular at home than you are here.'

The men started laughing, even Holmes.

'Only kidding,' said Crickmay with a grin. 'Actually, I've no idea if you've had any post or not. If not, apologies, old chap. I think you're wonderful.'

Longing for news from home was insatiable. The radio provided bulletins on what was happening in Britain. The mail was the chance to hear the voices of their loved ones, albeit on paper. Sometimes this was bittersweet. Danny had heard cases of letters arriving to crewmen from family members who had been killed in the devastating attacks on the country before the letters had arrived in North Africa.

There were a couple of letters for Danny. The second one was in handwriting he didn't recognise. He ripped open his mother's letter first. Inevitably it was written, for the most part, by Kate Shaw but his father, Stan, had added a postscript. Danny scanned through the letter and, once again, marvelled at how much space his mother devoted to questions around food. Come German bullets and shells, do your worst, thought Danny but God forbid the British army should fail to feed Kate Shaw's boy well.

Stan asked no questions. He knew Danny would not be allowed to make even the most innocuous of responses. Typically of the man, the father he knew, Stan confined himself to telling Danny that he was in his thoughts and that he believed he would see him and Tom again soon. Danny found his eyes stinging as he read the simple, heartfelt feelings of a man who had buried such emotions along with his friends decades before.

There was some news of Tom. It seemed he was in Tobruk and doing well, based on their last communication from the middle of summer. No allusion was made to the failure of Operation Battleaxe, the previous attempt at relieving Tobruk which had ended in failure just as Danny arrived in North Africa.

Danny opened the second letter, curious as to who else might have written to him. He glanced at the name and the address in astonishment. The cursive handwriting flowed elegantly across the page. He scanned to the bottom and saw her name: Sarah Cavendish. His eyes widened in shock, and he felt blood rushing through his body where it fizzed in his head like champagne. The letter was dated 7th August 1941.

He stood up immediately and walked away from the others. A letter like this could not be read near other people. He wanted to be alone to savour the experience, to define it and shape it so that in years to come nothing would sully this moment in his memory.

Dear Mr Shaw,

My father and I visited your parents yesterday. We've been visiting the families of everyone who has gone out to serve. It was humbling for both myself and my father to see the extent to which our village has risen to face this terrible menace.

I asked father, when we returned to the Hall, if he would allow me to write to each of the young men who have left the village to serve. He gave his assent immediately. Yours is the last letter I have written, Mr Shaw. Or perhaps I can call you Danny, as your friends and family do?

Robert speaks of you often. I think when he is old enough Robert will want to join up, too. I hope he doesn't. I hope this ghastly war will be over and this awful man Hitler is captured and put into prison forever. My father always comments on news relating to the different places that our boys are fighting. I follow everything now to do with North Africa whether it's a newspaper or the BBC news. I'm so frightened by it all but knowing where you are and what is happening makes things a little better.

When you returned earlier this year, I felt so very proud to see you, someone who is a friend to our family and who is serving this country. I can't imagine what you are experiencing in this war. It makes me scared to think of what might happen to you, to all of you from the village. I pray every night for your safe return.

Danny read the letter over and over again. Each time his eyes would linger over the underlined words. He knew that she would have written similar words to the other boys from the village but a part of him knew, with certainty, that none had been written with such emphasis. Danny found his chest had become tighter. This time it wasn't fear. He smiled to himself and returned to the others.

Whatever the significance of the letter and, yes, a young man dared to dream, the fact remained he was on another continent, facing an enemy out to kill him. He carefully folded the letter and put it into his breast pocket a smile across his face.

Craig glanced up at him when he returned. The shrewd eyes of the Ulsterman read in an instant what Danny was thinking. He smirked briefly then returned to his own world.

Chapter Ten

Gambut (fifty kilometres east of Tobruk), Libya, September 1941

Tears rolled down Gerhardt's face. He could hardly breathe in the heat. Even the slight breeze was warm. He was now on his knees bent double. Choking. Choking with laughter.

'I don't see what's so bloody funny about it,' said Manfred. He was definitely unamused. His stomach churned and he felt the tell-tale warning signals coming from his bowels.

'You're right,' agreed Gerhardt when he'd recovered sufficiently. He clapped his hand on Manfred's and sat up again. Both faced outwards onto the Mediterranean. The sea was the colour of a blue quilt and small choppy waves danced on the low swell. The sky was yellow-green, and no cloud interrupted its splendour.

Dozens of Afrika Korps soldiers shouted and frolicked in the waves. Some hardier souls ventured further out. Manfred could not risk this. Not in his condition. Of all the days to have the symptoms of dysentery.

'Have you been taking the onion and leek soup? It really works.'

'Yes,' replied Manfred irritably. He was not angry so much at his friend as the bad luck that had incapacitated him as so many others in the regiment had been hit. He could see a few pale, drawn faces on the beach. Fellow sufferers probably.

'A couple of days, you'll see.'

'It took Kohler a week when he had it,' said Manfred sourly. He wasn't in the mood for misplaced optimism.

'But that was before the miracle qualities of the soup were discovered,' pointed out Gerhardt. This was a moot point. Another soldier had recently claimed that he'd been cured taking the soup. Word spread to the regiment doctor. Soon the leek and onion soup had replaced traditional medicine for many sufferers. 'It works. Trust me. Jurgen in my tank swears by it.'

'He's a moron.'

'True, but you don't catch dysentery because you're stupid,' retorted Manfred.

'Well, you did. I told you to avoid Bedouin food,' said Gerhardt with exaggerated self-righteousness.

'I don't know why you're laughing so much,' responded Manfred. He saw his friend raise his eyebrows in a question. 'I'm probably still contagious.'

For the first time that afternoon Manfred began to chuckle. When he saw the dawning realisation on his friend, he rolled over on his back and began to laugh uproariously. Fate is a fickle friend, however. The relaxation induced by his physical response to Gerhardt's predicament produced the inevitable reaction. No sooner had he succumbed to the breathless hysteria of the situation than he felt the warning signals. His laughter turned to a groan.

'Oh, for crying out loud,' said Manfred rising quickly to his feet.

It was Gerhardt's turn to start giggling which even the sand kicked in his face by Manfred's running feet could do little to interrupt.

'Don't forget to wash your hands,' shouted Gerhardt.

Manfred's brief reply was muffled by the sand dune he'd dived behind.

Whether through boredom or a genuine interest in mechanics, Manfred often joined Kohler as he tinkered with the engine of the Mark III. Overath looked on in approval. Two heads were certainly better than Kohler's one, albeit mechanically minded head.

'The dust and sand are a killer,' said Kohler, examining the air filter. He held it up for Manfred to see.

'Stupid place to have a war,' agreed Manfred.

'It comes up through the cylinders and pistons. Wears them out.'

'Sounds like you when you visit Madame Jo Jo's.' Kohler either didn't get the reference or was too immersed in the engine. Manfred shrugged and gave his full attention.

'Do you know the engine only lasts twelve thousand kilometres here? In Europe, you would get fifty thousand or more, easy.' He looked at the air filter again. 'This engine is only so much use. By the time it's travelled from Tripoli to Egypt the damn thing's buggered.'

A German soldier dressed as a British officer walked past the two boys. Manfred paid him scant attention and then returned his gaze to the engine.

'I wish we could get hold of some of the English uniforms. I don't know what sadist designed our uniforms and diet here. Churchill clearly cares more about his men than Hitler does.'

Kohler looked sharply at Manfred in alarm. He whispered urgently at him.

'Don't say these things, even if you're joking. You don't know who's listening.'

Around them was a mixture of dress. Some men wore shorts and went without shirts. Some men, those going out on patrol, were clad head to foot. The risk of injury inside the tank or in the highly unlikely event of contact with the enemy meant that shorts were forbidden. Cuts in the desert healed very slowly and could be infected further by flies who may have spent a lazy afternoon near the latrine.

Behind them they heard a sergeant barking orders. As it did not appear to affect them, they continued concentrating on the engine. The commotion grew louder. The two boys looked up from the engine and saw a small crowd of Afrika Korps assembling by a Mark IV. In the centre of the group was Major Gunther Fenski. Beside him was an embarrassed looking Lieutenant Basler.

'Gather round,' said the grinning head of Manfred's battalion. Manfred and Kohler strolled over towards the group. Basler, their troop leader, seemed ill at ease. He was a serious man doing serious work. He was not renowned for having much of a sense of humour. He never joined in any joking. For this reason, he was treated with some suspicion by the others even if his fighting qualities were not in question. This was about to be made manifest if Manfred's suspicions were realised.

'This regiment,' began Fenski, 'has proven itself time and time again over the last few months. The enemy was sent scurrying back to Egypt.'

This brought cheers from the men. Fenski put his arms up and grinned broadly.

'Soon we'll send them back to England, to Australia, to South Africa.'

A loud cheer erupted as Fenski's voice rose to its conclusion.

'If I had my way, you would all receive medals for your heroism, for your sacrifice, for the way you've shown what our country is made of, for showing how we, with better leaders, would have won the last war.'

Stretching things a little bit, thought Manfred, but he found himself emotionally charged all the same.

'Today we honour Lieutenant Gunther Basler, and not just because we share a name.'

Perhaps not the strongest joke but even Manfred laughed good-naturedly. Fenski removed a box from his pocket. He showed the contents to everyone. A cheer went up at the sight of the honour; Fenski took out an Iron Cross and attached it to the collar of Basler whose face had a fixed grin that said, 'end this, please'.

Immediately a round of applause broke out from the ranks. A few shouts from the men called for Basler to make a speech. This amused Manfred as everything about the lieutenant's face suggested this was the last thing he wanted to do.

'Will you say a few words?' suggested Fenski, stepping back to give Basler the limelight.

Basler gazed at the faces in front of them. Despite his reservations about the supposed background of Basler, Manfred had to admire the sudden composure he was displaying following the obvious initial discomfort.

'Thank you for this great honour, Major Fenski.'

'Strictly speaking, it is we who are thanking you, lieutenant,' replied Fenski, nobly.

This was greeted with amusement by the crowd.

Basler nodded in acknowledgement before continuing.

'There are many men who deserve this more than I do. I, in fact all of us, are here because of what they have forfeited. If I cannot thank you for this great honour, then I shall thank them. Now get back to work.'

There was a mixture of clapping and cheering from the soldiers looking on.

'I think that's an order,' added Fenski with an amused twinkle in his eye. He led the soldiers in a final round of applause before the crowd dispersed back to where they'd come from. Fenski stayed with Basler.

'You'll never make senior ranks until you learn to accept praise without shame and take credit for things you've never done, Gunther,' said Fenski with a wry look at the lieutenant.

'I just want to make it out of here in one piece, sir.'

Fenski grinned and clapped the lieutenant on the back.

'You and me both, my friend.'

Chapter Eleven

El Alamein, Egypt, September 1941

The tent flap rippled in the light wind that wafted through the camp. Lister raised his eyes from the letter on the table and looked at the movement. He hoped it was not a portent of a sandstorm. There'd been no warning, not that there ever was. He got up from the table and called over Sergeant Graves. He gave some instructions and returned to his tent.

A few minutes later Captain Aston walked in followed by Majors Warren, Miller and Laing. Other officers followed. Captains Longworth, Cuttwell, Gjemre and Ainsley; Lieutenants Turner, Crickmay, Delson and Hutton. There were not enough seats in his tent, so Lister stood up. He briefly summarised the contents of the communication which was lying open on his table.

'Any questions?'

Major Miller spoke first. Lister noted the troubled look on Miller's face.

'Cunningham? Am I right in thinking he's new to desert warfare?' The question was diplomatic even if the implication was clear.

'Well both he and General Auchinleck will be new to this sort of theatre. We all were. If he's not already here, then he'll be here soon. I know Claude Auchinleck. He's a logistics man. He won't move until he's ready, whatever the politicos might want. This is good. You don't need me to tell you we're facing superior equipment, firepower and air power. He's the right man to even things up and give us a fighting chance.'

'But as the major says, neither knows anything about desert warfare,' pointed out Aston. The cheroot was fixed to the side of his mouth. It only just masked the supercilious look that accompanied the remark.

Lister looked at his captain and felt like pointing out that if Cunningham knew little about desert warfare, then it was twice as much as Aston. He smiled instead. Aston, warming to his theme, sensed that the other officers were agreeing with him even if they felt uncomfortable about his tone.

'And he knows nothing about the men around him. Their strengths or, more likely, weaknesses.'

'Changing horses mid-race is never ideal, I agree,' responded Lister, 'but we have to work with this. Now, I propose we let the men know that they won't see much of a change initially but, trust me, once Auchinleck is good and ready we'll be on the road to Tobruk. He's indicated as much. Consider this, gentlemen, by early winter we'll have over one hundred thousand men, eight hundred tanks and close to one thousand aircraft. Rommel may match us for men and tanks but not for planes. The balance is tilting again.'

The officers nodded towards Lister and then turned to leave the tent.

'What's going on over there?' asked Arthur glancing towards a large tent in the centre of the leaguer.

Danny turned in the direction Arthur was gazing. He saw Colonel

Lister with his senior officers as well as the lieutenants emerging from the tent in a group. The colonel was holding a piece of paper. Danny turned to Arthur and shrugged.

'No one seems too excited. I don't think it means we're attacking Jerry tomorrow. We'd have had more advance warning than this.'

'You think?' said Arthur sceptically. Danny smiled, well used to his friend's amused cynicism. The two men had long since given up wondering if tomorrow would be the day that they finally shipped out to engage the enemy. They were into the third month in North Africa. The most dangerous enemy they'd faced was flies.

'What do you reckon, then?' asked Arthur.

'We'll soon find out,' suggested Danny, as he saw the men heading in their direction. Lieutenant Turner whispered something to Sergeant Reed. Seconds later the order went out asking the regiment to congregate in the centre of the leaguer.

Danny and Arthur strolled forward until they were with Phil Lawrence. Arthur's raised eyebrows were met with a shrug by Lawrence. He'd no idea either.

'Hope they don't cancel my holiday in the South of France,' said Arthur to Danny. 'I was looking forward to that.'

'So were the ladies of Monte Carlo.'

'I'm a happily married man, I'll have you know.'

'My point exactly,' replied Danny.

Colonel Lister waited a couple of minutes. Then, after deciding everyone was there, he started to speak.

'We've had some communication from Cairo, and I suspect it means the wait may soon be over.'

There was a loud cheer at this, and Lister waited a few moments for order to be restored.

'There are a number of items to communicate. The army in North

Africa will now be known as the Eighth Army. I suspect our enemy will still think of you as I do, the Desert Rats.'

This brought another cheer from the assembled men.

'General Wavell, after performing the remarkable feat of kicking the Italians out of Libya, will move role to Commander-in-Chief in India. Replacing him is General Sir Claude Auchinleck who will be ably assisted, I know, by General Sir Alan Cunningham.'

'Missed out again, Sir Daniel,' whispered Arthur.

'It's all political, these days,' replied Danny. 'You have to know the right people.'

'We will have more men, more tanks, more artillery. This can mean only one thing,' continued Lister. 'I can tell you that General Auchinleck has already instructed his staff to finish the plan for relieving our comrades at Tobruk and clearing Rommel and his army out of Cyrenaica.'

Amidst the cheers Arthur glanced at Danny and Phil Lawrence and asked, 'Where?'

Lawrence shrugged. Danny whispered back, 'Eastern Libya.'

'Why didn't he bloody say that, then?'

Lister seemed to have finished his announcement. He turned and went back to his tent followed by his officers.

'Did you see the look on Aston's face?' said Lawrence.

'Didn't look happy,' agreed Arthur. Looking more serious he turned to Danny. 'Watch out for him. He's a bad 'un. He's your troop commander?'

Danny nodded, but he added that he didn't agree with their assessment of the captain.

'His brother is connected to my village. He was a war hero from the last lot. I don't know why everyone has such a grudge against him. Give him a chance, I say.'

103

'Remember what Lieutenant Turner said about him, or didn't say? I'm just telling you, Danny, watch out for him. You should hear what Captain Longworth thinks about him when he's out of earshot. I don't think the others much like him.'

The late afternoon sky was beginning to turn from blue into a greyish purple. It was still hot but noticeably less vicious than it had been a few weeks previously. The flies didn't care. They tortured the men on a continuous basis.

'I hope Auchinleck and Cunningham know what they're doing,' said Lawrence. He didn't want to raise the spectre of Rommel. It was there hanging over their thoughts whenever any conversation about the leadership of the Allies arose.

Such ideas were banished in an instant when Arthur was around.

'They can put Tommy Trinder in charge for all I care. Doubt he could be any worse than the jokers we had before.'

Chapter Twelve

Gambut (fifty kilometres east of Tobruk), Libya, October 1941

'That's ...'

'Yes,' replied Overath clanking up at Manfred. 'It is.'

Erwin Rommel had just stepped out of a high-sided armoured vehicle accompanied by a number of other senior officers. Greeting Rommel was the tall slender figure of Neumann-Silkov, the commander of the 15th Panzer Division. Neumann-Silkov was around fifty years of age with a prominent nose and skin stretched tightly over his face. He saluted Rommel and two other accompanying officers. One of the officers seemed familiar.

Lieutenant General Crüwell looked like a bank manager. That was until you stared into his eyes. The hard intensity spoke of a man who knew war. Like Rommel he'd fought in the Great War. Like Rommel he'd been decorated and promoted. He was now in charge of the Afrika Korps, second in command only to Rommel.

'You know Crüwell?' asked Overath.

'I haven't had him round for dinner,' replied Manfred with a grin, for which he was rewarded with a dig in the ribs. By the time Manfred and Overath had finished this exchange the officers had already moved towards Neumann-Silkov's tent.

All around this scene, Panzer crews pretended to be working on their vehicles. In fact, they were all watching the spectacle of the most senior commanders in North Africa, together in one place.

Manfred had met Neumann-Silkov briefly on a couple of occasions. Seeing all of these men together was thrilling for Manfred and a reminder that the business of war was conducted not just on the battlefield. It could be won or lost long before the enemy was ever engaged.

With something approaching embarrassment, Manfred realised he knew little of the men he would soon face in battle, even less about their generals. The quality of Allied leadership had often been discussed when they were out on patrol. It seemed abstract now. Only in battle would it become real. Tangible. Manfred absorbed everything he could about the tactics of the enemy, the quality of their armour and the character of their soldiers.

What of the men plotting the Axis defeat? Their names, their strengths, their weaknesses were unknown to him. One thing was clear though: tactically they had been bested by the men standing not thirty metres from him now.

Manfred felt a shiver of pride. To be on the same side as men like Rommel and Crüwell was to have an undeniable advantage. They were professionals. Their knowledge of war was not just a function of experience. It was as if they understood its capricious nature, its undulating rhythm, and its brutal sense of justice.

They'd already put the enemy to flight within a matter of months of their arrival. The combination of armour and men, no, the *integration* of better-trained men and superior armour with better strategy had proved irresistible. Would the enemy learn the lessons of the summer's bitter failure?

'I'm surprised Cramer is here,' commented Overath to Kastner. Manfred listened in, as he usually did, to their conversations.

'He doesn't look well,' agreed Kastner. Manfred recognised the craggy face of the regiment's commander, Colonel Cramer. He'd been wounded during the summer when the Germans had taken Sollum, a coastal town just inside Egypt's border with Libya.

'They're planning something,' said Overath. He handed Kastner a cigarette and the two men smoked while they considered what was afoot.

'It can't be Egypt,' said Kastner after a minute or two.

Manfred certainly didn't think so but did not feel confident enough to express his opinion. Moments later he regretted this as Overath confirmed Manfred's instincts.

'Not while the Tommies hold Tobruk. We can't have them attacking our supply lines from inside Libya. Tobruk first then Egypt is my guess.'

This would have been Manfred's assessment, too, and he felt frustrated with himself that he'd said nothing. But this had always been his way, hadn't it? If Erich had been here, he'd have offered an opinion whether informed or not. Manfred thought about the paradox of the German character and its army. He'd been brought up in almost military fashion. Obedience was demanded and beaten into you. Yet the army, while expecting obedience and respect for senior officers, encouraged individual self-reliance and autonomous thought, as long as it was not to the detriment of the whole.

Within the command structure there was an implicit acceptance that plans needed to evolve from the ground up, not the top down. Officers in the midst of battle had to be prepared to adapt the plan to the situation they faced. Manfred was certain that much of the Afrika Korps' success had come not just from superior equipment and strategy but also from more tactically astute officers taking advantage of changing events.

Manfred resolved at that moment to speak up more. In training he'd felt more comfortable in leadership because he was with his peers. Since arriving in North Africa this had largely disappeared; replaced by a feeling of inferiority, not just with older men like Overath and Kastner but also with Fischer who was his age. He glanced at Fischer who was now seated, drinking coffee. The Bavarian was treated by the two senior crew members as an equal. Kohler was disregarded somewhat. They rarely sought his opinion on anything that was not mechanical.

Rommel and the other officers disappeared into a tent. As they did so, Manfred heard Lieutenant Basler barking orders at the men who had stopped what they were doing to stare like football fans at their heroes on the pitch.

'Get back to work,' roared the lieutenant angrily.

Manfred joined Gerhardt at the other side of the camp where his friend's battalion had leaguered. Gerhardt had missed the arrival of the senior command and listened avidly to the news. They agreed they would soon be required to attack and take Tobruk. It was untenable that the enemy should have a bridge head in the country, particularly one which was a harbour that could constantly resupply the enemy with men and equipment.

The perimeter established by the Allies with minefields and barbed wire put the city out of range of the Afrika Korps' eighty-eights and, furthermore, made infantry and tank attack too high risk to consider. The regular bombing attacks by the Luftwaffe were proving costly. Too many losses. At some point they would have to go in. With the end of summer, they now had a window to attack.

'I think we'll strike soon. Within a few weeks,' said Gerhardt with all of the experience and understanding that only a young man can provide when so spectacularly devoid of any evidence to support his view.

'I agree,' said Manfred, adding an additional consideration that the army couldn't just sit on its backside day after day while the Allies bolstered their defences at the target. Before long, the two friends had single-handedly won the war in North Africa and were invading Russia from the Caucasus.

'It's all so easy,' said Manfred ironically.

'I know. Quite why our leaders haven't called upon us to direct the strategy is a mystery to me.'

'Complete mystery,' agreed Manfred.

With the war won and the world set to rights, Manfred made his way back in the darkness to the others. Basler was with Overath. They looked at Manfred as he arrived back.

'Where were you?' asked Basler.

His voice was serious, but Manfred detected some amusement in his eyes. He was immediately on alert.

'Sorry, sir, I had completed my tasks and went to see my friend in the second battalion.'

Basler nodded. Overath's face was unreadable, but he didn't seem happy. This was not unusual. His waking state tended to swing between anger and irritation with not a lot in between.

'You missed meeting Generals Rommel and Crüwell.'

Manfred only just stopped himself from letting out a yell of pain. Of all the times to take a walk. There was amusement on the faces of Kastner and Fischer which needed addressing.

'I've already met General Rommel, sir,' replied Manfred perhaps a little too casually.

This stopped Basler in his tracks for he was on the point of walking away.

'Really? When?'

'I asked him if I could join the Panzer regiment, sir.'

Basler eyed Manfred closely, unsure if the young man was joking or serious. In the end he decided to give him the benefit of the doubt. Manfred seemed in earnest. If there was nothing else to say, then Basler was certainly not the man to say it. The merest hint of a nod and he was off.

Manfred sat down aware that all the eyes of the crew were on him. This gave him some satisfaction although the missed opportunity to meet such men still burned. He wondered what had been said but knew he would never ask. In all probability, Fischer would find some excuse to bring it up. They had to fill the long hours spent in a stinking hot metal cage some way. Fischer and Kastner would, no doubt, speak about the time they met Rommel. He suspected they were just as curious to know about Manfred's experience, so honours would be even.

Later that night he heard the departure of the men who had come and lit a fire in the minds of the men in the camp. By then Manfred was lying on the hard ground, shivering in the night air, alone with the events of the day processing in his mind. They were one day closer to battle. One day closer to his possible death. Yet one thought above all festered in his heart and it wasn't the missed opportunity to meet Rommel. All he could think of was a moment when he'd wanted to speak and hadn't.

It was absurd.

How could he be willing to ride in a tin can towards the murderous fire of the enemy yet feel cowed when it came to expressing an opinion? We all crave love as a cure for loneliness but, at that moment, Manfred

110

realised he craved respect more. The esteem of men such as Overath, Fischer and Basler would be a shield from the fear he was feeling.

He heard a rustle near him. It was Fischer clutching something in his hand.

'I forgot to tell you, the mail came,' said Fischer, handing Manfred a letter. Manfred held the letter up to the lamp. It was his father's handwriting. He tore open the envelope and read the first line.

Dear Manfred,
It is with regret and much sadness that I must tell you of the
passing of your mother…

Chapter Thirteen

Gabr Fatma (forty miles south of Tobruk), Libya, 18th November 1941

A light rain fell late afternoon as three squadrons, around forty tanks, accompanied by the stink of petrol, rolled to a stop. Each took up their place in a square. Gun turrets traversed into position to cover the surrounding area. Two lanes were created to allow supply trucks access to the centre.

Danny was the last out. His muscles were fighting a rear-guard action against cramp, his bones creaked like a rheumatic old man, his face dappled black by a mixture of oil and sand. Oh God, the sand! Danny had long since decided he never wanted to visit a beach again; he'd never been to the seaside. The sand seemed to infiltrate every gap in his clothing. It itched damnably.

His clothes felt soiled from the sweat that had gushed from his unwashed body in the sweltering heat of the hull. What he would have given to be able to splash in the pond back home. Just the thought of immersing in the cold clear water made him feel like weeping. Another world. Another life. Would he see it again?

Danny joined a few of the others in stretching their arms and legs.

Blood slowly returned to his limbs; circulation restarted to the outer reaches of aching bodies. He looked around at Holmes as he heard the gunner's knees crack like the two-pounder gun.

'Bloody hell,' said Danny, grinning.

Holmes shrugged. Craig guffawed and called Holmes an old man. He was thirty, give or take.

'Where are we anyway?' asked Holmes gruffly. Nervousness, too, if Danny didn't miss his guess.

It had been a long march. They were through 'the Wire', into Cyrenaica. There was no question now; they were heading towards Tobruk. At that moment, however, the middle of nowhere seemed to be the most accurate description of their location.

It was hot, despite being November. After a few hours in the tank, Danny was sweating and exhausted. The air felt stifling rather than pleasant in his lungs. Shirtless he stood, scanning the barren-burned emptiness from the cupola. The view would never make itself onto a biscuit tin. Sand, jagged rock and more hard sand broken only by the odd crevice and some dark scrub. Even a poet would have been hard pushed to ennoble the bleakness of this landscape.

Stretching could only be allowed to carry on so long. There was work to be done. Sergeant Reed had already gone to join the troop leaders. In the middle stood the two captains, Aston and Cuttwell, plus the two lieutenants, Hutton and Turner. They had made a makeshift table and were all studying a map.

'The bastards are probably lost,' said the Ulsterman, Craig. No sentence of Craig's was complete without the addition of at least one swear word. When the mood or the situation took him, he upped the rate to an impressive every second word. At this point, the combination of his thick Antrim accent and profanity made him virtually unintelligible. This was beside the point as his passionate intensity spoke volumes for the meaning that the torrent of words was failing to convey.

The meeting was taking place in the middle of a hum of activity, coughing engines, and the smell of fuel. Everyone, Danny included, was immersed in their own jobs. Every part of the vehicle needed to be checked. Fuel, oil, wheels, guns and water. The daily examination of their tank was a never-ending task. Keeping it mobile was everything. It had to be ready the moment it was called into action. And one thing was certain: each passing hour brought contact with the enemy closer. The big push was imminent. A movement this size could not go undetected by the Axis forces. The money among the men was on an attack tomorrow. A fatalistic dread swept through Danny. Accompanying it was a sense that whatever happened tomorrow or the day after, it wouldn't be him. He would survive.

A few trucks from the echelon arrived containing supplies. Danny, Holmes and Felton were dispatched to fill the jerricans with water. There were around forty cans to load which was close to two hundred gallons of water. The tank drank it as fast as the men. All around them, the leaguer echoed to the dull thud of the cans being strapped onto every inch of spare space they could find.

An hour later, or was it two, they had finished. Danny noticed Arthur directly across from him. He strolled over to join him.

'Finished?'

'Yes. You?'

Arthur motioned with his head, and they wandered outside the leaguer. The sky was still blue but there was a layer of mauve that would soon take over. A few of the other men had the same idea, and groups had escaped the leaguer to light up, stretch their legs or avoid any more work. No one begrudged the men a break. They were joined by Phil Lawrence.

The three men strolled along the perimeter of the garrison. Two months of eating bully beef had slimmed Arthur's stockier frame to a degree he'd not known since his early twenties. This was something he reminded people about often. That he did so not with pride but with an almost visceral loathing for the food he had to eat provided some light relief from the tedium of the diet. His views on the V cigarettes were no more glowing.

'It tastes like camel diarrhoea,' was Arthur's expert view. Danny had tried these notorious cigarettes as almost everyone else seemed to smoke. He abandoned the project early. It was difficult to disagree with Arthur's assessment. Lawrence didn't seem to mind them much.

'An acquired taste,' he admitted.

'D'you think this is it?' asked Danny. The two men sat down and gazed out across an empty, alien landscape.

'You in a rush?'

'Only to go home.'

Arthur nodded and dragged on the cigarette.

'Blow that bloody smoke in another direction, would you,' growled Danny. He received another waft of it from Lawrence for his trouble. Arthur cackled at this.

'It's coming all right. Captain Longworth's been on our backs for the last few days. I can see why now. It makes sense. Tobruk can't hold out forever, can it? Something has to give. If I'd been Robert Menzies, I'd be on at Churchill every day to do something.'

Danny smiled and looked at his friend.

'You're a bit out of date. Fadden's the prime minister of Australia now. He's an Arthur, you'll be glad to hear.'

'Really? There you go. Arthurs always rise to the top.'

'Whatever you say, Private Perry.'

Arthur turned to Lawrence and asked, 'What time's it, Mickey?'

115

Lawrence held up his Mickey Mouse watch and showed them.

'Time to be getting back to do Minnie then,' responded Arthur.

'You're a romantic, Arthur,' grinned Lawrence.

Break over, the three friends trooped back into the camp. The sky was mauve bleeding into a pastel orange. The shadows were succumbing to twilight. Up ahead they saw the tanks arrayed in rows at the leaguer. The crews sat alongside their vehicles in groups, some still tinkering with the engines, others with the wheels and weaponry. Nothing could be left to chance.

Danny swatted a fly from his face and pronounced it a bastard from hell. A few of its Satanic friends soon replaced it. They parted at the leaguer. Arthur's tank was at the entrance. There was no parting goodbye. Danny kept walking towards his tank with Lawrence. Then they, too, parted company.

'Lover boy is back,' greeted Holmes. Danny saw Craig look up and smile. The war of words between Danny and Holmes was a daily affair now. 'How's your boyfriend?'

'He was asking after you. You'd be in there, y' know.'

Danny paused a moment and Craig, sensing an opportunity for mischief, filled in.

'If?'

'You weren't such a c…'

Holmes was on his feet immediately before Danny could finish the thought. Danny just strolled past him, smiling. He headed towards Charlie Felton. The wireless operator was playing with the controls. Finally, he found what he wanted. A presenter's voice came through clearly.

'We have a recording of a performance by the late Al Bowlly, made a few months before his death in April during an air raid.'

The crew quietened for a moment. Then he heard a guitar being

116

plucked before the crooner launched into the song 'Goodnight Sweetheart'. Danny felt a sadness descend on him. He sat down near Felton. Moments later, Holmes and Craig sat down near him. All listened to the South African, his words floating across the airwaves: across time.

'I saw him, once,' said Holmes, as the song ended. 'Went dancing with the missus at Theatre Royal Rochdale. He was performing. She couldn't take her eyes of 'im.'

'Ugly bastard like you, I don't blame her,' said Craig. He received a none too gentle punch on the arm for his trouble.

Danny said, 'I saw him too. It must have been days before he was killed.' His voice tailed off towards the end, causing Holmes to shoot him a look.

'While you ladies are dreaming of old Al, us real men prefer our singers to be blonde,' said Craig.

'Who?' asked Danny.

'Here we go,' said Holmes.

Craig smiled knowingly and said, 'Listen to Evelyn Dall sing "My Heart Belongs to Daddy", son. It'll make a man of you.'

After they had eaten, Craig was detailed to help Danny with clearing up. Danny noticed the Ulsterman was holding a book in his hand. It went with him everywhere. He caught Danny glancing at it. It was the Bible.

'Do you have faith, son?'

It was an odd question, at that moment, especially coming from the notoriously foul-mouthed Ulsterman. The certainty by which Craig lived his life was clearly built on a solid foundation. Danny guessed he was holding it at that moment.

'I went to a Church of England chapel,' replied Danny.

'That wasn't what I was asking.'

Danny thought for a moment before replying in a manner that only a young person could do before life, war or both find a chink in the walls we build.

'I have faith in myself.'

He saw Craig smile at this, but something told him it wasn't because he thought the reply either smart of funny. The look on Craig's face would rise up in Danny's mind again and again. A portent of his own folly, his own weakness and the fears that would one day stand in mute condemnation of youthful bravado.

Craig tapped the book and responded, 'Good luck with that, son. I suspect when the shells are raining down it won't be yourself you pray to.'

Danny smiled at this. It was a fair point, unarguable, even. As he did so, he spied Sergeant Reed arriving back. He rarely seemed to stop and rest. Always on the go, checking on the men, liaising between Colonel Lister and other officers. He liked the sergeant but had hardly spoken to him about anything not related to the war. This seemed to be his way. Fair enough, thought Danny. They weren't on a holiday. None of the others were any closer to Reed than he, but all respected him. Quite simply, having someone like this in your tank could be the difference between life and death.

'Shaw?'

'Yes, sarge,' said Danny standing up.

'You're on piquet tonight.'

Danny groaned inside but nodded to the sergeant. He picked up a sub-machine gun, a pistol to sound a warning and binoculars from Reed.

Sergeant Reed turned away from Danny and hopped up onto the

hull. Rising to his feet, Danny started out towards the perimeter to the sound of the cackling laughter of Craig who was clearly happy to have dodged any bullet. Ignoring the Ulsterman, Danny walked one hundred yards out to the designated position. It was a point located diagonally from the corner of the leaguer's square. Behind him and across the way he saw other men do likewise. Four of them in all. They would form an outer cordon which would provide the first warning in case of attack. Assuming they stayed awake.

He settled down for the evening. The role of piquet was one he had done once before. Normally it was assigned to the infantry, but the tank group was, to say the least, in an advanced position.

Evening was drawing in. Danny made a point of fixing specific landmarks in his mind to mark out distance. There weren't many. A distant hill. A piece of scrub. By Danny's estimation, they would be just about visible in the moonlight.

A previous piquet had burrowed a hole that could fit Danny snugly if not very comfortably. It gave him a view of the vast emptiness ahead. He hoped it stayed that way. Although months of inactivity meant he was up for the fight, if only to bring matters to an end.

Within an hour, it was dark. The moon reflected brightly off the sand. Visibility was good. The leaguer behind him had fallen silent. It felt like it was just him, the desert and nothingness. The lack of sound was eerie. The air seemed cleaner. Colder also. He pulled the blanket around him and stared into the emptiness, acutely aware of his smallness within the immensity that was the desert.

Silence.

He glanced back at the leaguer again. It was now a black silhouette. No lights were permitted. At a push, he reckoned he could get back to the leaguer within twelve seconds. He marked his route back. Best be safe. The direct route would require him to negotiate some potholes.

Perhaps fourteen seconds back. Traversing left and then right would give him a clear route back. No twisted ankle.

Silence.

But not really. He could hear *something*. Not a tank, thankfully. Was it the blood rushing around his body? The sound of life. His life. Yet he had never realised until this moment how fragile a thing it was. Despite his liking for Reverend Simmons, he had no great expectation about the existence of an afterlife. Therefore, he reasoned, on balance, it was better he survived this lot. He couldn't bank on choirs of angels ushering his arrival into Paradise.

He thought about Craig and the comfort he drew from reading his Bible. The contradiction in the Ulsterman was a wonder to perceive. He wore a grudge on his sleeve as a matter of honour and apparently brought a religious intensity to killing the enemy. Craig barely spoke to Felton who had, when they first met, the temerity to laugh at him when he talked about God.

Danny shook his head at the memory. Some things were best left alone. He looked out into the emptiness. Hope I don't fall asleep, he thought. As soon as this idea lodged, he found himself yawning.

Silence. Emptiness. Darkness.

Danny looked at his watch.

He'd been there five minutes. Only another six hours to go.

As Danny sat at the edge of the perimeter, the officers joined one another to hear Lister outline the plan for the next morning. The new plan. They listened in silence as Lister preferred questions to come at the end. It did not require a mind reader to guess what they were thinking, and Lister fought hard to prevent his voice revealing the scepticism he felt. Major Miller spoke first. It was clear from the nods around the table he was asking the question on everyone's mind.

'Sir, we seem to have caught Jerry somewhat unawares. If General Cunningham's plan expected contact by now, does that mean this plan is defunct?'

'So, it seems. I doubt General Cunningham anticipated that our arrival would go quite so unnoticed. Alternatively, Jerry knows we are here and simply doesn't want to be drawn into a pitched battle. Brings to mind Von Moltke's dictum that no plan survives contact with the enemy. It seems this can apply equally to lack of contact also.'

This raised a few grimly amused smiles around the table.

'All because he stayed put,' drawled Aston. 'Hasn't the bugger played cricket?'

This did raise some laughs although Lister was far from amused. Perhaps if it had been Laing or Miller he might have been. Not Aston, though. Instead, Lister glared at his captain. Was he being unfair? He could hardly blame him for displaying explicit disdain for a plan that had been questioned by more senior people.

'We have to draw him out, if only to get near enough to hurt his blasted tanks and then head straight for Tobruk,' continued Lister. 'Scobie is due to start his breakout on the 21st from Tobruk.'

At that moment there did not seem to be an alternative plan. They would have to make the best of it. Lister turned to his second in command, Major Warren, and his adjutant Captain Cuttwell.

'Warren and Cuttwell will provide you with the tactical details.' There was a sorrowful tone in his voice. He could offer them nothing better.

The other officers glanced at the two men and nodded. A silence followed. A concerned silence in which only the beating of hearts could be heard by each member of the group. There was little Lister could think of to defend the original plan. If what he heard was true, even General Cunningham's generals had had their doubts about the original idea. The new plan was the old plan, one day later.

Major Warren reiterated their objective. Using his stick, he tapped the map.

'We need to capture the Sidi Rezegh airfield. It's an important Axis supply route. Capturing it will force the Luftwaffe further away from the frontier.'

'We'll be blown to hell,' said Aston grimly.

Lister and Warren both glared at Aston. Wherever the truth lay, Aston, as ever, strayed beyond the line. The right of the officers to challenge and improve on an existing plan was fine so long as it did not descend into bellyaching. Lister could not abide the latter. Aston's input was invariably negative or worse, a sneer which did not offer a better alternative in its place.

'I disagree,' said Laing. He waved his hand over the map. 'Don't forget, Jerry may not know we're here. This could be an opportunity. We have surprise on our side.'

'Exactly, Laing,' agreed Lister. It was a good point although it was now questionable whether they were in a good position to take advantage. Regretfully, he added a note of caution.

'The divisions are rather dispersed now. The 22nd is down at el Gubi, and Norrie, Gatehouse and Godwin-Austin are all to the south-east. Not quite the concentration of armour General Cunningham originally anticipated would confront the enemy.'

Warren pointed to the map and explained the terrain in more detail.

'There are three escarpments running east-west. The northerly one is the Ed Duda ridge. It overlooks the Axis bypass road and Panzer group HQ. Scobie and the 70th Division will break out from Tobruk and attack this point. The middle escarpment is situated just south of the Trigh Capuzzo. It goes as high as six hundred feet in places.

There are certain key heights we need to claim, here at point 163, overlooking the airfield on its southern side and five miles east at point 175. These are naturally defended by defiles on either side.'

'Sir,' said Turner, stepping forward and pointing to the map. 'When we take the airfield and then succeed in linking with the Tobruk sortie, will we risk Rommel driving a wedge between us at the south of the airfield? This will split the 7th Armoured Brigade and the 4th Armoured Brigade. He can then attack us in detail.'

Lister nodded grimly. Turner had hit on the key implication of the dispersal of their armour. If the original plan was questionable because it relied on the enemy playing ball and showing up for the fight it, at least, had the merit of being a concentrated Allied force. Now, the enemy could pick off the three divisions one by one, as Turner suggested, assuming they could find them. Lister had experienced enough of the fog of war to know that this was not necessarily certain.

'All the more reason why we need to hold the airfield at Sidi Rezegh and the escarpment. This will be pivotal in relieving the siege on Tobruk. I think you could say that this is going to be bloody, protracted and, I suspect, messy.'

Major Warren and Captain Cuttwell briefed the officers on the tactical details. Lister immediately motioned for Captain Aston to join him. Aston strolled over. He could see anger in the eyes of his commanding officer. It reminded him of school. All those visits to old Palmer, the headmaster. Like Palmer, Lister was stuck with him just as he was stuck with being here. He glanced back and saw Turner eyeing him. If it hadn't been for that upstart, Turner, he could have been living the life in Cairo.

Lister glared at Aston. His tone was not loud but there was no mistaking his anger.

'Take that damn cigar out of your mouth. Your comments were as unwelcome as they were unhelpful. See that it does not occur again.'

Aston responded with the half smirk that a dozen school masters would have endured before, and an equally half-hearted, 'Yes, sir.'

Lister dismissed Aston and sat in his bivouac with his pipe. He was a worried man. How much he had been able to disguise his feelings was open to question. General Cunningham's plan was dependent on the Germans attacking the British position. This should have happened by now. Instead, their guns were silent. If the enemy knew they were here, they certainly appeared to be disinclined to do anything about it.

Lister was aware that the commander of the 7th Armoured Division, General Norrie, had concerns about the original plan. Never had the British army put together such a concentration of armour. Yet the 7th, the 22nd and the 4th Armoured Brigades had all pitched up to a battle with no one intent on fighting them. The new plan was, in effect, the complete opposite of the original Crusader intention: defeat the enemy armour and relieve Tobruk. Now, all of the 7th Armoured Division was dispersed. The brigades were heading off in different directions in search of a fight.

A brooding sense of apprehension overcame Lister that something had changed in the twenty-four hours since they had left camp in Egypt. Weariness and worry weighed heavily on his heart: a feeling that they were no longer the hunter.

Chapter Fourteen

Gambut (fifty kilometres east of Tobruk), Libya, 18th November 1941

Gerhardt dragged on a cigarette before handing it over to Manfred. They were both gazing out into the blackness. Only in the desert could either of them understand the noise that silence made. The moon provided some light: a chance to peer into the distance and wonder. The two boys sat on the crest of a hill and gazed at the valley below them. It stretched miles into the distance like a blue sea broken only by bits of scrub.

'They're out there somewhere,' said Gerhardt. As he said this, he hugged himself. The mid-November nights had a real bite to them. Each was wrapped up in an overcoat with a scarf and balaclava. The additional cruel joke played by this war was that it was fought during the day when the sun was burning hot, before things suddenly turned ice cold like a house with broken central heating.

'Yes,' replied Manfred.

They looked at one another. Both hoped that no sign of fear could be detected on their faces. As yet neither felt confident enough to admit to the fear they were feeling. Only the excitement. The anticipation.

That would change. The fear would become their constant companion and the anticipation would diminish with the pain, the fatigue, and the overwhelming desire to be somewhere else.

A gentle breeze carried faint murmurs of a sea far off. They turned and strolled back to the laughter, the coughing, the cursing, and the melancholic chat of men warming their hands on small campfires.

Of late Kohler had become closer to Manfred. They were the two most junior members of the crew. The least experienced, the most likely to be picked on. Manfred as the loader held the lowest position in the hierarchy. He had no problem with this. His time would come. He was as sure of this as he was unprepared to consider any thoughts of death. The fear was always there but it never developed into full blown anxiety about his impending demise. Instead, its recurring motif was how well he would carry out his duty. Being killed was the least of his worries.

Incompetence and cowardice were his twin enemies. Both would have to be overcome. But he could only confront them in the midst of battle. Would he be found wanting? His innocence would protect him at first. The lack of experience would shield him for a while. But after that? Who knew?

A tall figure came into view, walking along the middle of the two rows of Panzers. As he passed each group, he saw fires extinguished. He arrived at Manfred's tank. It was Lieutenant Basler. He glared down at Manfred and Kohler. He didn't have to speak; Kohler was already kicking sand over the embers. He moved along without saying anything.

Manfred crawled over to a position alongside the tracks and threw himself under a blanket, still clad in his overcoat. By now he had hardened himself to hunger. He was no longer distracted by the need for food. This detachment made him feel as if he was winning the battle against his body. Other battles lay ahead. If he'd ever had it, he no longer felt a wide-eyed commitment to the cause they were fighting for. Survival and courage were his goals. Perhaps in battle he would regain the moral purpose he was losing in the ennui of waiting day after day and night after night. His feeling of discontent would only be resolved when the day came that would give him a chance to prove his courage, not just to others but to himself.

Sleep usually came quickly. It was rarely deep. The cold made sure of that. Discomfort made it a fitful night. Manfred often woke at strange hours. He fell asleep again to the sound of snoring all around him. The next morning, he would still be tired. The eyes of his comrades always told a similar story.

As it turned out, the early morning alarm was the sound of an aeroplane overhead. Manfred sat bolt upright, too much sleep in his eyes to make out the shape in the sky.

'Ours?' he asked hopefully.

Kastner looked at him and said slowly, 'You need to learn the different sounds that planes make. It might save your life. Yes, one of ours.'

Manfred nodded and listened for the next few minutes as the plane flew directly overhead and then off into the distance. He focused on the hum of the engine, committing it to memory. He ignored the amused looks of Fischer and Kohler. They could laugh all they wanted. They'd probably had to do the same.

The sky was clear and blue. It was warm but nothing like the temperatures he'd endured upon arrival four months previously. This was bearable. It would have been uncivilised to have to fight in the midst of summer.

***

It was just after three in the afternoon. It was hotter inside the tank than out. The atmosphere in the cabin had the stale reek of engine fumes and the sweat of five men; the hot sweat of heat and the cold sweat of fear. It was something Manfred doubted he would ever grow accustomed to. He tried not to inhale too deeply because of the stench. They'd been travelling for over an hour and a half when a halt was called. Overath ordered Manfred and Kohler to check the fuel and the guns. Manfred sensed Overath was on edge. His sombre expression revealed so much more than words. There was only one thing that this could mean.

Manfred risked a glance towards the horizon. The haze was less intense which improved visibility. There was nothing to fear out there, hoped Manfred with the optimism of youth and inexperience. But Kastner seemed concerned. He put the binoculars halfway up to his eyes then settled down again and frowned. Overath remained tight-lipped. Manfred noticed the occasional exchanged glances. The shared understanding between the two men. The significance all too clear. Kohler came up alongside Manfred.

'I think this is it,' whispered Kohler.

'What do you mean?' replied Manfred, trying to keep his voice on a tight rein. One misplaced emphasis, a slip or a quaver would reveal too much of his nerves.

'I've been listening to the communications. The Tommies are making a bigger push than we expected along the front. They're coming for Tobruk. We've to hold them off. There are too many tanks for us to do it with the eighty-eights. We may have to go in, too, especially if they have infantry.'

Manfred nodded; he felt his stomach turn somersaults and fought hard to control the rising wave of nausea. It was interesting how much he'd wanted the chance to prove himself up until the moment arrived. Now he felt like running. Running as far away as he could. He wondered how the others felt. They knew what to expect. Hell, they even knew what to do. He was untried. Untested. But this would change now.

They started moving forward again. The set features of Fischer below and Kastner beside him required no explanation. Kohler had called this correctly. They were heading into battle.

Over the last few months everything he'd heard told him that they were in a superior vehicle. The fifty-millimetre gun was bigger, and their front armour was thicker. The Crusaders of the enemy had to get close to hurt them. Manfred felt sure it would be all right.

The tank trundled on. Despite his fear, Manfred found himself caught between exhilaration and anxiety. Oddly, the course of his fear was changing. His thoughts lay with things like the engine which sounded like it was straining, a fear that the torsion-bar suspension would break on the rough ground over which they were travelling. Every sound in the tank was a sign of something that could go wrong. He'd never thought of this before.

They reached a ridge and slowed down. Manfred noticed another exchange of looks between Kastner and Overath. Kastner glanced down at Manfred.

'Are you ready?'

Manfred nodded. His muscles tensed. For the last five months he'd trained himself and his muscles to load, load and load again quickly, efficiently and tirelessly. He was stronger and fitter as well thanks to a training regime that was initially laughed at by the rest of the crew, but they had eventually adopted also: press-ups, sit-ups. Every morning and every evening.

He was ready.

Part Three

Sidi Rezegh (Nov 19th–24th 1941)

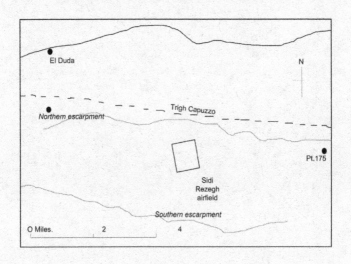

Chapter Fifteen

Gabr Fatma (forty miles south of Tobruk), Libya, 19ᵗʰ November 1941

It was just before eight in the morning. The night chill clung on a little, but daylight slowly warmed the bones of the 6ᵗʰ RTR. All around Danny engines coughed, metal clashed on metal, officers shouted orders, men cursed under their breath, arguments started, and laughter erupted like lava from a volcano. Reed called Danny over.

'Ammunition?'

'Checked.'

'Food?'

'Two days.'

'Water?'

The checks continued until Reed was satisfied. Felton gave Reed the thumbs up that he had contact with the other tanks on the wireless. They were ready to go. Craig joined Felton down in the hull. The engine spluttered bronchially to life. At the signal from Colonel Lister, the tanks set off in formation. They made a wide crescent with four hundred yards between each troop comprising three tanks. Lister's squadron headquarters moved in the centre about five hundred yards behind the centre troop. Overall, the formation covered nearly three miles which ensured good visibility of the front and the flanks.

In all, there were three squadrons of nine tanks and the four tanks of Lister's headquarters. Reed sat with his head and torso outside the cupola. Danny's view of the world was a good deal more limited. He confined himself to a view of the desert using the periscope.

Around midday they set off from Gabr Fatma at a stately twelve miles per hour with C squadron leading and Danny's B Squadron on the left followed by armoured cars and lorries. A little sand flew up in the air as the tracks crunched over the thick crust of the rough-cast desert.

The journey to the Sidi Rezegh airfield progressed without any contact with the enemy. They approached the southern escarpment through a valley. Progress was hampered by the soft ground caused by overnight rain.

'I thought this was supposed to be the desert,' complained Craig, 'not a bloody swamp.'

By early afternoon the sun was beating down on the metal relentlessly, and the tank felt oven hot. They had been on the road for nearly two hours; conversation had long since dried up. Whether through nerves, bravado or boredom, Danny decided enough was enough. He called up to Reed.

'Water?'

'No thanks,' said Reed.

'I meant for me, sarge,' replied Danny. He received a gentle kick from the sergeant whose shoulders he could see shaking.

'Cheeky git. Keep your eyes peeled.'

'I am, sir. I've spotted a bit of sand ahead. Have you seen it too?'

Danny received another kick for his trouble, but he didn't mind. It relieved a little of the tension that had been building inside the tank since they'd left. A whisper of excitement clung to the gasoline-filled air. Fear and adrenaline were building inside Danny.

'When do you think we'll finally meet Jerry, sarge?' shouted Danny up to Reed.

'Why are you so keen?'

'The bullets will be a lot less painful than these kicks, sir.' Danny successfully dodged the next kick from Reed, but Holmes punched him on the arm.

'Got him, sarge,' shouted up Holmes.

Reed guffawed before shouting, 'Carry on.'

Despite the distance between the vehicles, the soft sand being thrown up by the tank ahead meant that everyone was caked with dust inside the hull. It made for an uncomfortable companion to the heat and the smell of fuel. Two hours after setting off they took a break. All the men clambered weary-limbed from their vehicles.

'Brew up and be quick about it,' ordered Reed.

Danny hopped down from the top of the hull and brewed up some tea for the rest of the men. All around him, he saw men from the other tanks doing the same. Their movements were like a dance troupe. The operation was highly choreographed to ensure that tea was made as quickly and efficiently as possible.

Danny started the fire while Felton put the brew can on top. It took nearly ten minutes before the tea was ready. Biscuits were shared out. The break was no more than twenty minutes. In this time, they had to make and consume the tea, take care of any natural functions, and then kick over all traces of their stop before returning to the safety of the metal hulk and trundling off once more.

'Feel better?' asked Felton as they moved away slowly.

'Wonderful,' laughed Danny but his senses were alert for the menace

135

that lay waiting ahead. They bumped and rolled along the rocky, undulating road and soon everyone was miserable again.

Captain Aston looked at the procession with a wearied eye. He spoke into his microphone.

'I'm surprised we didn't take out a billboard in Piccadilly Circus to advertise our movements.'

The men below laughed. They enjoyed Aston's laconic, semi-rebellious humour.

'Want me to fire a few shells to announce to Jerry that we're on our way?'

'That's the spirit, Stone. Let the world know.'

Aston glanced to his left and saw that Lieutenant Turner was now running parallel with him. He gave a mock wave salute which Turner ignored. This amused Aston for some reason and put him in finer fettle than he might otherwise have been. Winding up the pious little pup always had that effect on him. It took his mind off his quaking innards.

Aston glanced along the line, left and right. Thirty odd tanks looked impressive, but he doubted how daunting the enemy would find it. They had hundreds of better made, more deadly Panzers waiting for them. It was enough to make a man sob. He listened to the Crusader labouring through the rain-softened ground and swore with feeling.

As he did so, he heard Lister's voice come over the radio. For a moment panic swept through him as he wondered if his profanities had been broadcast to everyone.

'Hello, Lister calling. Just heard confirmation that the 22nd encountering enemy force of guns at el Gubi. Heavy losses. The South Africans are in cars just ahead of you. They've had no contact with the enemy.'

'Bloody hell,' said Aston off microphone. 'That's the Italians, isn't it? How can they not beat them?'

'C Squadron will lead the advance,' continued Lister.

Major Laing confirmed reception of the order. Then Major Miller spoke to his B Squadron.

'Aston, Turner. You'll follow Squadron C, leading the advance of B Squadron on the left.'

'You heard,' said Aston. 'The fathead wants us out in front. Meanwhile he surrounds himself with a nice screen of armour. Next life I want to be a general. At least Turner will be alongside us. I'll let him lead.'

'Quite right, sir,' shouted the gunner, Wilson, from just below.

'This is it, chaps. You'll be in action soon,' said Aston, trying to control the quaver in his voice. He cursed Lieutenant Turner again. Had it not been for this petal he'd be behind a desk or, better still, with some lucky young wife in Cairo. He banged the turret, but not too hard.

Lieutenant Turner listened to the orders from Miller. Satisfaction glinted in the young lieutenant's eyes. He glanced over at Aston and grinned. He suspected that the captain would be none too pleased about leading the formation. This was comforting. He looked down at his gunner, Bill Wheeler.

'You heard that, boys.'

The two men nodded.

'They're out there. This time it's not a drill. We'll be engaging the enemy for real.'

'You'd have thought we'd have encountered someone by now,' shouted Wheeler. 'What's at Sidi Rezegh?'

'Sidi Rezegh is one of the enemy's airfields. If we can capture

137

it then it gives us a great platform to relieve the boys at Tobruk. Expect contact at the airfield,' replied Turner before adding, 'soon.' He looked at his watch. It was just before four in the afternoon. Very soon, thought Turner. He looked down at his finger. It was tapping impatiently on the metal. Or perhaps it was nerves. A quick glance down at his men revealed they, too, were fidgeting in different ways: stretching, scratching, yawning in Wheeler's case.

'Keeping you up, Wheeler?'

'Sorry, sir, it's the fumes.'

Danny's stomach felt as if a flutter of butterflies were mid-riot. There was a low rumble in the air now. Fighting was taking place somewhere in the distance. Each crew member shared that extraordinary feeling that only men in war can understand: that sense of fear and expectation as you wait for the enemy fire to strike.

The air seemed to evacuate the metal cabin. Danny felt his skin prickle in the heat. He glanced down at Felton. His knee was moving like a jackhammer. They exchanged glances. His eyes were bulging with fear as the sound grew louder over the whine of the engine.

At least it wasn't just him.

Soon the regiment had visibility of the Sidi Rezegh airfield. It lay in the valley just beyond the southern escarpment. Danny could see a few dozen aircraft. Incredibly they were all still on the ground. What were they doing? Just ahead he saw armoured cars racing towards the airfield. Whatever they were doing or whatever they wanted to do it was going to be too late.

'Reed here, we're over the escarpment and moving down the hill towards the south of the Sidi Rezegh airfield. We've encountered no tanks or anti-tank fire. I can see aircraft on the ground ahead.'

A few others called in and it was clear the squadron was now in the home straight. Ahead lay the prize. Surprise had been complete. There had been no reaction from the Axis troops stationed at the airfield.

Captain Arthur Crickmay watched the scene, three miles away, from the top of the escarpment. He was acting as crewman for Brigadier George Davy, the brigade commander. The sight of the tanks rushing down towards the airfield was breathtaking. Davy held binoculars up to his eyes and tracked from the Allied attack across the valley to the airfield.

'Looks like the Italians have woken up at last,' said Davy.

Crickmay swung around to check. In the distance he could see a few men running to the aircraft. Shifting his binoculars to the right, he saw the armoured cars screaming down the hill towards the airfield at close to fifty miles per hour.

'I see what you mean, sir. Bit late in the day, methinks.'

Davy put the microphone to his lips. The cavalry commander uttered one word.

'Gallop.'

Danny's heart was churning in his chest. Their tank was zipping along full pelt towards the airfield. He gazed through the periscope at the ground ahead. There was no response from the enemy. It seemed too good to be true.

'Ground better, making good progress over it,' said Reed over the microphone; then he saw them. 'Bloody hell.'

'Reed, what's happening? Do you see planes taking off?' It was Lister. An air attack might spell trouble for the armoured cars.

'Three aircraft, sir, taking off,' replied Reed.

'Confirmed, three Italian G.50s, sir,' said Turner.

'Only three?' said Lister, unable to hide the astonishment in his voice. 'What on earth are they playing at? Is this a trap?'

Then the guns started. Within seconds they could hear explosions around them. Danny winced as one shell exploded nearby. He quickly glanced around him, but no one seemed to have noticed his reaction.

Reed spoke on the microphone.

'Looks like the Italians have woken up. Traverse right and get ready to fire. We need to destroy those enemy aircraft on the ground and any guns.'

Danny heard the buzz of the planes as they approached. Fear and excitement gripped him. His muscles tensed. Then Holmes gave him a nod. Danny loaded a shell. He saw Holmes adjusting the aim.

'Gunner, open fire and keep firing until I tell you to stop,' ordered Reed urgently.

The howl of the G50s grew louder. Then he heard machine gun fire. The G50s opened up on the tanks. Bullets pinged off the armour like flies off a rhino.

Danny loaded another shell and then another and then another. The gun was belching shells as fast as Danny could load them. Outside he could hear the howl of the G50s and the rattle of machine gun fire.

Reed ducked into the turret and pointed to Danny.

'There's enough of us shooting at the airfield. Doesn't look like there are any other planes coming. Shaw, do you fancy taking a pot shot at the Italians? It's time you were blooded.'

'Yes, sir,' said Danny. All fear was gone. He accepted whatever fate had decided for him. He moved up through the cupola into the open air. The planes had done their first dive; Danny eyed them to see if they were coming back for more.

Danny grabbed hold of the Crusader's machine gun and made ready to fire. The distant buzz grew louder until the whine of the

G50s sent tremors along the ground, through the tank and up into Danny's arms. Or perhaps it was terror.

The low-wing single engine G50 was like a squat version of the RAF's more elegantly designed Spitfire. Danny watched them as they banked and shaped to make another pass.

Danny kept his eyes fixed on them while trying to shut the waling sound of their engine. He waited until they were fifty yards away. By now bullets were flying all around him. The three planes were not directly overhead, but they were flying exceptionally low. Had there been time, he might have admired the bravery of the Italian pilots. But it's difficult to admire something you desperately need to kill.

Danny pressed the trigger on the machine gun. A short sharp burst at the lead plane. He stopped quickly lest he run through all the bullets. He was sure he had hit the plane, but they reacted like they'd been stung by a wasp. Danny swung around ready for the next dive from the Italians. In the distance he could see them banking.

They came back. The first plane strafed the tanks and the armoured cars below. Danny fired off another short burst but as quickly as they'd come, they were gone. This time they were heading away from the airfield. The Italian pilots had, not unreasonably, weighed their odds of success against the desire to avoid capture and the destruction of valuable aircraft.

'They're gone, sir,' called Danny.

Reed immediately replaced Danny on top and radioed the colonel.

'Hello, Reed here. G50s have gone. None destroyed. No tanks or armoured cars destroyed.'

Lister ordered the regiment forward towards the airfield. Was it really possible they'd caught the enemy by surprise? It seemed too good to be true.

'You heard,' shouted Reed into his microphone. 'Let's keep going.'

The squadrons moved forward towards the airfield in what seemed like an air of unreality. At any moment they expected to see the enemy appear to bar their way. Yet every yard advanced brought no sign of any response. Danny glanced towards Holmes.

'Shouldn't we be getting bombed now?'

Holmes shrugged and replied, 'Don't complain, sonny boy. It'll come, trust me.'

Soon the squadron arrived at the airfield and saw around twenty planes sitting on the ground. Reed looked around, unable to believe his eyes. It had all been so easy. He heard Captain Aston radio in that they had taken the airfield, which seemed to him premature. Reed smiled grimly. Typical of Aston to impart this news. He was clearly aiming to be associated with the success.

'Well done, Aston. Await instruction. Over,' replied Lister.

With each passing minute it appeared that they had taken the airfield. A number of Italians appeared to be surrendering. Danny remained in the tank for the next few minutes wondering what the hell was going on. Finally, he heard Aston's voice on the wireless.

'Eighty prisoners, that is eight zero prisoners, nineteen aircraft, one nine, confirmed captured. Various transport. Over.'

'Hello all stations,' replied Lister. 'Any undamaged aircraft are to be demolished. Don't waste ammo on them, is this clear? Stay put at the airfield until further notice.'

Danny looked up at Reed.

'How do we destroy the aircraft, sarge?'

Craig let out a loud whoop of joy. Danny glanced down, a smile on his face.

'Do your worst, Craig,' said Reed with a grin.

The tank jolted forward, heading straight for the tail of one of the planes. Danny's smile widened as he saw what the Ulsterman intended.

'You're a vandal, Craig,' shouted Danny.

'I know,' shouted Craig exultantly. The whole crew laughed as the wheels crunched over the tail wings, helped by an infantry man balancing on the plane, pushing the back down.

Soon others were joining in the destructive mayhem. The wireless was full of cheering as, one by one, the G50s were destroyed. Danny caught sight of the pilots looking on in dismay.

It felt good.

A few hours later, Danny sat with his crew mates huddled around a fire eating a bully beef stew. It was night and they were all in a good mood. They'd accomplished the task they had set out to do and captured the airfield. Danny noted that Reed did not share the exultant mood of the group. This suggested he did not consider the task finished. Rather than join in with the good-natured ribbing that was taking place, Danny withdrew, taking his cue from Reed. He went in search of Arthur and Phil.

Arthur saw Danny first.

'So, you've won the war, then, I see,' shouted Danny when he spotted his friends.

Danny allowed himself a smile. Arthur continued. 'Had to happen. First sign of Daniel Shaw, esquire, the whole of the Afrika Korps collapses.'

They were joined a few moments later by Phil Lawrence.

'So, it's over then. We can go home?' asked Arthur.

'That's about the size of it, mate,' replied Lawrence. 'Blighty here we come.'

'Did you bag any planes earlier?' asked Lawrence.

'Bag any?' exclaimed Danny. 'We started the rout.'

This was met with good-natured albeit expletive-filled scepticism by his two friends. Danny gave up trying to convince them it was his idea and they turned to a more important topic. What would happen now.

'Any idea what's going to happen tomorrow?' asked Danny motioning towards the bivouac where Colonel Lister and the other officers were gathered together.

'Planning the celebration,' said Arthur laughing.

Lawrence smiled but he was thinking along similar lines. They'd succeeded in taking an airfield. There was the small matter of relieving Tobruk and removing the Afrika Korps from Cyrenaica and the rest of Libya. Arthur fell silent as he saw his two friends looking more thoughtful.

'Well, I thought it was funny, anyway.'

In the distance they could hear the rumble of heavy machinery. A number of patrols following the capture of the airfield had revealed German positions on the other side of the northern escarpment.

Colonel Lister looked around at his officers. They had achieved their objective and he could see in their eyes a note of triumph. And why not? They'd taken the airfield with the maximum amount of surprise and the minimum of inconvenience. Yet Lister felt perturbed. When a task was so easy it felt as if something had been missed. It felt incomplete.

'I've just been speaking with Brigadier Davy. Campbell, from the 7th Support Group, will join us tomorrow. We're to hold onto the airfield tomorrow and then breakout and try to reach point 175 to the north-east of the airfield. The airfield's importance to Jerry goes beyond the ability to launch air attacks. It means he can't use the Trigh

Capuzzo ridge which effectively severs his lines of communication with his troops at Sollum and Capuzzo. He'll want it back; you can be certain of that. We need Campbell's Support Group to dislodge those outposts, then we're on the perimeter of Tobruk. I'm sure Jerry will not sit idly by and wait for us to do our worst. I think we can all hear them now.'

No one spoke for a few seconds as they listened to the distant sounds of enemy armour moving. As if to confirm what they were thinking, some small arms fire broke out from both sides.

'It sounds as if we've found the fight we were looking for, sir,' said Major Miller.

'Yes, it does,' agreed Lister. He felt it important to be sincere, though.

'Unfortunately, when Cunningham first envisaged it, I suspect he didn't think we'd be quite so dispersed. In summary, gentlemen, this could become something of a melee.'

Chapter Sixteen

Gambut (fifty miles east of Tobruk), Libya, 19ʰ November 1941

The sun rose. And then it rose a bit more. Manfred looked at it, as he did every day, with some wonder and fear. There were two armies facing one another but they had a common enemy, too. The continent of Africa seemed to be conspiring to rid itself of the combatants. Rather like Aesop's fable of the north wind and the sun, it was using its weapons in a daily blitz. The heat of the day, the freezing cold of the night, as well as the occasional sandstorms, and, of course, the flies. The omnipresent flies that tortured you every day: finding their way into the food as you were eating; gorging themselves on the dead.

The sun-beaten landscape seemed to stretch forever. Silent, remote and forbidding, it promised only pain. Not for the last time did Manfred wonder what he was doing here. What was anyone doing here? No one wanted to be here. He doubted the Tommies felt anymore disposed towards this alien location than he did. He stared out into the nothingness with unblinking concentration.

Still holding his coffee cup, he drained it for what seemed like the fifth time. It was barely 0730. A whole day stretched in front as welcoming as the parched landscape before him. The men around him didn't seem to care. They insisted that this was preferable to the gut-wrenching fear of combat. He believed them but a part of him longed for something to happen. Three months and he'd seen nothing of the enemy. It seemed both sides had tacitly agreed it was simply too hot to fight. It seemed but a short step, to Manfred, to extend the idea.

'Brehme,' shouted Sergeant Overath. 'Get ready. We're pulling out.'

'What's happening?'

'We're pulling out. Save your questions,' replied Overath.

In a matter of moments, Manfred was inside the Panzer Mark III. He joined Overath and Kastner in the turret. Kohler and Fischer sat below in the hull. Overath stared down at Manfred and checked final details before they set off.

'Fuel?'

'Full up, sir, and we have reserve loaded also.'

'Water?'

Kohler called up and confirmed he'd loaded the water and two days of food supplies.

'Ammunition? It would help if we had something to shoot with.'

'All correct, sir,' said Manfred, by now used to Overath's dry sarcasm.

Overath grunted and glanced at Kastner. Seconds later the twelve-cylinder engine growled into life. This caused an immediate rise in the smell of petrol fumes. Manfred was used to this now, but it was no more welcome. Outside the tank they heard the sound of fifty other engines revving. They sensed the movement of the tanks and then, they began to move also.

One by one they moved out: five to ten metres apart. A cloud of dust was thrown up in the wake of the moving vehicles. The speed was paralysingly slow. Less than twenty kilometres per hour. Then again, what was the rush?

Ahead of them Manfred saw armoured vehicles pulling the enormous eighty-eight-millimetre anti-tank guns. Manfred looked through his viewer and felt a surge of pride in these weapons. Originally developed by Krupp in the thirties as anti-aircraft cannons, they had become a deadly killer of tanks in the desert.

'They've no chance against these,' Kastner had said. Manfred didn't argue. They were enormous. The barrel was over six metres long. It fired shells around fifteen thousand metres. It could kill a tank at a couple of thousand metres. Best of all, the Allies had nothing like this. It was like holding a child at arm's length and watching, amused, as flailing punches failed to land anywhere nearby.

The tanks would be arrayed behind the anti-tank guns in readiness to attack the infantry. As yet the Allies were not working in the unified way that the Afrika Korps had developed. The Afrika Korps operated like multi-function units rather than as individual parts of the armed services fighting alongside, but apart from, the other services.

Overath studied the maps he'd laid out earlier. Manfred glanced at them before returning his gaze to the gun barrels glistening in the sun. Within minutes of starting, the temperature in the hull had soared to levels that Manfred would once have found unbearable. Yet it was still early morning. It would get worse. The heat, the smell of men's bodies and the fumes made for an unhealthy cocktail.

They bumped and rolled along. The discomfort caused by the movement and the stench inside the cabin told its own story of how much he'd changed, reflected Manfred. Three months ago, he would have felt motion sickness and probably gagged at the air he was forced to inhale. Now the movement was a minor irritation against the many other things he would happily have complained about. He made no complaint, of course; privations were borne stoically. No one was exempt from the brutal life they were leading.

For over two hours they drove in this unremarkable and inhospitable landscape. The minutes ticked by slowly. Inside the tank, the air was thick and stifling. It discouraged conversation very quickly. For most of the journey from the camp to their destination the tank remained silent except for occasional warning shouts by Overath to Kastner to slow down as they pulled up too close to the tank in front. Overath was sitting atop, connected to the rest of the tank via a radio.

Manfred, as the newest crew member, was loader and supported Kastner who was the gunner. Overath wanted Manfred to take over the wireless and move Kohler to loading. He felt Manfred had less accented German and was clearer. But that was for the future. Manfred was still the new boy, untested in combat. Who knew how he would react when the shells started landing? For now, he had the easiest, albeit most physically demanding, job.

Around mid-morning the tanks stopped. The tanks were positioned at the crest of a hill. They were spread out as far as Manfred could see. In front lay the guns. They all stepped out of the tank for what could only be loosely described as fresh air. Manfred knew what was coming now and was already heading towards their provisions.

'Make some coffee,' ordered Kastner. 'We may not have a chance soon.'

Manfred frowned and tried to see what Kastner could see. Nothingness. The haze on the horizon was beginning to build. By midday visibility would be poor. He looked searchingly and saw nothing. His ears tried to pick out any telltale sounds. Nothing. Absolutely nothing. Manfred felt something build inside him.

Frustration.

He sensed Kastner smiling and turned towards him. The corporal pointed to his nose and looked slyly at him. This irritated Manfred but only for a moment. He took a mouthful of coffee and returned his gaze to the horizon, hoping the stimulating effects would help him pick out something. Anything.

'I can smell them. They're out there. Trust me, son,' said Kastner by way of explanation.

This was confirmed when Overath's platoon leader came over. Lieutenant Basler, the SS commander, motioned for Overath to join him in a rapid conference with the other tank commanders. They stood out of earshot for a few minutes giving Manfred time to distribute coffee to the others.

'The British are attacking Bir el Gubi. So far the Italians seem to be holding out.'

'Makes a change,' said Kastner, sourly.

Overath smiled at his gunner and then continued. 'Yes, it looks like the Italians are beginning to learn at last.'

'They're making for Tobruk,' said Fischer with all the Aryan confidence he could muster. He disliked the way Overath and Kastner monopolised conversation on battlefield situations. Manfred looked at Fischer wryly. Good for you, he thought. He knew what Fischer was trying to do. In a few months, with a few battles under his belt, he would make his presence felt, too. He was interested in how Overath and Kastner would react.

'Rommel doesn't think so,' said Overath dismissively. 'Maybe you should get on the radio and tell him he's wrong.'

This made Kastner cackle and Fischer reddened.

'This is another attempt to relieve Tobruk,' insisted Fischer. Interesting, thought Manfred. You don't lack confidence, do you?

Much to Manfred's surprise Overath's features softened a little and then he grinned. This appeared to surprise Fischer. The usual reaction of the two senior men to Fischer's suggestions veered between patient mockery or outright irritation, especially when he was right. Which was often.

'Apparently General von Ravenstein agrees with you, Fischer.'

'What are we going to do?' pressed Fischer.

Overath stopped and pointed into the empty vastness.

'Orders are to wait here. Finish your coffee then back into the tank. I want to be ready. For what it's worth, Fischer, I think you're right. I think something is starting. If it is, we won't get much rest for quite some time.'

Fischer looked pleased with himself. This was the normal for the Bavarian. Manfred once more found himself caught between liking the fact that it was possible to make a point that was listened to and irritation that it was Fischer who had made it. On balance he felt it was time to be less resentful of him and respect his abilities instead.

It might save his life one day.

Chapter Seventeen

Sidi Rezegh Airfield, Libya, 20th November 1941

It was still dark when the shooting started. Staccato-like infantry fire came from the northern ridge. Danny was safe from bullets inside the metal hulk. This was one compensation for the endless hours suffocating in the heat and the stench of the metal cabin. The gunfire acted as the regiment's early morning wake-up call. Danny woke with a start. The others began to stir. He climbed up into the turret and looked through the cupola at the night sky.

There was a hint of light somewhere. Not even dawn. He desperately wanted to lie back and re-join the dream he'd been having. The memory of the dream was fading with every passing second. It was always this way. The only remnant was the image of a young girl with green eyes.

All around him were the sounds of the British army waking. It was not a pleasant sound. Thanks to the various incidents of gunfire during the night, all were short of sleep.

Breakfast had to be made and Danny was the man to make it. He didn't need Reed to look his way again. He was on his feet in seconds. He started a small fire in order to brew tea thinking of an old aphorism: an army marches on its stomach. Danny smiled at this. The Eighth Army marched on tea.

The crew huddled around the fire clutching their cups. Little was said. It was too early, too cold and the sound of gunfire was too sobering to allow for any idle chit chat. Instead, they watched the bully beef being cooked with a feeling somewhere between revulsion and craving. Nearly all hated the food with a passion. Yet they knew a long day faced them. A day that would probably be spent under enemy fire. Right now, nothing else was more prominent on their minds. Holmes stood up and the other men looked at him.

'I'm going to take a spade for a walk,' said Holmes and put his cup down.

Danny and the other men grinned. Good idea thought Danny. I should do likewise. The stew was ready, and Danny played mother to the rest of the men before putting on a second brew. Reed had warned them there may not be many opportunities during the rest of the day. It was still dark when they finished breakfast.

The tea had worked its magic and Danny was more awake now but no more comfortable. His clothes had scratched thin lines in his skin. Sand and sweat made for uncomfortable bedfellows. He'd not had a chance to rid himself of the desert dust the previous evening. He cursed himself bitterly for this as the day ahead was going to be bad enough without him wanting to tear his shirt off and bathe. The guns in the distance soon dampened this enthusiasm for having a good wash.

Danny looked at Craig as if to say – what do we do now? Craig looked back at him and shrugged. All along the leaguer, Danny could see fires being extinguished. There was a low murmur of chat. Everything felt on edge. Even Craig seemed to be ill at ease. Danny quickly cleared up and stored their plates and cups. He just wanted to be doing something. It took his mind off whatever was coming. And if the atmosphere was anything to go by, something was coming.

Flares and explosions lit up the sky. Danny and the others were huddled inside the tank. He felt his stomach flutter as the sounds of gunfire acted as a malevolent dawn chorus.

'Should we be doing anything?' asked Danny.

'Don't allow any gaps for a stray bullet,' replied Craig.

The shooting continued for a little while and then as quickly as it had started, it stopped. Dawn was breaking and they sat inside the tank waiting. Danny glanced at Reed who was preoccupied with looking through his periscope every few minutes. As tempted as he was to ask, Danny remained silent. Whatever he was waiting for was coming soon.

Very soon, in fact.

The guns opened up. By now Danny recognised the difference between the big eighty-eights and the basic field artillery. The crump was definitely from a big gun. There was a moment of silence and then they heard the scream of shells. They ripped into the earth around them throwing up blossoms of sand and rock that rained on the armour of the tank. Danny was thrown to the ground narrowly avoiding a jagged metal edge. Ears ringing from the noise, he climbed unsteadily to his feet only to be thrown forward by the next wave of shells.

'Bloody hell,' exclaimed Felton over the noise. 'That's an eighty-eight.'

'Bigger maybe,' said Reed, eyes glued to his periscope. His comment was lost in the sound of the raging storm swirling outside.

'What's happening?' asked Holmes, in a voice that was shaken by more than just the physical impact of the shells detonating nearby.

'Just the guns so far. They'll be coming soon. The question is if it will be artillery, tanks or infantry,' replied Reed as the tempest subsided briefly.

At eight o'clock in the morning, Reed had an answer to his question when the shooting started again.

'This is going to be a fun day,' said Holmes motioning to Danny to load the gun. Danny immediately took the shell from his lap and opened the breech. Moments later he had another shell on his lap waiting to go.

'We're not just going to sit here and wait to be hit?' asked Craig.

Reed shook his head. 'I thought we'd be moving by now. At some point we must get to the top of the ridge at the north-east of the airfield. Unless we get tanks to the top of that ridge and over the Trigh Capuzzo, we've no way of linking up with the army at Tobruk.'

'Can't do it without the infantry boys,' pronounced Craig.

'Nope,' agreed Reed.

As the morning wore on, the stalemate continued. The Germans remained dug into their position, content to shell the valley floor. Neither side could move. Each was content to offer salvo after salvo from a distance. The temperature in the hull rose with the sun. Danny was bathed in sweat and frustrated. By now he just wanted to be doing something. Sitting here providing target practice for German anti-tank guns seemed bizarre. He wasn't the only one feeling strange.

'Aren't we going to move, sarge?' shouted Craig at one point. The querulous tone, the look of dismay. They were all feeling it. Reed held his hand up. He was listening to a wireless communication. When it finished, he indicated 'no' with a cursory shake of the head.

'Our orders are to hold the airfield. Anyway, I don't like the idea of getting too close to those eight-eights or hundreds, whatever they

155

are. Brigadier Campbell is coming here. I don't know if that means we attack today or leave it until tomorrow.'

'Doesn't sound like there's any tanks out there,' responded Craig.

Reed nodded. He'd noticed that, too. It could mean they were under attack from infantry and a handful of anti-tank guns. In which case why not have a pop at them from closer in? It was a strange situation. Perhaps the brass was afraid they would be walking into a trap.

'I agree,' he responded finally. He put his earphones back on and listened to any wireless traffic to understand better what the situation was. Whatever their original plan had been, Reed strongly suspected that it was now in flames. A hail of bullets pinged off the armour.

'I spy …'

Danny ducked down as the rest of the crew descended on him armed with berets. He didn't care. He was laughing and soon the others were, too.

Danny no longer noticed the bullets. It had taken one morning's contact with the enemy to become inured. They did no damage but were a constant irritant, rather like flies at the camp; at least you could swat the flies. Here Danny was unconvinced about the damage they were doing. It seemed to him the firing from the British was desultory and from the Germans, too, if the lack of activity was anything to go by. It was as if each side was keen to keep the other honest.

By early afternoon, it was clear they were going nowhere that day. Reed confirmed as much to them when there was a lull in the firing. Danny was tasked to brew up some tea with Felton's assistance while Reed explained the situation.

'As you know, we can't dislodge our friends on the other side of the escarpment without more infantry support. My guess is we're here tonight. Tomorrow we'll probably try to take the rest of the ridge up to point 175.'

'By which time Jerry will have worked out what's going on,' pointed out Holmes sourly, 'and arranged a big party in our honour.'

Reed nodded but said nothing. He held his mug of tea up to Danny by way of thanks. The taste of the tea and biscuits could not have been sweeter to him at that moment. In civilian life the taste would probably have appalled him. Here it was a feast that he'd been craving since mid-morning. The pangs of hunger, which hadn't really left him since breakfast, had become acute by mid-afternoon.

They quickly cleared up the brew. As they were doing so, Craig asked the question on all their minds.

'How long before we've more boiled shit to eat?'

Strangely while their situation was still hardly safe, the explosions from the anti-tank guns were a nuisance rather than a threat. The greater danger would occur when they moved forward to engage the enemy. Danny looked around at the bored faces of the crew. His mood swung between excitement and spasmodic terror. Only Craig could see how unsettled Danny seemed and guessed his state of mind.

'It's called digging in, son.'

Danny nodded and motioned with his head towards where the fire was coming from.

'Do you think they're doing the same?' He already knew the answer.

'Count on it,' replied the Ulsterman.

The night chill penetrated Danny's clothes, infiltrating his bones. He stayed close to the fire and listened to the forces radio. The music was classical and made little impression on Danny. He much preferred music from dance band leaders such as Ray Noble, Lew Stone and Roy Fox. The news, however, was always of interest. To hear what was happening back home could cheer or sadden in equal measure.

The voice of the radio announcer came on as the music finished. The news was to follow from the BBC centre in Cairo. Over the airwaves they heard the newscaster speak.

'The British army has launched an offensive in Libya against Rommel's Afrika Korps with over seventy-five thousand men.'

The group huddled around the fire and listened in stunned silence.

'Aren't the Germans listening to this?' asked Danny.

Reed threw his cup into the fire angrily.

'Of course they're bloody listening. Who the hell sanctioned that announcement?'

'I haven't a clue why they broadcast this news,' said Lister in answer to a similar question from Captain Aston at a hastily convened meeting. 'I suspect someone in Cairo is for the high jump. If Rommel didn't know we're launching a major offensive, he certainly does now.'

'Isn't that what General Cunningham wanted?' pointed out Aston, sourly.

It was of course, thought Lister bitterly, and not just because it was Aston who had made the point. But this was before the Eighth Army had scattered itself across the desert in Libya searching like an angry drunk for an enemy to fight. Lister ignored Aston's jibe. Rather than upbraid him publicly he was content to observe the looks on the faces of the other officers. They'd all arrived at an opinion about Captain Aston anyway. He doubted if theirs differed much from his.

'Any word on what is happening tomorrow, sir?' asked Major Miller. Lister noted the emphasis on the word 'is'. It was only fair. Unfortunately, he'd heard nothing concrete to tell them.

'Brigadier Davy is meeting with General Gott later tonight,' explained Lister. 'I'm sure I'll get an early morning call to tell me the outcome. Don't expect a lie in tomorrow, though.'

The officers, too tired to laugh, smiled. Major Miller was the first to react.

'My bet is we'll be asked to head over the escarpment and take the ridge north of Trigh Capuzzo.'

'I don't disagree Miller,' replied Lister. He didn't want to think about what they would meet on the other side of the escarpment. The crump of the eighty-eights or hundreds during the day held its own pledge.

After another meal of bully beef, Danny went in search of Arthur and Phil Lawrence. He walked along the row of tanks. A few were making repairs to the damage from the shelling earlier. It made Danny thankful that he'd escaped the worst of it. Men sat in groups, grousing about the food, talking about what they'd done that day, what they were going to do tomorrow or when they returned back home. There was silent reflection from some, laughter from others. This made Danny smile. Here they were, sitting in the middle of a desert. It was cold. They were facing an implacable enemy, yet these men continued to joke. One man had his hands clasped in front of him. Danny wondered if he was praying.

He passed a radio. It was tuned to the BBC. There was music playing. It sounded American rather than British. The stronger sound of saxophones and clarinets suggested Glenn Miller. Danny stopped to listen. One man offered him a cigarette, but Danny declined. He headed further along, passing men engaged in everyday activities: eating, brushing teeth or shaving. It was always important to look your best when facing death.

Up ahead he saw two familiar figures having a cigarette. Arthur turned to greet the new arrival. As ever, his smile was filled with an irrepressible good humour. Lawrence looked grave. This was unusual for the normally good-humoured corporal but then Danny saw the large swelling on the side of his head.

'I had an argument with the periscope,' explained Lawrence. This caused Arthur to start cackling.

'Cheers, mate,' said Lawrence dolefully. This made Arthur laugh more. Even Lawrence smiled.

'You both made it then,' grinned Danny.

'Course we did,' said Arthur. 'Never in doubt.'

They chatted for a few minutes about what they'd been doing that day which amounted to not very much. In place of facts they resorted, as men do, to exaggeration, jokes and insults. In such a way they nourished one another's courage, lifted their mood and banished fear, at least for a short while. It never really left, though.

Talk of the next day could not be ignored forever. It was their job now; all encompassing, utterly terrifying and ultimately heartrending.

'I'm not sure I fancy being target practice for the Jerry gunners,' admitted Danny. 'Do you know if anyone …?' He left the rest of the sentence unsaid. He was asking if any of the people they knew had been killed.

Arthur nodded.

'Ray Hill bought it this morning.'

'Really?' said Danny. He thought of the young man they'd befriended in Alexandria. 'That's a pity. He was all right.'

'He was,' agreed Lawrence, throwing away his cigarette.

'He won't be the last,' said Arthur.

They said their goodbyes. There would be no time the next morning. They'd be up, off and out. Danny walked back towards Reed and the others. He and his friends shared but one thought as they parted. They might not see one another again.

When Danny returned he saw Reed in conversation with Lieutenant

160

Hutton. The lieutenant departed as Danny arrived. Reed barely noticed Danny as he turned to the others and told them that they were still awaiting confirmation of the plan for the following morning.

A few minutes later Lister, accompanied by Major Miller, Captain Aston and Lieutenant Hutton walked up to Danny's crew. They were stopping by each crew in Miller's B Squadron. Danny and the others were on their feet in seconds.

'Hello, Reed,' said Lister. 'Remind me who we have here.'

Reed introduced all of the men. Lister shook hands with each of them and spoke briefly with Craig to ask him about his family.

'This is Private Shaw,' said Reed.

'Ahh yes, Shaw. I suppose you'll soon have an answer to the question you asked me a few months ago.'

Danny reddened slightly but grinned.

'I'm not sure I ever had the chance to apologise to Lieutenant Turner for putting him on the spot.'

'I rather think your friend put you on the spot,' replied Lister. The crew along with Lister and Miller laughed at the recollection. Captain Aston seemed bored. Or was it something else? Danny wondered if behind the superior, carefree air lay an altogether more human emotion. He, Arthur and Phil Lawrence hid their fears behind humour and moderate abuse. Lister and Miller always displayed refined good fellowship and optimism. In all likelihood, the affected ennui of Aston was nothing more than a wall built to hide his fears. It made Danny more sympathetic to the captain even if he didn't particularly like him.

The group of officers walked on to the next tank. Danny and the others sat down and looked at each other, uncertainty etched on their faces.

'I hope we're getting the hell out of here,' said Holmes. 'Bloody sitting ducks.'

Felton nodded his head in agreement. The men turned towards Reed who seemed on the point of saying something when Craig added his thoughts.

'I would be careful what you wish for.'

Danny noticed the stony features of Reed's face as he turned away and went to lie down on his makeshift bed by the tank.

'Put some music on, Charlie,' said Holmes.

Felton wandered over to the wireless and spent a minute or two searching for the BBC. Finally, some music came on.

It was a German song, 'Lili Marlene'.

'Have the Germans invaded Britain then?'

0230. It was cold and the sky was dagger black. Lister looked up as his majors trooped blearily into his bivouac followed by some of the other officers. One of them could not prevent a yawn. Lister glanced at him wryly.

'A bit of a bore, I know.'

'Sorry, sir,' came the sheepish reply.

Lister looked around him. All his officers were there: the three squadron leaders, Miller, Longworth and Laing as well as the troop leaders. A day spent absorbing shell fire had left them exhausted, but they were fighting men. They wanted to give the enemy a taste of his own medicine. Yet, still, Lister felt a foreboding. The enemy was now aware they were here. They would be ready.

'As you know, Scobie is to break out of Tobruk tomorrow. Sorry, today. Gott has ordered us to push north-west from the airfield towards Abiar el Amar. We and the rifle brigade will attack the enemy positions from the left while the Kings Royal Rifles attack from the right. We'll have artillery support from the Royal Horse artillery and the 60th.'

The men drew closer to Lister's map to see better. The lamp flickered a little as they moved. A shadow fell over their position on the map as Lister pointed to two different areas on the northern part of the escarpment that they would occupy.

'Once we've gained our objective,' continued Lister, 'we move forward past the Sidi Rezegh Mosque and link up with Scobie at 1400 hours.'

'What information do we have on the enemy strength, sir?' asked Major Miller.

'No information, I'm afraid. But Scobie has significant infantry strength. He will be, in effect, attacking their rear even though they are to the north of us. And don't forget he has the 4th Royal Tank Regiment to call upon, too. I think he'll make a dent. As you can see the situation is rather complicated. We are facing the enemy to the north. We know they are forming twenty miles to our south-west because the 4th Armoured Brigade encountered a bunch of Mark IIIs. Jerry, meanwhile, is facing us to his north, south and every which way. We won't have a lot of information when it kicks off. This lack of information is something that I suspect we'll need to get used to over the next few days,' said Lister more dejectedly than he'd intended. 'The key will be to maintain good communication and to think on your feet.'

The assembled officers nodded but it was clear from their faces that they were more than a little concerned by the rather complicated situation. Lister noted this but could think of nothing to allay their concerns. Instead, he concentrated on the plan.

'Now I will lead the advance to El Duda. Miller, you and B squadron will follow myself, and Warren over the Trigh Capuzzo. We'll seize the crossroads at Sidi Rezegh and link with the Tobruk sorties. Laing, you and C squadron stay south of the escarpment to provide flanking

163

protection. Longworth, you and A squadron will occupy point 167 and protect the left flank of the 60th. Are there any questions?'

The majors nodded, and the meeting ended a few minutes later as details of the advance were ironed out. Lister watched his officers depart. Their objective was clear but their concerns around the extent of enemy strength had been well made. Once they cleared the ridge and went into the valley what would they encounter? The lines of Tennyson rose into his mind as unwelcome as the last guests at a dinner party.

"Into the valley of death, rode the six hundred."

Chapter Eighteen

Trigh Capuzzo, Libya, 20ᵗʰ November 1941

That same morning, further to the west, Manfred sat in the hot wet metal box, bored, tired and hungry. The hunger was something he'd grown accustomed to. It was a permanent state for him and, if their conversation was anything to go by, for the other crew members. Every week they would have conversations about imaginary meals they wished they could have. The hunger and his general discontent were not helped by the fact that they seemed not to be doing very much.

'At what point do we just acknowledge there's no bloody Tommies around here?' asked Fischer.

This was not unreasonable, thought Manfred. Overath wanted to reprimand Fischer, but he agreed with him. They had been patrolling up and down the Trigh Capuzzo track for a few hours without seeing so much as a reptile on their journey. Instead, the crew were all hot, hungry and heavy-eyed through lack of sleep.

Over the wireless, they were aware of an engagement taking place about thirty kilometres to the west of their location at the Sidi Rezegh airfield and another further south at el Gubi. Fischer's comment from the previous evening hung heavy in the air. If the British had any intention of supporting a breakout from Tobruk then this was likely to be the start of it.

Overath glared down at Fischer and ordered him to keep his eyes ahead and his ears to the wireless. He then turned to Manfred and snarled irritably, 'And don't you talk, either.'

Manfred, who'd said nothing, remained impassive in the face of his sergeant. Moments later he glanced down at Fischer who was laughing. Manfred started to laugh himself. There was no point in getting too upset.

The morning dragged on, and silence descended on the tank. An armistice lest they get on one another's nerves. The heat and the torpor meant everything was done unconsciously. Manfred had next to nothing to do as he was neither a driver, a wireless operator nor the commander. To make himself useful he acted as another pair of eyes on the road ahead. His peripheral vision was limited. After a while he'd lost interest in even performing this task. Ahead of him was only dust and sand and nothing.

So, this was war. Waiting at a camp followed by yet more waiting while driving along an empty road. He'd heard from Fischer about the battle at the start of summer. This seemed to be another world. He almost envied Fischer his involvement. Almost. Unspoken was the realisation that the Bavarian had faced death. They'd all faced death. All except him. For so long his emotions swung wildly between eagerness and fear. Now the enemy was within touching distance yet all they were doing was driving around aimlessly. It was clear Overath thought this also but would not say.

More traffic on the wireless late morning revealed there was fighting to the south-west at Gabr Saleh. The 21st Panzers were unable to provide support as they'd run out of fuel. A gloomy silence engulfed the crew. They, along with the rest of the 15th Panzers, were patrolling a track that was singularly devoid of anything resembling the enemy. All of this only served to increase their sense of frustration. Even Overath could contain himself no longer.

'I don't think anyone has a clue what's going on.'

Finally, in the early afternoon they heard the news they'd been waiting for.

'Hello, this is Neumann-Silkov,' said the colonel of the 15th Panzer division. 'Drive south towards Gabr Saleh. We're to engage with the enemy.'

'How far away is Gabr Saleh?' shouted Kohler.

Overath checked the map. He studied it for a few seconds, then told Fischer on which course they should run.

'It's forty kilometres away. We should reach there before four.'

A wave of excitement went through the tank. For Manfred, it felt like his moment had arrived. A chance to face the enemy. But who was the enemy? The Allies or his own fear. Every passing minute was bringing him closer to answering this question.

An hour later, near four in the afternoon, Manfred and others could not just hear explosions. They could *feel* them. Manfred felt a thrill race through his body. Bit by bit the sound grew louder. It was clear that Kastner was now on edge. He kept glancing towards Manfred checking to see if he would be ready. They would soon come face to face with the Allies.

Overath spoke into the radio microphone.

'Approaching ridge. Can hear gunfire. No sign of British.'

There is probably a high correlation in one's life between saying something one moment and the opposite thing happening the next. This was Overath's experience just then. An explosion burst on the sand less than thirty metres away.

'What the hell!' shouted Kastner.

'I think that's the enemy we can't see,' said Fischer combining remarkable coolness with just enough irritating sarcasm to earn a glare from Overath. Moments later they heard a sickening thud against the front armour.

'Too far away,' said Kastner.

Manfred's eyes widened in confusion.

'Welcome to the war,' said Fischer in Manfred's direction. Manfred ignored him and, following a nod from Kastner, loaded the gun. It just bounced off, thought Manfred. He almost wanted to laugh. He felt giddy.

'Not very welcoming, if you ask me,' said Manfred with just enough coolness to earn a smile from Kastner.

Overath was looking through his periscope and holding his hand up to indicate he did not want any shells to be fired. Then he spoke into his microphone.

'I see tanks. I can't make out how many.'

Another voice responded.

'I can see at least thirty, three zero tanks. I think there are more behind the ridge.'

This was Basler. He was out in front. Manfred was further back, but they were now clearly in the range of the British guns.

'Keep pressing forward. We need to take the ridge.'

This was the 15th Panzer division leader, Neumann-Silkov.

Overath looked down at the rest of the crew. His features were tight but outwardly he seemed calm.

'You heard. Get ready to fire.'

'Keep moving forward,' ordered Overath, eyes glued to his periscope. 'Pick a target, corporal.'

Kastner adjusted the elevation of the gun.

Overath glanced down at his gunner. He and Kastner locked eyes for a moment. All around them they could hear the thunder of the guns and shells screaming overhead and explosions.

'Fire when you're ready.'

Kastner and Manfred exchanged looks. He saw that Manfred had the next shell ready to load. The Austrian turned back to his gun, eyes glued to his viewfinder.

Manfred felt as if he could see and hear everything around him: the chatter on the wireless, Kastner's breathing nearby, the sound of the engine straining as the tank moved slowly up the ridge, explosions rocking the ground outside.

The main gun fired, rocking the tank as it did so. Manfred had the breech open before Kastner could say 'load'.

Soon the gun was pounding out shells to a regular rhythm. Manfred loaded as fast as Kastner could fire them. Overath, manning the machine gun, was beating out a deadly hail of fire. Manfred marvelled at Kastner's imperturbable demeanour. The shells were firing at an astonishing rate, but the Austrian's movements were almost deliberate. The aim adjusted marginally after every couple of shots. All in the heat of battle. Bullets against the metal were a deafening drumbeat, and then something hit the front and bounced off. Manfred heard and felt it all, but he was in a trance. Open breech, lift, load.

Excitement, adrenaline and fear energised Manfred. Fear most of all. How would he react under fire? The answer, he realised exultantly, was the one he'd hoped for. He was barely aware of the heat in the cabin or the tiredness of his arms so disassociated had he become from his body. The crew were each doing their job. Working as a unit. Their training made thought secondary. They were one body, one mind, just an element of a whole greater than they.

Over one hundred Panzer Mark IIIs proceeded relentlessly up the ridge seemingly impervious to shell and shot. The weight of their numbers, the support from artillery and infantry, forced the British to pull back. Overath could see what was happening a few hundred yards ahead.

'They're pulling back. I'm pretty sure they're pulling back.'

Manfred felt like letting out a cheer but the intensity of Kastner, the focus of Fischer and Kohler muted his relief. And it was a relief that had nothing to do with mere survival. Kastner signalled for Manfred to stop loading. At this point Manfred became aware that he was bathed in sweat; they all were. His legs were aching, and he didn't want to think about what his arms would be like tonight.

He was hungry also. It seemed unlikely they would be eating for hours yet. The rumble of his stomach was only just drowned out by the sound of their engine and the sporadic sounds of battle.

Just before 0630 the fading light saw the battle peter out to its conclusion. Chatter on the radio confirmed Overath's view that the British were slowly pulling back down the reverse side of the slope. There was also news that a cloud of dust had been spotted coming from the west. This could only be British reinforcements.

Overath looked around at his crew. Streaks of sweat ran down his dust-covered face. But there was no mistaking the satisfaction he felt. It was not in his nature to dispense praise. He gave a nod instead. This was more than enough.

News from the wireless suggested that their commander, Neumann-Silkov, had sent an artillery screen to their western flank to discourage any British ideas of a surprise attack. Manfred was not sorry to hear that the attack would cease. The risk of running into the British in the dark was too great, potentially confusing, and would likely result in unnecessary casualties. The adrenaline rush of the afternoon had worn off completely now. He felt a fatigue he'd not experienced since that night he and Gerhardt had run around the square. Every muscle in his body was in pain and competing for sympathy.

'We're to pull back,' announced Overath, a little bit later. 'Command think it's too much of a risk to camp on the battlefield.'

The tank started to move back slowly. It was night now, but Manfred popped his head up above and could see the signs of battle everywhere. Smoking metal hulks glowing white from the heat of the fire within. Manfred was shocked by the devastation. The shots had seemed to ping off their tank making him feel invulnerable. The reality was somewhat different and more alarming. The British could do more damage than he'd realised. The thought that they were not quite so invincible jolted him. His next thought was for Gerhardt. Had he been in one of the tanks that had been destroyed?

From what he could see there were lights at ten or more of the Panzers. Perhaps they were recoverable. They passed a few that had been destroyed. The charred remains of some bodies lay around. Manfred ducked back into the tank. The chill he felt was more than just the night air. He saw Kastner looking at him.

'How many destroyed?'

'It was hard to see. More than ten, probably twenty.'

Kastner nodded. Overath glanced up.

'Thirty Mark IIIs were hit or destroyed, a few Mark IIs also. I don't know how many are dead. When we get back to the camp, we need to refuel and rearm. We also need to check the engine and the tracks. Then make me something to eat. I'm starving.'

Manfred managed to smile.

171

'Yes, sir.'

As they drove into their camp for the night the wireless crackled with the news that the BBC had announced the British offensive in Libya had started.

'They must be confident to broadcast that,' said Manfred.

'Or stupid,' said Kastner, drily.

By now everyone in the crew was ravenous. The thought of food, even if it was the usual tinned muck, was the only thing on the mind of each man. It was night when the regiment settled into its hedgehog position.

Overath went to Manfred as they sat and waited for the supply train to find the regiment in the desert.

'Do you know how many rounds you loaded today?'

Manfred laughed. 'Funnily enough, I wasn't counting.'

'Fifty-seven. Other tanks shot over sixty rounds today. You need to load faster.'

With that Overath turned and walked away, leaving Manfred feeling completely deflated. He couldn't see the grin on Overath's face, though.

Fischer punched him lightly on the arm.

'Do you know how many rounds we fired on my first time as loader?

'Tell me,' said Manfred sourly. 'One hundred?'

'Fifty-one.'

At 0230 Manfred found out how war has its own body clock. He'd bedded down for the night less than two hours previously having re-armed and refuelled.

'Get up, everyone,' said Overath. 'We have to head towards the Sidi Rezegh airfield. The Allies have taken it. We're joining the 21st Panzer group. We're going to take it back. We march at 0300 hours.'

Manfred silently groaned. He rose and felt the cold damp air bathe his skin. A swift glance towards Fischer and Kohler at least reassured him that he was not alone. They looked just as tired and just as disgruntled.

Chapter Nineteen

Sidi Rezegh Airfield, Libya, 21ˢᵗ November 1941

The wake-up call felt like it had come before Danny had actually been to sleep. He opened one eye and saw that it was still dark. He groaned. All around him he could hear similarly disgruntled noises. It never felt more like mutiny in the army than first thing in the morning. Especially when it was still dark.

The cruel reality of war wasn't just the fear of death. It was the constant company of hunger and fatigue. They never left you even when the fighting stopped. And then there was the cold. It woke up with you in the morning and settled down beside you at night. Danny's hands were numb. It took a minute to get the blood flowing. At that time in the morning, he didn't have a minute.

The sight of Reed turning in his direction had Danny on his feet in seconds and heading towards the provisions. He had a fire started in the blink of a bleary eye, despite his body feeling like it had been pummelled by Freddie Mills. His arms were dead. Even the cooking pots felt like lead weights. He saw Holmes looking at him wryly. Danny told him specifically and succinctly where he could go. Holmes erupted into laughter. Joined, it must be said, by Reed. The two men looked unsympathetically at Danny's struggle to subject tired muscles to his will. Moments later they were joined by Craig who decided to give it a commentary in a faux BBC accent.

'Shaw moving slowly on the outside. He looks done in and there's still a long way to go.'

The rest of the crew collapsed into hysterics. Craig had to pause in order to stop himself laughing and for his audience to recover.

'This horse looks like his race is run. Oh look, the jockey is taking out the whip.'

Reed took this as his cue to spur Danny along.

'Move your arse, you lazy little bugger,' shouted Reed between his chuckling.

Danny looked sourly at the others.

'Funny f…'

The response was lost in further laughter from the group.

'Some signs of life in this tired old mare but too little, too late. I think this old girl is bound for the knackers' yard or the charms of some Arab stallion.'

The last comment caused the group to collapse completely. Even Danny joined them. Breakfast, inevitably, was delayed while the group regained some form of composure. Of course, once they did, Danny came in for yet more abuse for delaying their grub.

On the stroke of eight in the morning they heard the first distant rumble of guns. For the previous two hours, Danny and the crew had made the tank ready. In the daylight it was possible to see the pounding that the armour had taken the previous day. The front had been hit a couple of times but, thankfully, nothing had penetrated. There were a few dents, nothing more. All along the sides of the vehicle was evidence of the fusillade of bullets that had peppered them.

'Bloody lucky to be inside this bugger,' pointed out Craig.

Danny nodded. He couldn't agree more. He felt for the infantry who would have been exposed to this intense fire. He was pretty sure his time would come, and soon. If this was what battle looked like with infantry and a few distant big guns, then close contact was going to be hellish. The thought prompted one last check of the tracks, the engine and the ammunition. Sergeant Reed glanced at him but said nothing. Danny suspected he'd just read the sergeant's mind.

When he'd finished the final check, he quickly rustled up another brew after getting the nod from Reed. The extent to which hunger was an issue was not something Danny had realised until yesterday. Halting for a quick cup of tea mid-battle was, unsurprisingly, out of the question. The gunfire intensified, and the explosions grew louder. He glanced at Felton. There was no mistaking the trepidation on his face. By now, even Holmes seemed even surlier than usual. He knew why. They were going 'over the top'.

It was a phrase he'd heard before. His father had never used it, but other dads had. It was the moment when a soldier left the relative safety of their dug in position to face the full wrath of bullets and shell from the enemy. So far, Danny had faced limited enemy fire. This morning he faced the prospect of experiencing what his father's generation had gone through. Reed, Holmes, Craig and Felton had undergone this baptism. The tension in the cabin was a testimony to the danger that lay ahead.

Lieutenant Colonel Lister listened to the wireless. His face remained impassive but inside he was in turmoil. His fears regarding the original Crusader plan and its slow disintegration were now being realised.

176

The news was not good. There was confirmation that one, possibly two, Panzer divisions were heading towards them from the south. This could only mean one thing. The Germans wanted their airfield back. Hardly unreasonable, thought Lister. An airfield was a bloody useful thing to have in the middle of nowhere, especially when you needed fuel, supplies or just wanted to take a pop at the enemy.

It was now clearer than ever that his men were going to be sandwiched between the enemy guarding the outer perimeter of Tobruk and the Panzer divisions heading their way from the south-east. Oddly, the enemy would also be sandwiched by the British divisions to the south of the Panzer groups.

It was shaping up into one bloody mess. However, his orders were clear even if they were not necessarily sensible. His men and Campbell's Support Group were to advance towards Tobruk. By the sounds of it, Campbell, the indestructible pirate that he was, had already started. There was something reassuring knowing that Campbell was the man General Gott had entrusted to lead this attack. He was the stuff of fiction. A man quite literally larger than life.

Somehow, thought Lister, with a man like this, there was hope. But one thought nagged him like his old doubles partner when he missed an easy volley. What sort of armour was approaching from the south-east? Lister hoped to God that the 4th Armoured Brigade could intercept them. Otherwise, the consequences would be catastrophic.

At 0830 they were riding towards battle. And a battle it was by the sounds of it. Reed confirmed that Campbell's Support Group had encountered the enemy and had even overrun some of their positions.

Danny was under no illusions about the day ahead: this would be very different from the previous one. Like a boxer, it would be hit and move. They would face anti-tank guns certainly and, potentially, tanks. The atmosphere grew noticeably more tense as they neared the battle. Still, it felt better to be inside the tank than sitting on the outside or in the back of a truck.

The regiment progressed slowly up the ridge that lay between the Sidi Rezegh airfield and the road to Tobruk. Behind the ridge, in the valley below was the Trigh Capuzzo, the desert track that ran from near Sollum on the coast through Libya, parallel to the Mediterranean.

'Slow down,' ordered Reed as they headed up the slope of the escarpment. Danny thought the order funny as they weren't exactly breaking any speed limits as it was. Then he realised that Reed was waiting for the smokescreen to thicken. Explosions rocked the tank as the German anti-tank guns made their presence felt.

Holmes gave Danny a nod and soon they began to retaliate. It was difficult to be certain, but Danny sensed that the enemy was primarily composed of infantry, artillery and anti-tank placements. The regiment moved slowly forward under the cover of the smoke-screen. Firing shells towards where they could see the enemy guns. Still no sign of any tanks.

The sound of gunfire grew louder. Aston looked through his binoculars and could see dust in the very far distance. He put the binoculars down and looked at the forty-millimetre gun of the Crusader. Right now, it felt like they were going into battle armed with a pop gun. His guts churned at the prospect of encountering the big eighty-eight-millimetre guns and possibly even Panzer Mark IIIs. He felt like praying. He tried to remember some long-forgotten prayers.

Then he heard a voice from below.

'Getting closer, sir.'

Damn right they were getting closer. How he wished he could join Longworth at the squadron headquarters a mile back. At least

Lister was with them at the front. He'd give the colonel that. Just as this thought entered his head, he heard Lister's voice crackle on the radio.

The damn fool was urging them to go forward. He felt like pointing out that certain death lay ahead. A glance down to the driver. He didn't have to tell his driver to slow down and make sure they weren't leading the charge. Best to let some other damn fool do that. Then he could come charging in at the end roaring his head off and waving his proverbial sword about. That kind of bluff nonsense had become his stock-in-trade. A few near-the-knuckle jokes and kick a nearby dead Nazi. Always worked.

The thought of Operation Battleaxe in early summer, the previous failed attempt at relieving Tobruk, was now on Aston's mind. It was the first time they'd had to deal with Rommel rather than a bunch of untrained and ill-equipped Italians. Rommel had kicked their arse then and there was no reason to think him incapable of doing so again. He'd survived that lot but saw a lot of men die in agony.

On the other side of the escarpment was the Sidi Rezegh Mosque, the tomb of an Arab saint. Age and war had heavily damaged the structure. Edmund Aston was sure of one thing. He would not be a martyr and he was certainly no saint.

The lead tanks were now nearing the top of the ridge leading down to a valley which would give them control of the Trigh Capuzzo road. However, it was plain that the Germans were dug in. The prize lay behind this screen, El Duda. Once they took El Duda it was but a matter of miles to Tobruk. Just ahead of the tanks, the British infantry were attempting to overrun these positions. The tanks at the front seemed to halt, slowing everything down behind.

179

Turner's voice came over the radio loud and clear. He was out in front and had a view of the one-hundred-yard-wide slope that led down into the valley.

'I'm through the smokescreen. Lots of enemy positions front and left. Small arms. All dug in by the looks of things.'

Danny watched as the 7th Support Group infantry inched closer to the German positions. The regiment moved forward with them in leapfrog fashion. The German weapons were doing no damage to the tank, but Danny suspected it was a different story outside the safety of his metal cocoon. At midday Danny heard the voice of Lister on the wireless.

'Campbell and the 7th Support Group have taken the escarpment. We're to go over and down into the valley.' The anxiety in his voice was clear. He knew that his men were probably going to face an anti-tank barrage, probably from eighty-eights. Danny recognised the sound all too well. It haunted him. It probably haunted all of them.

Reed picked up his microphone and waited for Aston or Laing to respond. Silence.

'Hello all stations,' responded Lister. 'Drivers advance.'

Captain Arthur Crickmay stood with Brigadier Davy observing the scene. Crickmay wondered what must be going through his commander's mind. He'd given the order to push ahead towards the meeting point at El Duda. It would require them to race across an open plain for a couple of miles in the face of intense enemy gunfire. He didn't envy his comrades in the 6th RTR.

Accompanying the tanks, Crickmay could see the infantry trucks and artillery. It was magnificent and terrifying. He didn't know how many guns they faced, but the enemy had time to get their sights and distance. Surely such a concentration of armour and men could break through. And they had Jock Campbell leading them. Crickmay dared to hope.

A flurry of explosions crunched around the advancing armour. The sickening realisation hit Crickmay that the big guns of the Germans were beginning to find their range. And then he saw one tank stop suddenly, smoke billowing from its hatches. Then another.

And then another.

Yet still they drove forward. Mad. Courage indescribable, unquantifiable. He felt a sense of wonder at the unfolding nobility revealed in the red-raw rush towards the enemy. One by one he saw the tanks give themselves up to the unforgiving cruelty of the desert.

Chapter Twenty

Forty kilometres south-east of Sidi Rezegh airfield, Libya, 21ˢᵗ November 1941

The 15ᵗʰ and the 21ˢᵗ Panzer divisions swept towards the Sidi Rezegh airfield at twenty kilometres per hour. Manfred felt energised despite the lack of sleep. The first day had gone well and he was almost jubilant that he'd performed well. Tougher days would follow. That was for the future. Now, he felt closer to being accepted by the crew around him.

Another reason for his air of confidence was the realisation that they were going to attack the airfield in force. They had infantry, artillery, anti-tank guns and around two hundred tanks. Superior tanks. Everything he had heard from the others suggested they were safer inside a Panzer Mark III than any Allied tank. The enemy would be caught between the Axis forces on the perimeter of Tobruk and the Panzer groups, moving towards them from the south-east.

What was happening behind did not worry him although he could hear from Overath's brief conversations on the radio that he was worried about the presence of the British they had beaten back the previous day coming back to re-engage them on their flank. This would present a major problem if they were attacking the army holding the Sidi Rezegh airfield. At best, it would become something of a jumble. At worst, it could inflict untold damage to the tanks which were a finite resource for the Axis forces. An hour after their departure from Gabr Saleh, Overath's voice came over the radio.

'Tanks, left,' said Overath before adding, 'British.'

Manfred was jolted by this and went immediately to check.

'They're burning by the looks of things,' added Overath. 'Fischer.'

He didn't need to finish the order; it was apparent that Fischer was steering towards them.

'Hurry,' shouted Overath.

Manfred was confused by what was happening. For once, though, silence was the best policy. They drew to a halt outside one tank. Overath immediately hopped out followed by Kohler from the hull. Fischer was grinning. Again, Manfred was awash with curiosity but remained quiet. A minute or two later, Overath jumped through into the turret clutching his booty. Tins of fruit and vegetables, some chocolate and a can of beer spilled from his arms.

'God save the King,' said Overath in English. With a wide grin.

It was eight in the morning when Manfred heard anti-tank guns in the distance. The crew glanced at one another. Were these their guns or British? Sitting in a hot, stinking tank it was impossible for Manfred to know. He glanced towards Kastner.

Kastner shrugged. He didn't know either.

'Big help, you are,' said Manfred.

'You're welcome,' replied Kastner, laughing sourly.

'They're ours,' said Fischer confidently. 'The British only have their two-pounder guns and they don't sound like our eighty-eights. It can only be our anti-tank guns.'

Overath chimed in at this point.

'The British also have their twenty-five pounders, so aside from being completely wrong, Fischer's right. They're ours. I don't think there'll be much left of the Tommies by the time we get there.'

Manfred wasn't sure whether to be heartened by this or disappointed. By now, he was up for the fight. He didn't want to say this, of course. It was better to leave these kinds of pronouncements to Fischer. Once more, he felt alive in a way that would have been unimaginable a year ago. All of his senses were activated. Perhaps too much so. The excitement that drove waves of adrenaline around his body dulled his discomfort with the ever-present sand infiltrating every part of his clothing. But when the battle was over and the adrenaline wore off, fatigue, pain and the constant irritation of sand on skin took over.

By 0800 hours, they had first sight of the tanks. The voice of Lieutenant Basler popped over the airwaves.

'I see thirty tanks ahead. Three zero tanks. There must be more somewhere.'

There weren't.

The 15th Panzer division and the 21st Panzers drove through them laying waste to the British tanks and splitting the Allied artillery in two. Once again, Manfred felt his luck was holding. Puffs of white smoke mixed with the sand being thrown up by the large number of tanks. Kastner fired off shells as quickly as Manfred could load them.

By mid-morning the rout had finished but the long march followed by the engagement had its own cost.

'We're running low on gasoline,' shouted Fischer.

If their tank was running low on fuel then, in all likelihood, the whole division was. The order from Neumann-Silkov to disengage

184

came around just before midday. The Panzers began to pull back to the eastern end of the valley. This made sense. Low ammunition and a lack of fuel would jeopardise success in their ultimate objective: the capture of the airfield.

As they pulled back to the eastern end of the valley, Manfred marvelled at the carnage they'd created. Burnt-out tanks, mostly British, were scattered across the plain. It had been a slaughter. He didn't pay much attention to the charred bodies littered around the shredded metal remains of the Crusaders.

To Manfred, it merely proved the superiority of the German war machine. For the first time, he could see why Fischer had such an air of confidence. He didn't pause to think about why Overath and Kastner seemed less enthusiastic. Their caution in the face of such overwhelming evidence of German dominance seemed as unfathomable as it was unpatriotic. Fischer, as ever, was ebullient.

'My God look at that,' exclaimed Fischer, like an excited schoolboy at a funfair. At this moment, Manfred felt he understood the Bavarian better. There had always been something of the kid about him. A kid on holiday. Although Manfred, too, felt thrilled, a voice inside him counselled against too overt a display of this. This would be his way. He got on with his job. He disposed of the empty cartridges and checked the gun while the tank joined with the supply echelon. He glanced at Kohler who was busy cleaning the bow machine gun, then attended to the antenna. The day never seemed to end.

The next hour was its own type of melee. Refuelling and rearming fifty or more tanks crowding round the ammunition and petrol trucks nearly caused a second conflict to break out. Manfred, whose job it was to get the replacement shells, watched it all with wry amusement. Overath had told him to wait. So, Manfred waited. Kohler, who was in charge of fuel, did likewise. The two boys sat and shared a cigarette, enjoying watching the frayed tempers of their tired Afrika Korps comrades become increasingly frazzled.

'It looks like they're rationing the fuel,' observed Kohler. He pointed to a big argument between an enormous sergeant called Muller and another sergeant handing out the petrol cans.

'I haven't seen it like this before,' said Manfred.

Kohler laughed. But there was a harshness to the laugh. Manfred realised that he wouldn't have seen it previously because he'd never been in this situation before. He reddened slightly.

'It's always like this,' said Kohler. 'Every bloody time.'

Manfred was about to comment on why they didn't just bring more fuel when a thought struck him. A chilling thought. What if we just don't have enough fuel? The sight of the temperature gauge rising amongst his colleagues became something else to him now.

It was a harbinger.

The Afrika Korps was the greatest fighting machine on the planet. Manfred had absolute certainty about this. In Rommel, they had a leader who had taken them to victory from France all the way down to North Africa. Yet, without fuel, they were nothing. This was why they were here. It wasn't Britain who would defeat the German nation. It was gasoline. Unless they had access to gasoline, Germany could not win the war. Their greatest enemy was also their greatest ally.

Oil.

'This doesn't look good,' said Kastner eyeing Lieutenant Basler walking along the makeshift leaguer picking out tanks.

'What's going on?' asked Manfred, picking up on the direction of Kastner's gaze.

'On your feet,' ordered Overath as he, too, noticed the SS lieutenant heading their way.

Moments later Basler was at Manfred's tank. He looked annoyed.
But then he always seemed irritated by something. Manfred stood
up and looked at the SS man. Up close Manfred was surprised at
how young he seemed. Mid-twenties, at a guess. His skin had been
darkened by the African sun and with his dark hair he might have
passed for a local were it not for the eyes. They were ice blue but there
was a fire in there, too.

'You men are to join me. We've had reports of a patrol of
armoured cars to the south. They're clearly doing reconnaissance.
We can't let them know where we are and risk air attack or their
guns targeting us. To the vehicles. We're to follow Captain Kummel
to engage. We march west back towards where we came from.
Follow me.'

Manfred and the rest of the crew immediately kicked over the
traces of their fire and made for the tank. Minutes later a party of
around twenty-five tanks headed towards the southern ridge where
the armoured vehicles had been sighted.

Overath sat on top and invited Manfred to join him. Manfred
looked at the line of tanks throwing up the sand into the air. They
would soon be visible to the enemy. And the enemy would run. What
else could they do? He doubted they'd give chase. It would be too
much of a risk. At best they might get close enough to hit a few. Job
done then head home.

'What do you think, Brehme?' asked Overath.

Manfred looked at Overath and wondered what the hell was the
answer to a question like that. What did Overath want from him?

'I think we've been fortunate so far. The enemy has not been
concentrated. They don't seem integrated, either. We fight alongside

187

infantry, artillery and with an anti-tank screen. The Tommies all seem to be fighting their own war.'

Overath nodded but did not respond to Manfred's point. Manfred took this to mean agreement. Whether or not this was what he'd been asking was another matter altogether.

They rode together in silence. Manfred did not have binoculars so contented himself with looking around their flanks while Overath kept his vision straight ahead. It made a pleasant change from the cramped cauldron of the cabin. But up top had its own challenge. His hat could barely cast enough shadow over his face. He felt his neck burning. The sky was no longer so overcast. The clouds had cleared. There were no birds or planes just stretches of blue. The only sound was the rumble of tanks and clanking wheels. It was difficult to see too far ahead due to the heat haze which intensified as midday approached.

This was an issue. It would make it more difficult to pick out the British vehicles. The noise, the dust cloud and the size of their party would be less difficult to spot by the Allies. Ten minutes later Overath asked Manfred to send Kohler up.

'Go to the wireless,' ordered the sergeant as Manfred stepped down.

Manfred took up Kohler's position as the vehicle trundled forward. Fischer, sitting nearby, said nothing. A frown was starched into his skin. The wireless crackled suddenly. It was Basler, who was out in front along with the leader of the party, Captain Hummel.

'Enemy spotted south-west. Six zero, zero metres.'

Hummel came on the radio at this point.

'Turn, march. Spread out and attack cars.'

Fischer nodded in response. As he did so, Manfred heard the crump of guns in the distance. Manfred's ears had become more attuned now. They did not sound German.

'My God,' said Overath on the microphone.

'What's happened?' shouted Kastner.

'They've taken out Wult. Direct hit. Start firing.'

Manfred had already loaded the first cartridge. Seconds later, although it felt like an eternity, Kastner fired. Manfred had the second shell into the breech by the time Kastner informed them he'd missed.

Shells were raining down around them. Manfred winced as the explosions rocked the tank.

'Why aren't our eighty-eights shelling them?' shouted Manfred opening the breech for another cartridge.

'We've driven out of range,' responded Overath grimly. 'We're on our own.' He added a few other choice words to describe his feelings on the wisdom of this march.

As he said this, another explosion burst in Manfred's ears. The percussive force of the barrage sent shockwaves through Manfred's body. Nearby, another Mark III in the troop was destroyed causing all it shells to explode in rapid succession in a manner that reminded Manfred of firecrackers, only louder and deadlier. His stomach knotted in fear as the firestorm continued unabated.

Basler came on the radio.

'Stop. We're going straight into their anti-tank guns. Reverse.'

Fischer responded immediately and shifted the gears into reverse cursing loudly as he did so. Overath had, by now, ducked into the turret. His presence steadied the nervousness that had descended like a dark cloud on Manfred and the others. In a calm voice Overath spoke to Fischer.

'Steady, Fischer, we don't want to crash into our tanks.'

'Yes, sir,' replied Fischer who took his cue from the cool demeanour of the sergeant. His voice betrayed no anxiety. Manfred glanced down at him. He had to admire how quickly he had recovered his composure. The storm outside was intense, but the Bavarian barely blinked with each explosion. They continued their steady progress backwards despite the vicious harassment they were experiencing. The constant buzz of the radio revealed how more and more tanks had been destroyed.

Then an enormous explosion rocked them. Manfred was sent crashing backwards. His head cracked against some metal knocking him out momentarily. He came to and it seemed like the tank was spinning. The noise he could hear was the beating of his heart. Two things dawned on him: they had been hit, and he was alive.

Above he could see blood spilled like paint across the inside wall of the turret. He was drenched in it. And something else. There were hot bloodied clumps on his face and uniform. His ears felt like agony. The noise momentarily ceased. It felt like he was in a cave listening to distant echoes.

He looked around. Fischer was shouting something at him. He couldn't hear anything, but could see Fischer gesturing him to get out. He saw Kohler escaping through a hatch; Fischer was motioning for him to follow. He raised himself up from the floor. For the first time he became aware of the extraordinary heat inside the cabin. Glancing down at his uniform, he saw that it was soaked red but he could not detect any injury save for the throbbing of his head. It felt like he was moving in sections.

Smoke filled the tank and the smell of petrol was now overpowering. Despite the smoke stinging his eyes, he managed to crawl over to the hatch. His hands felt sticky and there was some sort of soft material all over the metal floor which caused him to slip and bang his knee painfully on the breech. He threw himself towards the hatch ducking his head just in time to avoid the edge. Moments later he landed on the sand. Two arms reached under his armpits and dragged him away from the metal coffin.

Fischer had saved him. The Bavarian continued to pull Manfred away from the burning hulk. Small explosions were detonating inside as the ammunition went off with a series of popping noises. Fischer released Manfred onto the sand.

'Can you move?'

'Yes, I think so,' replied Manfred.

He got gingerly to his feet and followed Fischer and Kohler. They fell into a depression in the sand which provided some cover from the crack of gunfire around them. Manfred looked at Fischer. He was a bloody mess but seemed unhurt. So too Kohler.

'The sergeant?' asked Manfred. Fischer shook his head. Then Manfred looked down at his hands. The stickiness was blood and there was something else. It was all over his uniform. A scream formed in his throat, but he managed to control himself.

All over his hair, his face and uniform were the remains of Overath and Kastner. Fischer and Kohler were looking at him. Then Kohler turned away and began to retch. Manfred felt like weeping but the sight of Fischer staring at him stiffened his resolve. Slowly he began to wipe his face and body of the blood and tissue.

Behind them they heard the sound of the tanks receding into the distance. None felt like giving chase. The impact of the explosion had been delayed but Manfred realised his body was aching all over. He could barely move his legs.

'What do we do now?' asked Kohler, who'd recovered sufficiently by this time.

Manfred pointed in the direction of the tanks and Fischer answered. 'We walk.'

They waited until the gunfire had subsided, then helped each other up like old men. Around them lay the burnt-out wrecks of the Mark IIIs caught in the firestorm. Although none wanted to look at their old tank, they realised they needed water. Slowly they trudged over and took whatever water and food they could find in what remained. Fischer bathed Manfred in some water to remove blood and tissue. Manfred nodded to him as the grim assignment was completed.

They spent the next ten minutes taking whatever they could salvage for the march ahead of them. The cans would weigh heavily on fatigued arms. Manfred and Fischer said nothing as they contemplated this but Kohler by now was in a mood to grumble. He complained about all the things that his two companions were feeling.

'How far do you think?'

Fischer replied with a figure clutched from the air. 'Five, maybe ten kilometres at least. We went out of the range of our guns. I don't know what we were thinking.'

Kohler let out a string of oaths as they passed the twisted metal remains of the troop. In the pitiless heat of the mid-afternoon sun this seemed a suitable eulogy for men who'd ordered them to march into deadly fire.

'My God, five kilometres in this heat,' continued Kohler. 'This is terrible.'

Then they heard the sound of a vehicle. It was a low hum at first and then it became louder. They looked around them but could see nothing. Manfred felt a surge of hope mixed with apprehension. By now, Kohler was shouting. 'Help! Help!'

'Shut up you fool,' snarled Fischer.

Kohler looked at him askance.

'What do you mean?'

'He means,' replied Manfred, 'that they could be Tommies.'

In this Manfred was wrong. A vehicle eventually appeared over the ridge and made straight for them. On the side of the vehicle was a flag. Manfred recognised the colours. It was South African. Within a few minutes Manfred and the others were staring at half a dozen guns trained on them.

'Any of you speak English?' asked a sergeant.

Chapter Twenty-One

Sidi Rezegh Airfield, Libya, 21st November 1941

Danny fought back a rising tide of fear. His breath grew shallower and shallower. He glanced around the tank. Aside from Felton and himself, the other members of the crew were highly experienced. He thought of his friends. Phil Lawrence was probably nearby. Arthur, meanwhile, was part of A squadron, so not involved.

The crump of guns in the distance was followed by the scream of shells. The air seemed to rupture around them. Within seconds they were rocked by explosions. The shock waves shook the men inside the tank.

'Welcome to the war, son,' shouted Craig over to Danny.

Danny offered a smile and hoped he didn't look as white as Felton. The tank was moving fast. He was tossed against the side. A swift glance up at Holmes revealed the gunner's eyes fixed on his gun sights. Danny grabbed a shell. The weight stopped his hands shaking.

They advanced down the reverse side of the escarpment. For the first hundred yards it seemed the shells could have been landing in another country. Then Danny heard a different sound. The sound of shells hitting armour and the appalling realisation that the series of shattering blasts following this was the sound of the tank's shells exploding. Soon, he saw sand erupting just in front and then all around.

The German batteries spat angrily at the cavalry charge. The steel rain rent the earth. Tanks shuddered as explosions threw up sand and rock. Danny willed himself to look through the periscope. The sight was hell itself. Fire, smoke and death. Ahead he could see a Crusader in flames. Then two. Then three.

Lieutenant Turner spoke again.

'I can see the enemy. Figures two zero, zero, zero yards away on far ridge there are guns,' said Turner before adding almost unnecessarily, 'anti-tank guns.'

Lister responded seconds later.

'Hello all stations. Lister here. We must keep going. Our objective is two thousand yards ahead.'

Aston let out an oath which came over loud and clear on his microphone. This was followed by several more when he realised that he had been caught out. To cover himself he urged Turner to keep advancing.

'Driver advance,' ordered Aston deliberately so that every tank could hear him. He didn't have to add, stay behind Turner. The lead troop moved forward onto the plain. Behind them, British anti-tank guns opened fire, some stray shells landing near them.

Danny felt his body shake. He wasn't sure if it was terror, or the shock waves made by the gun fire rupturing the air around them. They were well within the killing range of these monster guns, spoken of in tones of hushed awe by the men that had faced them before. He thought of his brother, Tom, and wondered if he was out there as part of the

195

breakout from Tobruk. And good old Carruthers, of course. He was likely to be in the artillery. If he was still alive, that is.

He stopped himself from thinking more. Any thoughts of death were always cast out of his mind immediately. There was no point in dwelling on it. He gazed out in front of him. An explosion in front of the tank threw up grit. He instinctively jerked backwards.

They were all silent now. A homage to the rage of shells plummeting around them. A prayer for their survival. Even Danny was finding God at that moment, remembering Craig's comment from a lifetime ago.

Bravely, or foolishly, Sergeant Reed put his head up to make a quick scan of the enemy positions. He kept the hatch open just enough so that his eyes were level with the cupola, and he could see what was in front. A screaming shell forced Reed back into the turret, head down. A thin, mirthless grin appeared on his face; a riposte to the fearful sight he'd witnessed outside.

'I was curious,' said Reed. Danny saw the look that passed between the sergeant and Craig.

In the distance, through his viewing hatch, Danny could at last make out the sinister shapes of the enemy through his periscope; the heavily camouflaged guns which were now spitting shells at a shocking rate. One fireball after another soared into the air and landed with a terrible thud on the ground in front of them. They were weaving in a desperate attempt to avoid being hit. A shell burst nearby lighting up the cabin and throwing Danny against the side. He felt a sharp pain but quickly resumed his position.

They had to cross over a mile of open ground, without cover, without much hope of avoiding a hit. Danny's tank was in the third row of B squadron. To his left he saw Aston's vehicle trundling alongside them. Turner was out front, moving rapidly. At least their speed

196

made them a difficult target. Danny saw one tank go up in a huge gout of flames. The orange flame stood out against the blue sky, a harmony of science and savagery.

The first row and then the second were bearing the brunt of the onslaught. One by one he saw them stop abruptly and burst into flames. He saw Major Miller's Crusader go up. They'd lost the leader of B Squadron. No one could possibly survive although he saw some men diving out of the hatches. He couldn't look. His eyes flicked ahead to the belching guns.

The sickening reality of war was laid bare for Danny. The Crusaders, when they managed to work, were no match for the terrifying power of the anti-tank gun, even from a long range. As soon as tanks went over the top and down the slope they were knocked out. It was like a shooting gallery for the Germans.

'Don't stop,' ordered Reed. What else could they do? Either direction was suicidal. The ground in front of them was moving. A man-made earthquake created waves on the ground. Shards of rock were being thrown up all around them.

Danny saw carnage everywhere he looked. The sound was a percussion of rage. Explosions mixed with the chattering of machine guns. Flashes of tracer flew through the air, pinging off the tank. Holmes was firing back now. They were in the game at last. Able to return fire with fire.

'Keep loading,' shouted Holmes to Danny.

'Keep firing,' said Danny through gritted teeth.

Reed let out an oath which was unusual. Moments later the tank was hit at the front. The clang echoed around the tank. Danny's heart stopped beating then restarted as he realised that they were alive. He sucked the air into his lungs and regretted it immediately. It was rank with fumes and the acrid smell of cordite.

'This is suicide,' said Reed. There was no fear in his voice, just wonder mixed with dismay. An acceptance of his own mortality.

Below, Danny heard Craig call out the name of the Lord in a manner that seemed at odds with his deeply held beliefs. Something hit the tank on the right. Then the left. No damage. Every explosion seemed to rock the tank to its rivets. Danny felt numb from the pounding. Every near miss passed along the earth and through the tank like stones thrown into a pond.

They'd passed over the Trigh Capuzzo and were nearing the ridge where the gun emplacements rained shells on them. Not only were they getting close, but they were also beginning to do some damage.

'Got one,' shouted Holmes triumphantly. They were now within close enough range to do some serious damage. The tank jolted upwards as it reached the escarpment beyond the Trigh Capuzzo, throwing Danny backwards. He scrambled forward again rubbing his head which had just bashed against the wall of the tank.

'I'm hit,' came a voice on the radio. It was Lister. The lieutenant colonel had taken part in this cavalry charge. The radio went dead. This was a new kind of shock for Danny. The lieutenant colonel had been at the forefront of this mad cavalry charge. Now he was perhaps dead. Danny hoped he'd escaped the tank.

Danny was still mechanically feeding shells into the gun barrel. He was past thought. His movements were robotic. Reed was speaking into his microphone, but Danny couldn't hear what was being said. Everything was blocked out for him save for the racing of his heart and his breathing. He felt a touch on his arm. It was Holmes. He motioned for Danny to stop. They were taking evasive action.

'Reverse,' shouted Reed. The attack was failing. They had travelled too far and there was no support. They'd lost their commanding officer as well as the leader of B Squadron. Yes, the attack was failing.

Catastrophically.

The radio crackled. It was Aston ordering the tanks back. They couldn't hope to hold the ridge. The whistle of shells continued; the stomach-turning wait before the shells exploded their confirmation that it wasn't you. This time.

The engine whined and groaned as Craig reversed the tank, keeping the hull facing front where it was most heavily armoured gave them a better chance of surviving a hit. It felt like they were in the midst of a hailstorm such were the number of hits on the tank.

'Faster,' shouted Reed, struggling to keep the fear from his voice.

Danny held his breath as he felt the tank jerk backwards. It was moving and he breathed a sigh of relief. Reed released a torrent of oaths. Danny put his eyes to the periscope.

At this moment they stopped.

'What the hell is going on?' shouted Reed.

'The bastard engine's conked out,' responded Craig.

'Keep firing,' ordered Lieutenant Turner. What else could they do? It was only by a miracle they'd not been hit. He'd heard Lister's last message. The news elsewhere suggested Miller had been hit also. He wondered how many of the tanks were left. When they crested the ridge, the full folly of what they were undertaking hit him. They couldn't possibly hold the position. Ahead was the heavily fortified German redoubt. The result of the night-long rumble of noise was now in full view.

Without artillery and infantry support, this attack was destined to end in failure. Thoughts raced through the mind of Turner as he realised the extent of the overwhelming folly they had embarked upon. It was Balaclava all over again. A charge towards guns. Turner felt a freezing wave of panic pass through him. What were they to do now that they'd reached the ridge? The wireless was full of sound, but Turner could hear nothing. It was chatter mixed with terror. And then the question was answered for him. He heard Aston calling for them to retreat.

The tank slammed into reverse. They had practiced such a manoeuvre often. Down the hill incline they raced. Puffs of smoke from the redoubt preceded explosions in front and to their side. Shell splinters hit the armour plating. Dull metallic clangs reverberated around the compartment. A glance to the right revealed a tank crew scrambling out of the tank hatches as wisps of smoke appeared in the turret.

The battlefield was shrouded in a deadly mist. Blackened burning tanks bore testimony to the battering they had taken. It was a mess, a bloody mess, thought Turner angrily. Then the mist seemed to clear. Blue sky appeared and Turner knew it would only reveal his position. Sure enough, more puffs of smoke sprouted in the distance. His eye caught a menacing dark shape against the sky. Transfixed he watched it for what seemed like minutes. He wanted to move but his feet were anchored to the spot. He hoped the shell would pitch up short.

It blew his tank to bits.

Reed looked down frantically at Craig. This was not the time for their Crusader to prove its unreliability.

'It might have been a shell,' shouted Craig. The engine was not responding. It was dead.

A nearby explosion shook the tank. They had to evacuate. That much was certain. Reed and Danny immediately turned their attention to what was in front of them.

Danny looked through his periscope. He saw the tank ahead of him halt suddenly. It erupted into smoke and flames. In the confusion,

Danny struggled to remember who was inside. Then he saw the turret separate from the tank. It flew twenty feet into the air. With a sickening feeling in the pit of his stomach he realised the detached turret was heading directly for them.

'God almighty,' said Reed, who was also aware of the impending collision. Holmes looked at Danny.

'What's happening?' shouted Holmes, confused, scared and aware something was happening. Something terrible.

'Duck,' said Danny. There was no way they could avoid being hit. Then all went black.

Chapter Twenty-Two

Fifteen kilometres south of Sidi Rezegh Airfield, Libya, 21ˢᵗ November 1941

The big sergeant spoke English, but the accent of the soldier was different from that of Diane Landau, the English girl Manfred had been at school with nearly ten years earlier before her family fled from Germany. The man before him could not have been more different. He was big. Very big. Even Manfred found himself looking up at him. The South African had a gun and was pointing it at the three boys. Manfred almost smiled. The gun seemed unnecessary. It would have taken at least three of them to overpower him.

Manfred glanced from the sergeant to the jeep they were travelling in. There was a machine gun mounted on the back of it. The South African manning it seemed to be built on a similar architectural scale. The key thing that Manfred noticed was that there was no room in the jeep for them to be taken away. He thought it unlikely that the South Africans would want them to sit on their knees.

The November sun was still hot enough to burn Manfred's skin. He needed a hat. Every second's exposure increased the sense of his skin reddening. The big sergeant was waiting for an answer. Who speaks English? Manfred did. By admitting so a number of thoughts went through his mind. It could mean survival. The South Africans may want to take a prisoner. This could mean interrogation unless they observed the Geneva Convention. He wondered, and then doubted, how much his own side were doing so. But admission could mean survival; sitting out the war, bored and healthy versus risking your life every day for years to come.

He stayed silent.

They heard a voice from the jeep.

'What do you want to do with them?'

This seemed to jolt the South African awake. He looked at Manfred and the others, a grim smile on his face. The situation was almost absurd. Eight men in the middle of a desert. A question of life and death swirling in the airless air.

The South African glanced down at the jerricans on the ground by the Germans. He motioned with his gun for Manfred and Fischer to step back. They did so and the sergeant walked forward and lifted one of the cans. It was clearly full. He set it down again and then turned and walked to the jeep. They had a brief conference; then the sergeant returned.

He studied the three German men before them. Men? They were children. Sergeant Pieter Coetzee had three children. All of them were around the age of the boys before him. But they were at war. There was a job to do.

Kohler was the only one who could not return his gaze. He would do. Coetzee stepped forward and put a gun to Kohler's head.

'Do you speak English?' barked Coetzee at Kohler.

'Nein,' cried Kohler. He repeated it again. Coetzee believed him. Besides which, he had a feeling about the other two boys. An instinct told him that one or both could speak English. The key was to get them to admit it. He hated this war. Hated it with every fibre of his being. It didn't matter though. They had to win. He wanted to return to his family in Johannesburg. The sooner the better.

Keeping his Webley revolver trained on the temple of Kohler, he fixed his gaze on Manfred and then Fischer in turn. Cocking the hammer with his thumb he spoke.

'One of you speaks English. If you don't tell me, I'll shoot your friend.'

'Stop!' shouted Manfred in English. 'What sort of animal are you?'

Manfred heard a noise of disapproval from Fischer, who was seconds away from launching himself at the big South African. Then the South African began to laugh. He took the gun away from Kohler's head.

Manfred looked first at the South African and then Fischer. He was confused. Fischer wasn't. He was shaking his head. Without knowing why Manfred felt like an idiot. He felt his anger growing. He glared at the South African.

Coetzee began putting bullets into his gun. Manfred felt a wave of humiliation as he realised the South African had held an empty gun to Kohler's head. He couldn't bring himself to look at Fischer. He didn't need to. The heavy sigh from Fischer sealed Manfred's mortification.

Gun loaded, Coetzee pointed it at Manfred.

'Come with me.'

'Where?' asked Manfred, as if he had a choice. The question was academic, and Manfred realised it probably had not added to his credibility with Fischer at that moment.

The South African looked at him. Under the cap, Manfred saw a pair of blue eyes study him shrewdly. Manfred suspected he was thinking the same thing that Fischer was at that moment: this boy is an idiot. Manfred reddened under the intensity of the

South African's gaze and the knowledge that Fischer was present to witness his folly.

'What about them?' said Manfred, desperate to gain some sense of control in a situation that was well beyond this.

It was clear the sergeant was becoming irritated by the young German. The reply was curt.

'I don't shoot unarmed men. They have water. Food. They can walk.'

This ended the discussion. The sergeant's patience had worn out; Manfred realised he had no choice but to go. He glanced at his companions and shrugged. Fischer nodded. Kohler ignored him. He had his own shame to deal with. Manfred didn't envy him the company of Fischer while they tried to find their way back home. Fischer sensed Manfred's unease and said, in German, 'They won't kill you. Don't tell them anything.'

Manfred nodded as he walked forward with the South African.

He heard Fischer say as he left, 'We'll be all right. I've been through this before.'

A few moments later Manfred was climbing into the jeep. Fischer and Kohler watched the jeep head over the ridge. Kohler looked to Fischer.

'We walk then?'

Fischer shook his head. 'No. I want to try something first.'

The speed of the jeep felt strange to Manfred after so many months in a slow-moving tank. Ahead of them lay an empty space that stretched for a mile or so ending in another ridge. Manfred suspected the Allies were stationed just behind there. He could see some dark shapes moving around.

The jeep drove along the hard sand. Manfred was wedged in between two men. Most of the men in the jeep were older than him. If their looks were anything to go by, they were hardened fighters. The leathery skin and the resoluteness in their eyes told a story and issued a warning to the young German. They were not to be messed with.

The sergeant, sitting in the front, turned around and held out an open cigarette packet to Manfred. It seemed a genuine offer, so Manfred took one and the soldier to his right who had been smoking helped light him up.

'You learned English at school then?'

Manfred thought it unlikely that the future of the Afrika Korps hinged on his answer but felt caught between being too friendly or appearing like a surly young man. He'd also heard that the Allies generally played fair. In fact, it was a regular story in the camp that both sides displayed courtesy towards prisoners and the wounded. Manfred guessed he was about to find out if this was true.

'Yes, at school.'

This seemed to satisfy the sergeant and they travelled along in silence for a few minutes. The open-air jeep allowed no escape from the sun but the breeze in Manfred's face cooled him a little. He sensed the sergeant was about to speak to him again. His head turned slightly to the side, and he said, 'We're South African. All from Johannesburg. Where are you from?'

'Near Heidelberg.'

'Don't know it,' said Coetzee.

'There's a university there,' said the soldier driving the jeep. Manfred couldn't see his face, but he sounded younger than the others. There was a stripe on his arm.

'You were at university?' asked Coetzee.

Once again, Manfred saw no reason to avoid answering.

'No, I joined the army.'

'Bet you wished you'd gone to study instead,' laughed Coetzee. The others laughed also. Manfred smiled. He was now a prisoner of war, caught in an inhospitable land soon after witnessing the horrible death of his comrades. Yes, right now university seemed a more pleasant option. Not that there would have been any choice. All he'd done was anticipate a demand that would have been made of him anyway. As he sat with these tough South Africans, Manfred realised that his country would need more and more young people like him if they were to win.

They reached the crest of the ridge. On the other side Manfred saw a number of tanks and what looked like a brigade of armoured cars. There was also some artillery. A chill went through him as he realised that it was these weapons that had destroyed their squadron. Manfred cursed the fool's errand they'd been sent on. The jeep pulled up outside a tent and Coetzee hopped out. He pointed to Manfred.

'Come with me.'

There seemed nothing better to do at that moment and the tent was potentially his destination. Manfred wasted no time in climbing out. At least he would be in the shade. Oddly, he felt quite calm. He'd never considered what it would be like to be a prisoner of war. The possibility had seemed so remote. Insofar as he'd given any thought to death, he'd always considered this would be the most likely way his war would end. Even being wounded seemed, to Manfred, an abstract idea. It was life or death. Anything in between was intangible.

The sergeant led him into the tent. Inside was a man in his forties. Manfred did not recognise the rank but as he was in a tent and twice his age, he was probably the senior officer.

'Sir,' said Coetzee, 'we found a number of Panzer crew who survived the engagement. We've taken this man back for interrogation. We established that he speaks English.'

207

The officer kept his eyes fixed on Manfred. There was a bang on his head. He wondered briefly if this had been Coetzee or one of the other men. Probably not. It didn't seem to be his style.

'Very good,' said the officer. He stood up and Manfred could see he was not quite as tall as him. He walked near Manfred and introduced himself.

'My name is Lieutenant Colonel Newton-King. And you are?'

'Private Brehme, sir,' said Manfred standing to attention.

Newton-King nodded to Manfred.

'You're with the 15th Panzer Division, I'm right in thinking?'

Manfred said nothing in reply. He knew his only response needed to be his name, his rank and his serial number. Manfred could hear his heart beating. It wasn't just the heat that was making him feel light-headed. The officer studied him closely. Manfred held his gaze, determined not to blink. He felt a trickle of sweat descend his forehead. He hoped that it would not drop into his eyes. Thankfully it diverted at the last minute and continued its journey down the side of his face.

Recognising that Manfred was not going to say more, the South African officer nodded and returned to his seat. He did not seem angry about this.

'How many tanks did you lose?'

Manfred saw no reason not to answer.

'Five, perhaps more, sir.'

'You lost your comrades?'

'Yes, my sergeant and corporal.'

Newton-King nodded again and picked up his pipe. There was silence in the tent for a minute while Newton-King looked at a piece of paper in front of him.

'We've been hit pretty hard ourselves by you chaps. Very well. Sergeant, take him away. Get something to eat.'

'Yes, sir,' replied Coetzee.

The big South African did not seem pleased by this. Manfred wondered why. They left the tent and for wont of anything else he could do, Manfred followed him over to a bunch of other soldiers.

'What are we going to do with him, sarge?'

Coetzee looked at Manfred and shrugged.

'It doesn't look like he's going to talk, and you know what the colonel is like.'

As Manfred did not know what the colonel was like, he was all ears. Unfortunately, the thought was not elaborated on by the others. Coetzee looked at Manfred again. Manfred tried to read what was behind his eyes. The others were looking at Manfred, too, in a sort of bewilderment about what to do.

'We can hardly take him with us, sarge,' pointed out a corporal.

Coetzee looked at the soldier, irritation across his face.

'I'm aware of that, Gerrie. I've an idea.'

'What's that?' asked the soldier.

'You'll see. Take your gun and come with me.'

Soon Manfred, Coetzee and the soldier were back in the jeep and driving back in the direction of where they'd come from. Manfred felt nervous. If they intended murdering him, for he viewed it this way, then they would clearly not want to do it in the camp within earshot of the colonel or full view of the camp. They drove for a mile along the track they'd come from. At a certain point, perhaps halfway between where they'd picked him up and the camp, Coetzee told the driver to stop the car.

'Out of the car,' said Coetzee.

Manfred looked at him for a moment, unsure of how to respond. The South African seemed unwilling to expand on his order. Manfred jumped out of the jeep and looked at the two men.

'Walk,' said Coetzee. He pointed towards the ridge which was half a mile away. 'Go on. Walk.'

Manfred glanced at the ridge and then back to the two South Africans. Overhead the sun was beating down on him and he could feel his skin burning again. He desperately wanted to be under cover. He looked again at the South Africans. To help him in his decision, Coetzee pointed the gun at him and then motioned for him to start moving.

Manfred turned his back and started to walk. He heard the car start again. He walked slowly and steadily in the direction of the ridge. His senses were alive in a way he could not remember before. If an insect had tripped up in the sand at that moment, he'd have heard the sound of it swearing. His shirt was soaking wet yet still he could feel it scratch his skin. He wanted to scratch. Even more than this he wanted to run. But where to?

His heart was racing like an engine, sending blood surging around his body making him light-headed. They hadn't driven away yet. He tried to drown out the sound of their intentions. The click of the machine gun.

He felt he was going to pass out.

Chapter Twenty-Three

North of Sidi Rezegh Airfield, Libya, 21ˢᵗ November 1941

'All stations. Aston. Move back. Move back now. We can't hold ridge.'

When he put down the microphone, Aston's feelings on the attack poured forth in a series of obscenities that would have earned the acclaim of a trawlerman. His driver had already been slowing down to make ready for the order to retreat.

Then the tank stopped.

'What the hell's happened?' screamed Aston. His worst fear had always been the reliability of the Crusader. This was not the time for it to be confirmed.

The engine coughed into life. Aston offered up his soul to God in thanks. The tank jerked backwards, sent on its way by a hail of bullets tattooing the front armour.

The men exchanged looks. They'd got away with this one but how long could their luck last?

Aston peered out of the small gap in the cupola. His mouth dropped in shock at the sight of Turner's tank erupting into flame.

'What's happened?' called someone from below.

'Turner's gone,' announced Aston in a stunned voice. There was no sense of satisfaction; instead, fear engulfed him. Then he realised the turret of the tank had been detached by the force of the explosion. He saw it smash into another Crusader just behind them.

'Is that Reed?' he asked, almost to himself. A voice from below confirmed it.

'Yes, that's Reed.'

Aston looked down at the driver. Nothing had to be said. The terror in both men's eyes transmitted the order and its reception.

'Sir, three men have escaped. We should pick them up.'

Stopping would be suicidal. Aston's immediate reaction was to tell his gunner to go to blazes.

'Keep reversing but slow down. At this speed they could walk and catch us up. Don't let the engine stall.'

Cursing, quite literally, like a trooper, Aston raised his head briefly through the cupola. He motioned for the three men to jump on.

Blackness.

Sounds of shouting.

Danny felt himself being pulled. Muscles seemed to strain and tear. The pain woke him. He was outside on the sand. All around him he could hear explosions. The smell of cordite, petrol and something else he would one day learn was the smell of burnt flesh, infected the air. His eyes could not focus, and they were stinging with sand and smoke. Finally, some vision returned to his eyes. He looked up and saw Craig.

'You all right, son?' shouted Craig.

Danny couldn't speak but nodded.

'Can you get on your feet? We need to move.'

Danny found he could move his legs and quickly rose to his feet.

His head was ringing like he'd been hit repeatedly by a cricket bat. He glanced around him, but Craig was pulling him away.

'No time. Move!' shouted the Ulsterman.

Danny realised Felton was on the other side of him holding his arm. They were running, half dragging him away towards a tank that was reversing. It slowed down and Danny could see someone appear and wave them to climb aboard. The sounds of battle were dulled by a combination of the pain in Danny's arms and the ringing in his ears.

Moments later he felt himself picked up and then he was on top of the hull. Craig and Felton were beside him. The tank picked up speed and Danny was nearly thrown off. He grabbed hold of some metal and held on for dear life.

Up ahead he could see their tank. It was in flames. Lying beside it was the turret of another Crusader. Danny remembered they'd been hit. His mind was scrambled. Something important was missing. He stared in horror at the sight of a dozen British tanks in flames. There were puffs of white smoke in the distance; then he would hear a sound overhead. He ducked when he heard it, like that would help.

Something important was missing. What the hell was it?

Finally.

'Where's sarge?'

He turned to Craig. The Ulsterman looked grim.

'Dead.'

'Holmes'

Craig shook his head. Danny couldn't believe it. Two men dead from the tank within minutes of the attack commencing. The death of Reed seemed extraordinary to him. Of all the men he'd met so far, he admired the sergeant most. He had an air about him that all the men recognised. Even Holmes seemed to defer to Reed for reasons

213

that went beyond rank. It felt to Danny as if his war was over before it had even started.

He looked back towards the stricken metal shell that had been their home. For the first time he became aware of a gash on his forehead. He put his hand to the wound. Craig smiled grimly at him.

'Sorry, we banged your head as we pulled you out.'

'Idiot,' responded Danny. 'Thanks.' He meant it.

The remainder of the regiment continued reversing as shots sang all around them. What a mess. He turned to Felton to say thanks. As he did so, a shell burst at the side of the tank. Felton looked shocked for a second and then he slumped forward into Danny's arms. The back of his head was a bloody mess. Craig's eyes widened in horror. Danny's throat was too parched to cry out. He resisted every impulse to throw the dead body off the hull. Instead, in the midst of the mayhem, he gently laid the body out on the top of the hull.

Craig and Danny kept their heads down. They passed one bombed out armoured vehicle after another. The charred remains of men lay abandoned like leaves in autumn. Every yard backwards was accompanied by eruptions close by. Shards of shell stung the side armour. The two men glanced at one another.

Both Danny and Craig could do nothing but hold on. Tears were streaming down the face of the Ulsterman. Tears for a fallen comrade. Danny heard him whispering repeatedly a long-forgotten psalm as a choir of whistling shells fell around them.

'...though I walk through the valley of the shadow of death, I will fear no evil; for Thou art with me; Thy rod and Thy staff, they comfort me.'

Minutes later they were cresting the northern escarpment and heading towards point 167 to meet with the remainder of A squadron who had not taken part in the action. Some degree of safety was in sight.

But for how long? The other tanks were now visible. The intensity of the fire had subsided. They finally drew to a halt.

How many had survived? Danny raised himself up and looked around. From out of the hatch emerged Captain Aston. Danny was aware of other crew members scrambling out from the hatch located in the hull. Three men came to help Danny and Craig down from the top of the hull.

'Thanks,' said Danny. He saw Craig move towards Felton. Danny joined him and the two men took their fallen comrade down from the front of the tank. Stretcher bearers appeared. Felton departed. Danny and Craig stared at his departure in silence. Danny felt a hand on his back. A soldier was speaking to him. He half recognised him, but his mind was too scrambled from what he'd been through.

'What the hell happened, mate?'

Unable to speak, Danny shook his head. Aston appeared behind the soldier. Grime streaked by sweat covered his face. He was smoking a cheroot.

'Do you need a doctor?' asked Aston glancing at the side of Danny's face which was caked with blood. The captain seemed in possession of himself but there was a tremor in his voice.

'No,' replied Danny but Aston was already walking away towards Squadron A's tanks.

Aston joined the remaining officers huddled around a tall, well-made man wearing corduroy trousers. This was the head of the Support Group, Brigadier Jock Campbell. Aston was the last to join the group of officers. Campbell nodded to Aston as he arrived. A quick glance around confirmed there were not many officers left. He and Longworth were the two most senior officers. His first thought was to pray that Longworth was the more senior of the two. With a sinking heart,

Aston realised he was going to be pitched right back into the fight. Carousing in Cairo seemed a lifetime ago.

Aston looked into the clear blue eyes of Jock Campbell. The eyes betrayed no fear. He was as tall as Aston. A light, clipped moustache stood out against his sun-reddened face. His tone, when he began speaking, was calm, but urgent.

'The situation is fraught. We've lost a lot of officers, men and armour. As far as I can tell, Lieutenant Colonel Lister, and the commanders of B and C squadrons have all been killed or captured. The 6th RTR has seventeen tanks left. They will now fall under the command of Captain Longworth. Captain Ainsley, can you take some tanks to confirm if there are Axis tanks advancing on the airfield? We cannot lose our hold. I'm going down there now. Longworth, assemble whatever we have left and get them ready as quickly as you can and get them down to the airfield.'

This effectively ended the meeting. Campbell climbed into the waiting staff car and sped off, leaving the remaining officers to organise the remnants of the regiment. The list of killed or captured made for sobering reading.

Ainsley handed the list to Aston, who shook his head but said nothing. Longworth's face was ashen.

'Have we rescued any men?' asked Longworth dejectedly.

'I picked up some of Reed's men,' said Aston.

Longworth looked up hopefully at this. Reed was highly regarded by all of the officers. Aston shook his head.

'No, Reed's gone.'

'Are any of the reserve tanks ready?'

'No, sir,' replied Ainsley.

'Then can we find tanks for the other men?' pressed Longworth.

Aston nodded. So, too, did Ainsley.

'My tank was hit; Mackenzie and Woodburn were wounded,' said Ainsley.

'My loader Dalton,' said Captain Aston, shaking his head. 'Dropped a shell on his ankle. I think it might be broken. Bloody idiot.'

It would be fair to say the other officers looked aghast at this incompetence. Aston felt that some of the disgust was directed towards him. He quickly moved the topic on, while they had time in the midday lull.

'What of the other sectors? Do we know what's been happening?' asked Aston.

Longworth's face looked grim. It was clear that things elsewhere were not going well.

'A division of Panzers to the south-east was engaged by the 7th Hussars. I gather their losses were heavy. The 60th artillery are up against a Panzer division. The Germans are in charge of the eastern end of the southern escarpment. It's not looking good. I've told Davy we're too spread out. He thinks we're winning,' said Longworth with a note of incredulity.

Pent up feeling against the ineffectiveness and unreliability of the Crusaders, their equipment and the cluelessness of the commanders threatened to derail the meeting until Longworth held his hand up and asked for quiet.

'I know how you feel. The Germans have better tanks and better guns. There's nothing we can do about that at the moment. Better tanks will come, I'm sure of that. For now, we have our job to do. Hold onto the airfield. The New Zealanders are coming from the east and Scobie's making good progress from Tobruk. We've also got the 4th and 22nd coming from the south. They'll give Rommel something to think about.'

'How many tanks do we have left?' asked Aston. 'Including the 2nd RTR.'

'Less than thirty. We're trying to see what we can salvage,' replied Longworth. He shot Aston a glance. If there was a way of introducing a downbeat note into proceedings, Aston was your man.

There was no way for Longworth to sugar-coat the level of damage the Afrika Korps had inflicted on them in the morning. The meeting had reached its conclusion and Longworth gathered up his maps. He recapped on their new objective.

'It's going to get even messier now. I don't doubt for a second the enemy will anticipate our moves. Divide Reed's men amongst yourselves,' said Longworth. 'We have to move to a new position to the south-west of this one. I'll radio the details. All right. To the tanks, everyone.'

They broke up with Ainsley and Aston walking alongside one another. They discussed who they would take. Although all the men in the tank would have been trained for each of the different roles, it was best to have experience where possible.

Danny and Craig were handed some biscuits and tea. When Danny had finished these he went in search of his friends. He saw Arthur and Lawrence walking towards him.

'Thought you were a goner there at one moment, my lad,' said Arthur.

'You look in a bad way. What happened?'

Danny was unable to speak at first. Arthur and Lawrence could see the deep sorrow on Danny's face. He felt Arthur pat his arm. His relief at his surviving and the adrenaline surge he'd experienced during the day had evaporated. His fatigue was deep, his sadness for the lost colleagues deeper still, and a feeling of guilt rose within him.

'Sorry, mate,' said Lawrence. 'You don't have to say anything.'

'No, it's all right,' replied Danny at last.

Danny talked a little of what had happened. When he reached the point at which they'd been hit, he stopped for a moment to collect himself.

'It's so quick. You've no time to think. I don't know what we were doing. It was suicide.'

His two friends nodded. Word of the charge had filtered through to A Squadron. It sounded hellish. There was little they could say to console their young friend. However, Danny felt a little better for having spoken of what he'd experienced, if only because he thought it might help his friends in a similar situation. They were grateful. When a tank was hit and began to brew up, they had seconds to escape.

'I see you're with that bugger Aston now,' said Lawrence.

'I don't know. Anyway, he's not that bad,' replied Danny, in defence. 'If he hadn't collected us, I wouldn't be here now.' His two friends exchanged glances and said nothing more on the topic of Captain Aston. They parted with their usual farewell.

'Keep your head down.'

Danny trotted back towards Craig, who was sitting down, alone, holding his tea, and smoking a cigarette.

'Any word of what's happening?' asked Danny. Craig shook his head and pointed to a spot behind Danny.

Danny turned just in time to see two officers approach. Captains Aston and Ainsley were deep in conversation. They both glanced in the direction of Danny and Craig.

'Well, Danny-boy, I guess this is it,' said Craig. 'We're about to get new tanks. On your feet.'

Craig leapt to his feet and threw away his cigarette. Aston spoke first.

'Which one of you can load?'

'I was loader in Sergeant Reed's tank,' said Danny.

Aston glanced up at the wound. He raised an eyebrow which Danny correctly interpreted as a question.

'It's a scratch, sir,' said Danny, conscious it hurt like hell.

'And you?' asked Ainsley, directing his gaze towards Craig.

Craig replied, 'I'm the driver. I've been on wireless and a gunner also.'

Ainsley nodded. It made sense as to why they had not been killed by the turret from Hutton's tank.

'All right,' said Ainsley, looking at Craig. 'You come with me.'

This left Danny and Captain Aston standing together.

'Follow me …' Aston paused a moment and waited for Danny to fill in his name.

'Shaw, sir,' said Danny.

'Yes, yes, I remember.'

Chapter Twenty-Four

Manfred stumbled forward. Tears stung his eyes as he heard the sound of the South African jeep recede into the distance. He felt exhausted yet he'd barely walked more than a hundred metres. He reached the crest of the ridge and slid-walked down the sand.

He needed shade.

It was hot but not unbearably so. The problem was the sun. His fair skin was never designed to be in this country. Manfred didn't want to survive a tank battle or being a prisoner of war, albeit for minutes rather than years, only to die of sunstroke.

Ahead, he could see the twisted metal remnants and his heart lurched at the sight of the devastation. We are not indestructible, he realised. If they can get close enough, they can kill us. Five smoking hulks bore testimony to the folly of travelling beyond the security of their anti-tank guns.

Just at that moment he heard a sound. It was a clang. The thought hit him that someone was alive inside one of the tanks. A surge of energy coursed through him. He ran forward towards the nearest

Panzer. It was blackened from the explosion. It was no longer so hot to touch. Manfred opened the hatch and glanced in. A wave of revulsion went through him. Death was spread all over the interior where once there had been life. He knelt on all fours and began retching. Somewhere behind him he heard another clang.

He rose groggily to his feet and stumbled in the direction of the sound. It grew louder as he approached the last Mark III. He'd heard that there were people who dwelled in the desert who made money from robbing the dead and the dying in the desert. Anger swelled within him. He would not allow this.

Clambering on top of the hull, he reached the turret and ducked his head inside. Just as he did so he heard a single, all-too-German word. There were two men inside.

'You're back,' said Kohler in English.

Manfred didn't know whether to laugh or cry. He was certainly in shock. He'd no idea Kohler spoke English. There was no reason why he shouldn't, of course. It was a lesson Manfred supposed. Not to judge people so readily. He'd never thought of Kohler being intellectually the biggest gun among the crew. In truth, he thought him a bit thick. Who was the idiot now?

Fischer turned around and looked up at Manfred. If he was surprised, he was doing a remarkable job of hiding it. If anything, he was more interested in Kohler's progress on trying to fix the tank. In fact, within seconds he'd lost interest and looked at Kohler.

'Any luck?'

'No. I can't do anything,' replied Kohler.

They looked at one another, then both turned up towards Manfred.

'I don't suppose you overpowered those South Africans and stole their jeep, English boy?'

Manfred wasn't sure whether to be stung by their mockery or accept it as a good-humoured welcome back to the team. He took it as the latter and grinned.

'Yes, sure. I took them prisoner.'

Fischer held his arm up and Manfred helped first him then Kohler out of the tank.

The three of them jumped down and looked around at the carnage. Manfred slapped a can of water which was strapped to the side of the hull.

'We should take some of these.'

Fisher pointed over to a pile a few yards away. They'd already begun to take supplies for the long walk back to the camp. Manfred nodded and unhooked the water from the tank. He grabbed a ground sheet and laid it out. With the help of Fischer and Kohler, he added to their supply stock. Soon they had taken as much as they could reasonably carry with them.

'Shall we?' asked Fischer. They began to walk in the direction they'd come from.

'You look ridiculous,' said Fischer. The three boys were clear of the destroyed tanks and following the tracks of those that had survived the onslaught.

Manfred grinned and had to acknowledge that he did look a little strange. He'd taken off his shirt and was wearing it over his head like an Arab headscarf. It meant his lower back and arms were exposed to the sun. At least his head and shoulders were covered; Manfred deemed them the most important areas to protect.

'You mean I don't seem like an Arab?' asked Manfred.

Fischer stopped for a second and looked at the pale white skin, the blond hair peeking out from the khaki shirt and the blue eyes.

223

'Would you be offended if I said, no?'

Manfred burst out laughing. He put the can down, did a twirl and then held his arms out.

'I thought I was blending in quite well.'

Fischer laughed and sat down. It was time for a water break. Manfred and Kohler joined him, and they gorged themselves thirstily on the water. In fact, Manfred had been thinking of nothing else for the past twenty minutes. His arms were aching from the weight, the first hint of a blister or three were appearing on his heels and his eyes were stinging from the sweat pouring down his forehead. While satiating his need for liquid seemed eminently sensible, he hadn't wanted to be the one to suggest it. He wondered idly if Fischer had used the joke as an excuse for them to rest and drink.

'We should do this every thirty minutes,' suggested Manfred.

'Let's make it twenty,' replied Kohler. There was no argument from Manfred or Fischer on this. Kohler had, by now, adopted Manfred's form of headdress. In the end, Fischer did so as well. This gave Manfred some quiet satisfaction, but it did not last long. His mind turned to another problem.

'How far do you think we must go?'

'I think we travelled six or seven kilometres. It'll take an hour or two to get back to the camp. If they're still there.'

Manfred nodded. He'd been thinking on similar lines. Neither mentioned the likelihood that the regiment would have moved by the time they reached what was their original camp.

A few minutes later they were on their feet again and walking. The sun glared down at them angrily. If God had meant Germans to be in this hostile landscape, he'd have given them different skin. This was the real enemy, Manfred realised. Overcoming the Allies was one thing; mastering this harsh, unforgiving environment, another. The

Germans had no answer to the weaponry it could deploy; a merciless sun that burned your skin, that made metal unbearable to touch and tanks furnace hot.

Then there were the nights where the chill permeated your clothing and took up residence in your bones. The lack of food or water or civilisation. This land, this region wasn't just inhospitable; it was alien.

Oddly, Manfred felt a little bit more relaxed than he had ten minutes previously and it wasn't just because they'd refreshed themselves. It was something more basic, more important yet utterly trivial. It was Fischer who'd instigated the break, not he. Even Kohler had waited for Fischer. This meant he was human. Not some sort of Aryan superman.

Manfred was one of them now. He'd faced the enemy. More than this, he'd faced his demons and won. He'd not lost face. Either in the tank, facing the South Africans, or under the merciless intensity of the desert sun. The episode with the South Africans had not diminished him as much as he'd thought it might.

'If we ever get out of this, I'm going to take up skiing,' said Manfred.

'You'll love it,' replied Fischer.

Of course, he would be an expert, thought Manfred, regretting having mentioned it. For once the jealousy was only passing.

'Where did you learn?' asked Manfred in need of something to take his mind off the walking. He was surprised by how little he knew about the Bavarian. For all his conceitedness, Fischer was actually quite private and rarely spoke about his life before the war.

'I'm from Munich. We went to the mountains most weekends. During winter I virtually lived on the slopes. Maybe if we hadn't had this war I'd have competed at the Olympics.'

'Really? You're that good.'

'Yes. That good,' replied Fischer. Manfred supressed a smile. He did not doubt Fischer was *that* good but hearing him say it amused him. 'Maybe when this is over, you'll come down. I'll teach you.'

'Would you?' asked Manfred.

'Of course. Let's get through this first.'

Manfred nodded. He looked ahead. The mid-afternoon haze had lifted. It was possible to see quite a long way ahead now. Not that there was much to see in the flat, featureless landscape. Fischer seemed to have the same thought.

'Not much sign of life, is there?'

Although he thought he knew the answer, Manfred asked the question anyway.

'Do you speak English?' asked Manfred in English to Fischer.

Fischer laughed and replied in English, 'Yes, of course.'

They walked along in silence for another minute. A thought was gnawing within him. He remembered Fischer's reaction when Manfred had, he thought, saved Kohler's life.

'Why didn't you say then?' asked Manfred.

Indeed, why didn't he say? Or Kohler. Neither had spoken. Even Kohler, a gun pointed to his head, had stayed silent. Did that make him naïve? Stupid? The truth was walking alongside him. Kohler, alive. But he would have lived anyway. They both had guessed, gambled even, that the South African's threat was not real.

'I didn't believe he'd kill Kohler.'

'Do you think I was acting to save my own skin?'

Fischer looked at Manfred and grinned.

'Were you?'

The answer to that was more complicated. Manfred was silent for a few moments while he considered how to respond.

'They might have tortured me,' pointed out Manfred although he didn't really believe this himself.

226

'I doubt it. The war in the desert has been fought with some decency on both sides,' replied Fischer. Then the Bavarian stopped. This forced his two companions to do likewise. 'I don't think you're a coward, but you should have known better. Their jeep was full. They didn't want the hassle of dealing with us any more than we would have wanted to take them back to camp with us. They wouldn't have murdered us any more than we would have murdered them. The best policy was silence.'

Manfred looked surprised at Fischer. This appeared to amuse the Bavarian. The idea that he would speak almost well of the enemy was unexpected. Manfred had always assumed that Fischer was a Nazi to his core. He looked the part and certainly sounded it. But, then again, didn't he look every bit the Aryan boy? Hadn't he been in the Hitler Youth? Why should Fischer be any more of a Nazi than he? Manfred's feelings towards his leader had changed since he'd become a soldier. His allegiance was no longer an unquestioning obedience. There were doubts now.

He thought of the young Jewish girl, Diane Landau, again. And Anja. Yes, the doubts had been there from the start, he realised. Back then, he'd denied it to himself. Now, such questions could be asked openly because here, in the desert, there was no one to censure him. Fischer began a story about his first experience of conflict in the desert.

They started to walk again. Kohler remained silent but it was clear Fischer wanted to say more.

'We never spoke of this back at the camp but in the middle of June when the British came to relieve Tobruk the first time, I was in a different tank. It didn't last long, a few days maybe, but it was intense. We fought against their tanks. We took out so many of them, but they kept coming. You'd see one tank explode, or another brew up. Their men would escape. We let them. They let ours go, too.'

'I heard Seeler say that they killed our men,' said Kohler.

'Seeler's an idiot.'

As ever there was utter conviction in Fischer's words. To be fair, Manfred did not disagree. Seeler *was* an idiot.

Fischer had not finished, however.

'On the second morning of the battle my tank was hit. Previously when we were hit, we ignored it. But the others knew straightaway that the fuel had been hit. They were heading for the hatches before I'd time to ask what had happened. I got out just in time. The tank was in flames; then the turret went ten metres into the sky. Damn near caught me on the way down.

'We'd all escaped unharmed, but the battle was going on around us. We could see the Tommy tank that had destroyed ours fifty metres away. They drove past us, and a hand came out the side and waved. Then they gave us this kind of two-finger salute.

'We jumped onto a couple of tanks that were moving backwards. My God I prayed like I've never prayed before. All around me I could hear shells screaming overhead and then exploding nearby or hitting our tanks. I thought I was finished. The sound of the explosions. I'll never forget it.

'I was with a gunner called Kruger sitting on one tank and the rest of my crew were on another. I saw the Tommy tank first. It was coming over a ridge from our side. I shouted a warning to Kruger. They had us side on. I jumped off the back of the tank. It was no more than a second later it was hit. I jumped into a hole made by one of the explosions. The tank brewed up quickly. I saw men coming out of it on fire. They hadn't a chance, Brehme. I went to see them after, but they were all dead. I saw things inside that tank that I never want to see again. I wanted to cry.

'The Tommy tank left me alone and drove off. Then I saw others

228

pass me. Within a few minutes they were gone. I was on my own. There wasn't anything I could do other than see what I could salvage from the tank. There was a lot of water and food, but I couldn't carry it all. I took a sheet and wrapped up as much as I could. It weighed a tonne. But I was able to drag it on the sand. I started to walk back in the direction of where we'd had a camp. I think it was around four in the afternoon. The heat was much worse than now, trust me.

'I'd been walking for an hour or so when I saw two men in the distance. I shouted and waved to them. They waved back. It was only when we got near each other I realised they were Tommies. I couldn't believe my luck. I stopped and they ran towards me. It wasn't like I had anywhere else to go and they would have caught me anyway. May as well let them come to me. I was tired enough.

'Of course, they couldn't believe they'd met a German. Neither spoke German of course. Typical British. They expect the mountain to come to Mohammed when it comes to language. And they call us arrogant.

'They were friendly which was a surprise. There was no interest in fighting the war. We sat down and had a meal. They had some rations. Their food is better. They didn't think much of it though. Then they tried what I had. It was funny. One of them spat it out. They're in a desert, abandoned and at risk of starvation and they reject our food. That tells you something, boys, trust me.

'When we'd finished our meals, I gave them some of my water; then we wished each other luck and went in different directions. They waved. I waved. It was madness really. They were just like you and me. We argued a bit about Hitler. They said a lot of things against him. But they had no idea what it was like in Germany for us and our families. I think they were a bit surprised when I told

229

them. Maybe they have a better idea why we had a right to become strong again.

'I followed the tracks and found a lot of destroyed British tanks. I even had a look at them myself. Very poor quality. Small guns and much more like a tin box than the Panzer when you rap the front of it. The sound and the feel are different. I think we're lucky to have the tanks we have. It was getting dark, and I was feeling a bit nervous. I'm not normally afraid of the dark, I would add, but when you're in the middle of nowhere, and it's complete silence around you, I can tell you it gets you thinking.

'I was walking in the tracks themselves because visibility was non-existent. Then, finally, I saw it. Lights in the distance. Not many. A few campfires. I walked back into the camp. It was quite a welcome but there was sadness, too. We lost a lot of people. But we beat them. Sent them back to Egypt.'

'I think if I were a cat,' concluded Fischer, 'I would have lost eight of my nine lives.'

Manfred smiled and looked up at the sun. It was lower in the sky and the mid-afternoon heat was not unpleasant. But they were alone. There was nothing around them except desert. A plain, pitiless landscape where nothing could live.

'Don't speak too soon, Fischer,' replied Manfred. 'We're not home yet.'

Home. Where was that now? The tank? The camp? Germany?

They forged ahead as the gloom descended on the desert. They were silent now. Thoughts of where they would camp were uppermost in their minds. The race was on now, against nightfall. They would have no tracks to guide them in the dark. Finally, Fischer held his hand up like he was leading a cavalry troop. Manfred and Kohler exchanged glances and a roll of the eyes. Fischer peered into the gathering gloom. The curtain had come down on this adventure, at least for the moment. The three boys allowed the blackness to enfold them.

'What do you think, my friends?'

Manfred started to laugh. It was a nervous reaction to the events of the day. It seemed to surprise Fischer. He spun around.

'I hope you're not afraid of the dark.'

Manfred's answer succinctly suggested this was not the case. Fischer grinned, his teeth gleaming like pearls at the bottom of the sea. Kohler started to laugh but seemed less sure of what the joke was. By now Manfred was giggling uncontrollably which set Fischer off. Both had to sit down such was their merriment. It was free and pure. The laughter of youth, unrestricted by responsibility. The laughter of people who had a whole life ahead of them.

Chapter Twenty-Five

Sidi Rezegh Airfield, Libya, 21st November 1941

Danny looked around him as he followed Aston back towards his new tank. Arthur gave him a salute and Danny managed a grin. A number of C Squadron tanks had survived the charge. Only two from Danny's. Somewhere in the distance he could hear the rumble of guns. He looked down at his watch and saw it was broken. The face was cracked, and time stilled. He took it off and threw it away. He thought about Phil Lawrence's ridiculous Mickey Mouse watch.

He and Aston walked in silence towards the tank. Both were still too much in shock from the morning to speak. Aston glanced at Danny. He remembered the cocky soldier from a few months previously. Not so cocky now are you, son? thought Aston. They arrived at the tank which was being refuelled and replenished with ammunition.

The Crusader was in a pitiful state. The dents, the dust and the sense of death hung over it. Aston stared at it in silence and wondered how the hell they'd escaped the carnage.

'Listen up, men,' said Aston. 'This is Shaw. He's our loader now. You can introduce yourselves in the tank. Is it ready yet?'

Twenty minutes later, just enough time for Danny to gulp down as much water as he could and grab some biscuits, they were ready to leave. They climbed into the Crusader. It looked identical to the one Danny had recently vacated feet first, unconscious. He recognised a couple of them from the football games back at the camp.

'Shaw, this is Stone, our gunner,' said Aston. 'Shaw, you take orders from these men until I say so.'

'Yes, sir,' replied Danny. He eyed Stone who grinned and held out his hand. Stone then indicated the men behind him.

'That's Dave Bennett on the wireless and Alex Wilson our driver.'

Danny quickly shook hands before Wilson moved to crank up the tank for moving out. Ten minutes later they were on the move again. The smell of fumes and men was no different from his previous one, yet Danny felt like he was in an alien land. After five months with the other men, this was different.

He'd had no time to grieve for his dead crew mates. But a feeling of desolation hit him now. Although he'd never had much time for Holmes, the thought of how he'd met his end was distressing. The loss of Reed affected him particularly. There had been a quiet certainty about the sergeant that Danny had admired. There was no more competent soldier than Reed. None braver. Yet nothing could have saved him. The insanity of what they'd undertaken was laid bare. He tried to draw solace from the fact he had survived. This was doomed to fail.

While he was busy checking their new vehicle, Danny noticed that Stone was studying him. There was a shrewdness to the Londoner that made him feel like he was an open book. He felt wary at first. Then Stone spoke.

'Sorry about your mates. Can't be easy.'

Danny nodded. It wasn't easy.

233

'Reed was a good man. The captain,' said Stone, glancing upwards towards Aston, 'tried to get him in his tank six months ago but Lister wasn't having it. He promoted him and gave him his own tank instead.'

Danny noted that Stone didn't say 'Lieutenant Colonel'. It was just Lister. This didn't feel right, but he said nothing. He'd heard stories of the insubordinate nature of this crew. They took their lead from their commander. A part of him felt uncomfortable about such an attitude of defiance. He believed in the command structure of the army. Why else would he ride into battle fully aware of the risks involved? Another part of him questioned what they were doing. Riding into enemy gunfire seemed no more intelligent now than it had when his father had watched friends and comrades walking to their death in a hail of machine gun fire.

'He was a good man,' confirmed Danny at last.

No one in the tank felt like talking. This suited Danny. He wasn't in the mood to get to know his new comrades. On first acquaintance, they were a surly bunch. There was a sly look about the gunner, Stone, that was the opposite of Holmes. He knew Holmes didn't like him. He made no attempt to hide this. To be fair, Holmes liked no one so Danny was not a special case.

Craig was a cynic. He woke up cynical and went to bed secure in the knowledge he was right to be so. As with Holmes, Danny always felt he knew where he stood with the Ulsterman. Charlie Felton was more open because he was in the same place as Danny. New, inexperienced and not trusted.

The men of this crew seemed more guarded. They usually kept themselves to themselves in camp although Stone and Wilson played football occasionally. Collectively they had the same cynicism as Craig but without the dry humour that accompanied it. Danny concluded from this that his best policy was to keep his head down and do his job while avoiding conversation which showed dissent with any senior officer.

The radio crackled and Danny heard Longworth's voice over the airwaves.

'Longworth here. Report positions.'

Aston's reply was off air and off colour, but it made them all smile, Danny included. He looked at Aston again and had to admit there was a charisma about the man, a certain devil-may-care aura. Although Reed had never said as much, he knew the sergeant didn't have time for Aston. Separately, Danny had heard he was a bit of a bellyacher. Yet here he was, albeit inside twenty tons of metal, ready to face German gunfire.

And the German gunfire started again and did not stop for the duration of the afternoon. The radio was their lifeline to what was happening in the world outside, yet the story was confused. The exasperation in Aston's voice was all too clear as he sought to make sense of a battle which was as chaotic as any he'd ever experienced.

'What's happening, sir?' asked Danny as there was a brief lull in the barrage.

Aston was on the point of providing an unsympathetic and brief response to the question when he saw the rest of the men looking his way. He held his natural inclination in check and gave the best summary he could on his limited understanding.

Danny smiled at this and found himself warming to the aristocratic captain. The situation was ghastly, no question. But something of the captain's acerbity was comforting. Aston's face, like all of them, was caked in sand. They were dirty, tired and more than a little bit frightened by the shells raining down on them. But Aston's summary of the situation helped, oddly, in staving off the sense of displacement they had sitting in their metal box.

'Listen up,' said Aston. 'As you may have gathered, it's all a bit of a mess. I don't think Campbell knows what's happening; I suspect Gott and Davy even less. We're under attack at the airfield. You may have noticed one or two bombs headed our way.'

Danny and the other men laughed. They had certainly noticed. Aston took out a map and set it down for all to see. His hands were dirty. Grime-encrusted skin and fingernails were not quite what one would have associated with a nobleman's son.

'It's a bloody mess. Jerry has taken the north-western end of the escarpment, but we're in control of the south. The enemy is also to our east at Abiar el Amar and to the north at El Duda. Behind them, Scobie at Tobruk is threatening their rear. To our south Gott and Davy are being threatened by more tanks. We're going to join Campbell and the Support Group and try to hold Jerry off at the eastern side of the airfield. We have artillery and infantry there but may come up against tanks. Get ready for another pounding.'

There was an audible groan from the men.

'It's worse than you think. I heard from Longworth that the 60th artillery barely has any guns left. I don't know how long we can hold on. The best we can hope for is that it's long enough for either darkness to fall or they run out of petrol or ammunition or both. Not the best strategy I've heard lately. To cap it off, and there's no sugar-coating it, we're slap bang in the middle of this show. It's all a bit like a Battenberg cake at the moment.'

Well, he certainly hadn't sugar-coated it, thought Danny. Oddly he felt better for knowing. It was clear that Aston was not a man for dispensing false hope. This was a strange form of reassurance.

The tank bumped along in the direction of the airfield. The sounds of battle grew louder. By now, Danny was too numb to feel terror. Could what they were about to face be any worse than what he'd been through already? He was aware of a dull throb in his head where he'd banged it earlier. His stomach was empty, yet he felt no hunger. His mind was filled with a sense of wonder at what he and the men around him had been through, and what they were being asked to do now.

Late afternoon, the twelve remaining tanks of the 6th RTR, trundled towards the Sidi Rezegh airfield. Danny could see the square, clean pattern of the airfield filled with destroyed planes at the boundary. In the middle were some burnt-out armoured vehicles and tanks. A black pall of smoke filled the air.

The 60th Field Regiment were firing their guns, but they were greatly reduced in number. There was a staff car in front of them. Danny could see an officer waving the tanks forward holding aloft a blue scarf. Who the hell is that, wondered Danny? They were passing burning vehicles as they sped down the hill.

'Campbell must be mad,' uttered Aston incredulously. 'He's running around in that bloody staff car. He's even waving a scarf. You'd think he wants the Germans to aim at him.'

A blue scarf thought Danny. This wasn't in any training manual he'd read. Still, it seemed to be working. The tanks were racing forward behind this extraordinary man. Beside him, driving, was a fair-haired man. They were heading directly towards dozens of Panzer Mark IIIs in the distance.

'The man's insane,' said Aston staring ahead at the same sight as Danny.

Aston glanced down at Wilson, the driver. A tacit signal was exchanged. Danny sensed they were slowing slightly. He felt a touch on his arm from Stone. Danny reacted immediately and loaded a shell into the gun.

Shells were now raining down, a cacophony of clanging against

237

their armour. Danny risked a glance through his periscope and saw sadistic flashes of fire from the approaching Panzers.

He heard Stone fire off the first round. Danny tracked its progress and saw it hit the target.

'Shot,' yelled Danny in joy before the crushing dismay as realisation set in that the shell had merely bounced off the Panzer III armour. They were too far away.

Aston had seen the same thing and gave vent to his feelings about the inadequacy of the British guns with a volley of oaths.

Danny tugged the next shell out of the bracket, pulling down the ejection leaver and forcing it into the barrel with enough force to close the breech in a single movement. He tapped the gunner to give the 'gun ready' signal. Stone fired again but Danny was barely aware as he was already tugging at the next shell.

Out of the corner of his eye he saw Wilson. His foot was coming off the accelerator. He was aware of the increasing intensity of Aston's swearing at the enemy, but he and Stone were a blur of activity: load, fire, load, fire.

'Oh God,' shouted Aston. 'This is carnage.'

Danny couldn't see what was happening but guessed their charge at the vast army of tanks was exacting a horrible toll.

But it was not all one-sided.

Stone's shells were striking home to great effect if the gunner's 'got 'im' was to be believed. Danny hadn't time to admire Stone's handiwork. His movements were piston-like, efficient and potently in sync with the deadly purpose of the tank. He was part of a killing machine.

The hit they took probably saved them. The tank shuddered as it was struck sending a shock wave through each man. It stopped them in their tracks. The acrid smell of cordite came first; then smoke began to fill the hull and then the turret. Flames followed but by then Wilson was screaming what they all knew. The tank was brewing up.

'Bale out,' screamed Aston, already climbing out through the cupola. Danny followed Stone out of the top. The heat of the metal singed Danny's hands as he climbed out. He felt breathless, dazed and deafened. Only his racing heartbeat confirmed to him he'd survived. One thought was on his mind. Get clear.

All five men were out of the tank and sprinting for cover. Seconds later the tank exploded as the shells inside detonated. Danny hit the ground and covered his head. Earth and bits of metal rained down. He spun around and saw the smoking ruin that was once the Crusader tank. Behind him he heard the others shouting. They were racing in between the destroyed tanks. It was a slaughter. At least half a dozen of the remaining tanks of the regiment had been destroyed. It had taken the Germans less than a few minutes to wreak this havoc.

Danny got to his feet and sprinted behind one tank and dodged towards another. The other men had disappeared now. Glancing to his right he saw an explosion take out soldiers manning a twenty-five pounder. He ran over towards the gun to see if he could help any of the wounded men to safety.

Arriving at the gun he saw that the two men were, in fact, dead. He collapsed to his knees and retched at the sight of the injuries. The barrage continued. Shells whistled overhead. He ignored them. He looked up into the sky and saw the black smoke blotting out the sunlight.

Explosions erupted across the airfield. He turned around and looked at the burning misshapen hulks dotted around the airfield. He heard shouts in the distance, but Danny was past caring. A wordless acceptance that death was near.

A car pulled up near Danny. He turned around and saw an officer stride over towards him.

'Artillery?'

'Tank.'

'Do you know how to operate one of these?'

Danny looked at the tall officer and then the twenty-five-pounder gun. He nodded and then jumped to his feet. The officer was already on his way towards the gun. Danny made straight for the shells.

'Load,' ordered the officer.

Danny levered the breech open and heaved the cartridge into the jacket of the barrel. He closed the block quickly while the officer adjusted his aim.

'Have you pushed the crank forward? We don't want the shell coming back out,' asked the officer, still considering his aim.

'Yes, sir. Crank is locked.'

Seconds later the officer fired off a shell towards the tanks in the distance. This ranging shell gave the officer an idea of the adjustments needed. The empty chamber fell backwards from the gun. Moments later the officer nodded to Danny. At this point Danny already had a fresh cartridge ready to load. The officer adjusted the aim.

'Name?'

'Shaw, sir. 6th Tanks.'

This was met with a curt nod then the officer fired again. It landed just in front of one of the oncoming Panzers. This led to a stream of un-officer-like dismay at his rotten luck. As Danny loaded the next cartridge the officer noticed some stragglers taking evasive action from a gun that had been hit.

'Over here,' shouted the officer. The officer turned again to Danny. 'This fires five rounds a minute. Keep firing at those bastards over there.'

240

The group of soldiers were now racing over. The officer pointed at the two men.

'Help Shaw fire this. Keep firing until you run out of ammo. Then throw sticks at them if you have to; just stop them reaching the airfield.'

The tall officer grinned and strode off back to the staff car. He took off holding up a blue and white scarf.

A sergeant stepped forward. He was in his early thirties covered with sweat-streaked dust. His arm was bandaged. The other man seemed like he'd been beaten up in a fight after pub closing time. They looked at Danny holding the cartridge.

'What are you waiting for, son? You heard what the brigadier said.'

There was no time for conversation or greetings. In a moment Danny was loading another shell. Then another. And they were doing damage. Danny saw one tank shatter and then another. Another gun was in action nearby. Danny glanced over and saw an officer pulling a dead body off the portee to get the gun firing again.

Bullets punched the bank in front of the gun while Danny and the two men blazed away. When Danny glanced back at the other gun, he saw the officer lying dead. The other two men continued firing. Behind him he heard a grunt and saw the sergeant collapse. He'd been hit by shrapnel. Death had been instantaneous.

The other soldier stared in speechless horror at the fallen sergeant.

'Get down,' shouted Danny. He leapt forward to rugby tackle the soldier just as an explosion hit the gun. Stinging shards of steel ripped through the air. Danny felt pain in his leg as his body collided with the second soldier. When he raised himself up and looked down, sightless eyes stared back at him.

Tears of frustration stung Danny's eyes. He turned to the gun. It was now disabled. He glanced over towards the other gun. The two remaining men had withdrawn. Their gun had been turned into a twisted, smoking heap of metal.

Bullets tore into the sand around Danny. He had to find cover. He spotted a destroyed tank further back. Slowly, he crawled towards it. Overhead he heard the Allied twenty-five pounders firing on the approaching tanks. This, at least, was giving the Germans something to think about. The hail of bullets around his gun subsided.

Danny, sensing the attention of the tanks was now diverted elsewhere, pulled himself up from the ground and sprinted towards the rear of the tank. Circling around to the side he saw that the hatch was open. He glanced inside to see if there were any survivors. Shock and nausea overcame him. He fell backwards immediately from the hatch and began to throw up.

It was not the sight of the burnt blackened bodies nor the sharp smell of smoke and charred flesh. On one of the burned stumps there was the unmistakable shape and metallic colour of a watch. Despite the damage, he could still make out on the cracked, dust-covered watch face a small cartoon figure with big black ears, white gloves, big red shorts and two white buttons.

242

Chapter Twenty-Six

Sidi Rezegh Airfield, Libya, 21st November 1941

Danny looked up to the skies and was surprised to see it was raining lightly. Amid the bombs and the bullets, he'd not noticed the weather turning. Stomach sore and legs stinging from the piece of shrapnel, Danny got to his feet again. The attack seemed to have abated. The guns, if not silent, were not beating out shell after shell as they had earlier. Danny weaved in and out of the destroyed vehicles in the direction of the guns that were still in operation.

He heard someone calling his name. A look to his left revealed the gunner, Stone, motioning for him to come over. Danny jogged towards the spot where he and the rest of the tank crew were sitting. Captain Aston held binoculars up to his eyes. His gaze was fixed on the horizon.

'I think we've stopped them for the moment or perhaps they're running low on ammo.'

There was no question that there was a lull in the battle. The light was beginning to fade. The sound of shelling had all but stopped. There was still the low rumble of explosions elsewhere but they, too, were slowly subsiding. The group gazed down at the burnt-out hulks of the Crusaders. The 6th RTR had been annihilated.

'What happens now, sir?' asked Stone.

Aston laughed drily.

'Damned if I know, Stone. We haven't got a pot to piss in never mind a tank.'

The group stared out at the airfield in silent shock at the slaughter of their regiment. Sand was caked over Danny's face and his eyes felt clogged. His calf muscle burned from where the shell fragment had hit him. The smell of burning permeated the atmosphere. Danny began to shiver as the images of his friend swam into his mind. He was filthy, starving, angry and broken-hearted. The bile rose from within him, and he fought hard to stop himself throwing up again.

Stone put an arm on his shoulder.

'It doesn't get better.'

Danny looked at Stone and forced a smile. The others were on their feet now, and Danny rose with them. They trooped slowly past the remaining twenty-five pounders of the 60th Field Regiment. Past the twisted metal of the disabled guns. Stretcher bearers carried corpses away from the scattered devastation.

'Where are we heading, sir?'

'Good question,' said Captain Aston. He turned to Stone and pointed out some orderlies. 'Be a sport and see if you can find out where Brigade HQ is.'

Stone trotted off and spoke to a group of men near a wounded corporal. He returned a few moments later and nodded upwards.

'That way.'

The remainder of the 6th RTR rallied at the Brigade HQ to the south of the airfield. The arrival of Aston with Danny and the others provided some degree of consolation on a catastrophic day for the regiment. Danny glanced around and spotted Arthur at the side of one of the few tanks left.

'Arthur,' shouted Danny.

His friend turned and stared at him in shock. Danny tried to smile but his heart wasn't in it. He must have been quite a sight. Arthur ran over with one question on his lips.

'Phil?'

Danny couldn't speak. He shook his head. Arthur nodded and led him over to the tank.

'Sit down,' ordered Arthur. 'I'll make you some grub. Have you eaten?'

'I haven't eaten since this morning,' replied Danny. It felt so long since he'd brewed up the tea and handed out the biscuits and marmalade. So much had happened. He watched in silence as Arthur made the tea. Finally, Arthur brought over a cup and a tin with warm bully beef which Danny scoffed down in seconds.

'You saw him?' asked Arthur.

'Yes. I don't know how we survived. It was over so quickly.'

Arthur listened in silence as Danny related the events of the afternoon. A light drizzle fell on them but neither noticed. Danny withheld the detail of what he'd witnessed in the tank. It would be his memory alone. When Danny had finished, neither said anything. Each was left with their recollection of the corporal who had first greeted them at the camp. A sense of despondency hung over the men. Arthur's voice was barely recognisable to Danny.

'All gone, in the blink of an eye. I heard that the 6th held back a whole division of Panzers. I hadn't realised what it was like. You boys are bloody heroes, mate.'

'Not many of us left are there, though?' said Danny glancing around at the remaining Crusaders.

'We have about four tanks that are still working. One of them is mine. I was with Captain Gjemre. We were out with ordnance.'

'You were well out of it, mate. It was hell.' Out of the corner of his eye Danny saw Alex Wilson, the driver in Aston's tank, waving over to him. 'I'd better go here, Arthur. Duty calls.'

Danny rose gingerly to his feet. He looked up to the sky and let the drizzle wash over his face. He wiped his cheeks and limped over to Aston's group. The others made space for him.

'What's happening?' asked Danny.

'The captain's off to find out where we're going to be deployed tomorrow. There are not enough tanks to go around. The regiment's finished for the moment.'

Danny saw in the distance two tall figures walking towards their group. Captain Aston was walking with the officer Danny had met earlier by the two pounders.

'Who's that with the captain?' asked Danny.

'That's Brigadier Campbell,' answered Stone. 'Jock Campbell. Why?' asked Wilson.

'I met him earlier.'

Danny didn't offer anything else, and the others were too weary to ask more. Instead, they watched the two men talking. Behind them stretcher bearers carried a steady stream of dead and wounded. Aston pointed to their group as they walked. The two men halted and Aston saluted Campbell as if they were about to part. Then Campbell peered at them in the gloom. He turned to say something to Aston, who glanced back at the group. Aston shrugged and then the two men started walking towards where they were all sitting.

'On your feet, boys,' said Stone.

246

Danny felt his calf muscle cramping. It needed a supreme effort to get to his feet. He grimaced as he rose. Wilson noticed Danny's discomfort and offered a helping hand. At that moment Danny craved nothing more than sleep. His mind was muddled like he was drunk. The earth seemed to be pulling him down into its embrace.

'Thanks,' whispered Danny to the driver. Wilson winked back to him and kept a steadying arm on his back. Danny shivered a little and became aware of the cold for the first time.

'This is Brigadier Campbell,' said Aston. Danny and the others stood to attention and saluted. It amazed Danny he could even lift his arm.

Campbell looked at the weary men before him. Few of the tank crew members remained of what had once been the 6th RTR.

'I know of the sacrifices you and other men have made. The enemy threw everything at us, but they didn't succeed. We held on to the airfield thanks to what you did today. Make no mistake, they'll be back again tomorrow and the day after and the day after that until we kick them out. They've given us a bit of a battering today, but we got a few blows in too. The 4th and 22nd Brigades are coming up, so they won't have it all their own way tomorrow. In the meantime, we must fight on.'

'Yes, sir,' said each man.

'There aren't enough tanks left, so we're going to have to redeploy some of you elsewhere for now.'

They all nodded. This was less of a blow for Danny, but he suspected the others would be sorry. The sense of brotherhood among tank crews ran deep. Although he'd felt like an outsider initially, it didn't take long for the bonds of comradeship to be forged. This process had already started after what they had undergone.

Campbell turned to Danny. His eyes narrowed.

'We met earlier, didn't we?'

'Yes, sir.'

'I thought so. It was good work down at the gun. How do you fancy joining one of the columns for the time being? It'll give you a chance to hit the Jerry hard and distract them while we sort out this mess and can get you a new tank.'

The Jock columns were small fighting patrols developed by Campbell comprising of a troop of armoured cars, two or three troops of guns and a company of infantry that fought guerrilla style warfare in an effort to harass and distract the enemy.

For the first time that day Danny managed a weak smile.

'I'd love to, sir.'

Chapter Twenty-Seven

South of Sidi Rezegh Airfield, 22nd November 1941

Manfred and the others made an early start as none of them had slept well. A rapid breakfast and they were on the march again. Supplies beginning to dwindle. Manfred could, at least, console himself with the thought that it was a lighter load. The bayonet-black night when they set off slowly gave way to mauve and then pink. An hour after setting off the sky was a cloudless blue. The air was still fresh but that would change soon.

They followed the deep rutted tracks for another two hours until they arrived at the camp that they'd left the previous day. It was deserted save for the debris of occupation. The boys stopped and looked around.

'They're not here, then,' said Fischer. There was resignation in his voice.

'Maybe we should look to see if they've left anything behind,' replied Manfred looking around at the remains from their former camp.

Fischer nodded but was lost in his own thoughts. Kohler sat down, close to despair. Manfred glanced down at him but felt little sympathy. They were all in the same boat, lost in the middle of a sandy ocean.

Manfred slowly spun around, scanning the horizon. The emptiness was a presence in itself. It surrounded you. Embraced you. Slowly, it suffocated you. First it tested your physical resolve with heat. Then it went for your mind. Chipping away bit by bit at hope until fear set in followed by surrender.

It was likely Kohler was experiencing a sense of desolation. Manfred felt it, too, but was still strong enough to fight it. Or perhaps it was a desire not to succumb in the presence of Fischer. The key to survival was to deny the dark thoughts. Despair blunted your senses, undermined your endurance, and acted to deny your survival instinct.

They parted for a few minutes and made a search. Manfred found the traces of a few campfires. All were cold. The camp had clearly been abandoned the previous afternoon. They joined one another in the centre and looked around them.

'Where to now?' said Manfred. It wasn't really a question so much as a thought spoken loudly. He spun slowly around. There were so many different sets of tracks now it made it difficult to decide which direction was best.

Fischer grinned at Manfred and shrugged his shoulders. The Bavarian's smile was oddly reassuring. Manfred sensed there was no sense of panic. He was relieved that he, too, was not yet feeling any panic. There were choices. None great. All wrong in their own unique way. They sat down and discussed all the stupid things they could do at that point. The discussion was as calm as it was surreal.

'If we go back to where we were, we can replenish our supplies. Well, you never know, we might meet our side out there.' Fischer's arm made a wide sweep.

'Or Tommy,' pointed out Manfred with a grin.

'True, we'll say we speak better English than our friend,' said Fischer in English.

'How do you do?' said Manfred in English also. They both collapsed laughing. Kohler looked at them askance.

When they'd finished laughing, they returned to the subject of their options. By now they could hear the rumble of guns in the distance. They tried to gauge from which direction the sounds were coming from. The emptiness of the desert was its own neutrality. The source of the sound was not obvious, and they agreed the best guess was to their north-west.

'So, we'll march to war, then,' said Manfred.

Fischer grinned and said, 'Must be mad.'

They looked down at their supplies. If they were lucky, they'd have enough until evening. This didn't need to be voiced. If the bombs or the bullets didn't get them then starvation and thirst would. Maybe Kohler was smarter than they were. Maybe despair was the only correct reaction to their situation. With the decision made they headed in the direction of Tobruk. Kohler rose slowly from the ground. If he was reluctant to continue walking, particularly in the direction of the fighting, he was even more reluctant to be left on his own.

Thankfully, there were sufficient tracks for them to follow. Clearly some of their comrades, if not the whole division, had set off in this direction. It made sense. If they were right, and their training had given them an acute sense of direction, then they were heading towards the most logical place where there was fighting: Tobruk. At the very least they would run into the Sidi Rezegh airfield, around twenty or twenty-five kilometres away, sometime that night. They were sure to meet friend or foe there.

They walked in silence for a while. Each felt a sense of foreboding that only torture could have forced them to admit openly. As if their predicament were not bad enough, they would have to contend with the elements. The heat was intensifying now.

Manfred glanced at Fischer as they ploughed forward. He realised that his own sense of worried calm was a long way short of the panic their situation might otherwise have triggered. With an unusual insight for one so young, he also appreciated that his presence was acting in a similar manner for the Bavarian. Whatever happened now, they had a shared experience that would forge something that was not solely friendship. They were reliant on one another to survive with their sanity intact, if not their bodies.

One positive sign was the sounds of war were louder. They were heading in the right direction. The observation of this amused both of them greatly.

'I never thought I'd miss the sound of shelling,' observed Manfred.

'The sweetest sound in the world,' agreed Fischer, laughing.

'I wonder who's winning?' said Kohler. This was actually a good point, thought Manfred. Who was winning? They might return to the frontline and risk being taken prisoner. He stopped any thoughts of defeat. The only way they could lose is if they did something stupid like attacking a few armoured cars with a squadron of tanks, for instance. Manfred shook his head. Such a waste.

'Nobody would be my best guess,' suggested Fischer.

In this he was right. Ahead of them lay day three of one of the most complicated battles in history. Each side had contrived to surround one another in an intricate war of attrition brought on by lack of communication, stretched supply lines and poor planning. But the three boys trudged on, unaware of the unfolding mess in front of them.

By now, they were footsore and leg weary. Their youth had taken them this far. It would be their spirit that carried them the rest of the way. The heat was endurable, but the intensity of the sun made burning an increasing risk.

'Let's go over there,' suggested Fischer, pointing to a cleft in the ridge just ahead which could provide some shade from the rays of the sun. They had agreed tacitly to manage their diminishing reserves more carefully. Their next meal would be the last. The water would last until tomorrow if conserved. They'd been walking less than a couple of hours.

Conversation had dried up. None would admit what they were thinking; an overwhelming desire to avoid, at least, one more day of conflict. As they sat in the shade, Manfred saw Fischer look at the photograph of a girl. Unable to stop himself he said, 'You're a lucky man. She's beautiful.'

Fischer burst out laughing. In fact, he was helpless with laughter and Manfred wondered if the desert was beginning to exact its toll.

'What's so funny?' he asked, finally.

'It's my sister,' said Fischer.

'Ahhh, sorry.'

'No, don't apologise. I know it's different with your country bump-kins, but in the city, we tend not to sleep with family members.'

Both Manfred and Kohler erupted into laughter. It is a remarkable fact of life that crude humour can become a crutch for young men even in the direst of circumstances. The next few minutes passed cheerfully in a bout of raillery that encompassed exaggerated allusions, both positive and negative, on the respective attractiveness of each to the opposite sex before moving on to regional rivalries.

'At least we have culture and education. You're just a bunch of uneducated, beer-guzzling sausage stuffers, too drunk to handle the poor women down there.'

'I defer to your experience,' said Fischer, making a mock salute.

Manfred decided to move the topic on. This was certainly not an area that he'd great experiences to share.

'How far do you think we've walked?'

Fischer looked at his watch and made a swift calculation.

'Ten to twelve kilometres.'

Kohler stood up and climbed onto a clump of rocks and stared out at the never-ending plain broken only by the occasional wadi bed. He shook his head as Manfred raised his eyes hopefully. 'How long do you think we should stay here?'

'I was thinking about this,' replied Fischer. 'My guess is that we are at least another ten to fifteen kilometres from our lines. I am assuming, of course, we are on our side of the airfield. If you think about it, our guns can pick off the Tommies from four kilometres away. The guns will be screening our tanks, so they are further back. We can't be more than three or four hours walk away. This is nothing,' replied Fischer, airily.

Three hours sounded a lot to Manfred, thinking about the blisters on his feet. Each step was increasingly painful. It wasn't just his feet. The pain in his heel and toe had forced him to change his walking gait. The result of this change was to strain rarely used muscles causing cramp. Thankfully, he'd been able to avoid collapsing on the ground but that would not be far away, no matter how long they rested.

There was a tacit acceptance that they should wait until the latter part of the afternoon before setting off again. The sounds of war were beginning to peter out when they resumed their walk. The guns were their guide, their compass. They trudged forward, thankful that the heat was becoming more bearable.

Time dragged.

The sun could still burn but there was probably another two hours of light. They could manage that, so they set off again. The remaining daylight would give them sufficient time to reconnect with the rest of the army or, at least, have visibility. The rest had helped their mood if not Manfred's concerns about his legs. After walking some way, Fischer noticed the strangeness of Manfred's gait.

'What's wrong?' asked Fischer.

'Blisters,' said Manfred.

Fischer nodded and replied, 'I can feel two coming also.' As he said this, he heard a particularly loud explosion. They were getting nearer. To whom, God only knew.

Manfred grinned and indicated the direction of the loud boom. 'Could be worse, I suppose.'

'True.'

The proximity of the battle was now uppermost on their minds. They were obviously getting closer but could not see anything as the valley was not an entirely flat plain. There were ridges that denied a full view of the horizon. Soon, they could see a pall of black smoke rising into the sky.

'What are the chances we meet our boys or theirs?' asked Fischer. It was more rhetorical, but Manfred had been thinking about nothing else.

'We should be on the right side of the battle. My only worry is that the desert is swarming with British. They come behind our lines. They call it the Long-Range Desert Group.'

'Yes, I've heard of them,' replied Fischer. He could think of nothing to say about them, so the subject dropped. They trooped along in silence. The sounds of fighting provided a fanfare for their reappearance.

'Do you think they'll have the red carpet ready?' asked Manfred.

Fischer laughed and replied, 'Either that or being shot for desertion.' He saw the look on Kohler's face and laughed even more.

'Bastard,' grinned Kohler. 'You had me there.'

A few minutes later they heard a different sound. It started as a low hum but soon became a growl. It was coming from the air.

The three boys looked at one another. An aeroplane. But whose? They cast their eyes around them for a place to hide but there was none. They were in the open. Completely exposed.

'Take the shirts off our heads,' ordered Manfred, who removed his makeshift headscarf.

Fischer and Kohler quickly followed Manfred's instruction. The three of them continued walking, their shirts stuffed into their trousers. Then Fischer began to laugh. At first Manfred was confused; then he looked at his companion. Then, he began to laugh, too. It was funny. Two blond-haired boys in the middle of the desert. No pilot in the world could mistake the two boys below for anything other than prime examples of the Aryan race.

'How do you do?' said Manfred in English.

'Jolly good,' replied Fischer. 'Would you like some tea?'

Kohler looked at the two of them as if they had gone mad. He shifted his gaze from the two boys to the plane then back.

That was it for Manfred. He collapsed onto the ground laughing hysterically as the growl of the plane's engine grew louder and louder. They could see it clearly now and it was heading directly for them. And flying low.

Fischer was spluttering with laughter trying to say something else. As the plane drew nearer, he staggered in front of Manfred and cast a shadow over him. He managed to say something at last that was recognisably English.

'Cheerio, old chap.'

Chapter Twenty-Eight

South-east of Sidi Rezegh Airfield, Libya, 22ⁿᵈ November 1941

The plane roared over Fischer's head. A whoop of laughter ensued from both boys.

'He nearly took your stupid head off,' shouted Manfred, still laughing.

Fischer shook his fist at the pilot. The plane was a Hurricane. The British fighter plane that had caused significant problems for German shipping in the Mediterranean and now in North Africa.

'Road hog!' shouted Fischer towards the departing plane. Moments later they could hear it firing on their comrades. Another plane had joined it. This silenced the two boys and they looked at one another with a degree of shame. Somewhere up ahead, comrades of theirs, perhaps no older than them, would be dying.

Fischer collapsed on the ground dejectedly. Manfred patted him on the arm. Then he took his shirt out and put it around his head and shoulders. Nothing was said. Instead, they listened to the rattle of the machine guns. As quickly as it started it was finished. The planes circled around once more but flew off and headed back to where they came from.

'You're both mad,' said Kohler. There was nothing funny about their current situation. He was irritated by the light-hearted manner adopted by the others. He marched on ahead. Alone.

The two boys helped one another up from the ground and started back on their march after Kohler. Gradually their amusement dissipated. They began to discuss whether they should arrive in time to help or wait until the firing had finished. Ahead they could see their own lines. At least their assessment was correct.

The question was now urgent. The last thing they wanted to do was to be mistaken for the enemy. This was not entirely without reason. Manfred suspected that many Panzers had been destroyed by their own guns in the fog of war. They were now in the middle of a wadi, a valley bordered by ridge less than two kilometres ahead upon which they could see armoured trucks. Further ahead of the trucks would be the tanks and the screen of eighty-eights. The chump of the big guns and shells filled the air.

'What do you think?' asked Manfred. They couldn't avoid the subject any longer.

Fischer looked at his watch. For the first time Manfred noticed it. A Patek Phillipe. Swiss. Expensive.

Fischer grinned at Manfred.

'Twenty-first birthday present. My father represents them in Germany. It's after five. I say we wait until things calm down.'

Manfred collapsed onto the ground without saying anything. His feet and legs were in agony now. He wasn't sure he could have walked much further even if he'd wanted to. The thought of being on a tank tomorrow was now haunting him. He just wanted to rest, sleep for a week, have a long bath and shave. His face itched damnably as a result of the sand and three days without shaving.

Half an hour later the sound of battle receded as the light began to fade. The three boys looked at one another and got slowly to their feet. They began to slog forward through the hard sand. Manfred noticed for the first time that even Fischer was finding the going hard. At least it wasn't just him.

As they neared the ridge a shot rang out. A bullet pinged into the sand nearby. They ducked in case more followed. Then a voice shouted out, 'Identify yourselves.'

'Don't shoot,' shouted Fischer. He remained crouched but waved. 'We're German. Our tank was destroyed yesterday.'

'Come forward slowly.'

The three of them had no problem obeying this order. Their movements were paralysingly slow. In fact, so much so that the order was rescinded, much to their amusement.

'Hurry,' shouted the sentry.

'Make up your bloody mind,' responded Fischer. Something of his old arrogant self was returning.

They reached the ridge and began to scramble up the face. It was an undignified end to a traumatic twenty-four hours. At the top they were greeted by a number of infantry soldiers. Their guns were trained on the three boys.

'Myself and my Arab friend wish to join the glorious Afrika Korps,' said Fischer sourly. Manfred had to choke back the laughter. The soldiers seemed less than amused by this, but they were in no doubt that they were dealing with Germans.

Manfred added, 'Where do I sign up?' Kohler looked askance at his friends, fully convinced they'd gone mad.

'Funny bastards,' said a corporal. 'Come this way.'

The atmosphere relaxed a little. In truth, there could be no mistaking either Manfred or Fischer for anything other than German. However, the boys would still need to be processed. Even in the middle of hell,

259

German organisational discipline did not falter, reflected Manfred.

They were led to a bivouac where a senior officer sat at a desk. He looked up at the new arrivals surrounded by three of his men half-heartedly pointing guns at them. The officer was in his mid-thirties and an infantry captain. The sight was not entirely unfamiliar.

'Sir, we found these men. More stragglers. They came from the south-east,' said the corporal.

The captain stood up. He seemed about a foot shorter than the boys. Manfred wondered idly about the inverse relationship between height and seniority. The walk and the evident fact they'd survived had made him feel light-headed. This realisation woke him up. The last thing he wanted to do was to collapse but my God he felt like it. He could feel his legs stiffening with every passing second of the wholly gratuitous inspection.

'What happened?'

Thankfully, Fischer had also woken up to the seriousness of their situation. He began to speak, summarising with great clarity the events of the previous day. This unquestionably tallied with what was known. The captain nodded and turned to the corporal.

'Get these men in a car and back to their Panzer group, Corporal Huber. Actually, no. Feed them first.'

Neither Manfred nor Fischer said anything. Their eyes remained directly ahead. But Manfred could have cheered the little captain at that moment. They were dismissed. The corporal led them out of the bivouac. Manfred exchanged a glance with Fischer and Kohler. Fischer's face was a mask hiding his exhaustion. Kohler looked like a wreck, but they were back. They were alive. Old rules would apply, perhaps.

Forty minutes later, with darkness falling rapidly, the three found themselves in a jeep heading towards the tank leaguer just south of hill 175, a natural defence to the east of Sidi Rezegh airfield. The corporal who'd found them was their driver. His initial suspicion had long since disappeared. Like them, he was tired, determined to get things over quickly and return home in one piece.

'You wouldn't catch me in one of those death traps,' said Huber.

The boys laughed. Manfred replied, 'Safer than being in the open. You could get killed out there.'

It was Huber's turn to laugh. In fact, the four of them were laughing as they drove near the leaguer. They were stopped at the perimeter and then ordered to drive to the tent of Major Fenski.

Huber pulled up outside and the three boys followed him into the tent. Fenski was studying a map with a number of senior officers including Lieutenant Basler. The corporal handed Fenski a note from the captain. Basler looked up, his eyes hostile and accusing.

'I recognise these boys. They were in Overath's tank,' said Basler. He walked over to the three boys and studied them. He could see they were exhausted, sunburned and caked with dust.

'Had a nice stroll in the sun, then?' asked the lieutenant walking forward, fixing his eyes on them. There was no attempt to hide his suspicion that they had tried to run away.

Manfred and Fischer looked to one another while Kohler stared fixedly ahead. Anger surged through Manfred, and he saw that Fischer was almost shaking with rage. As if sensing their anger, Basler's tone softened a little. An admission he'd misread the situation.

'Just you three? There were no other survivors?'

Manfred shook his head and briefly explained what had happened.

'The South Africans took me to their brigade camp a few kilometres away. They questioned me. I said nothing. I sensed they were not going to torture me. Then they took me away from

261

the camp and dropped me a kilometre away from where they'd picked me up.'

Basler smiled grimly. He switched his gaze to Fenski and said, 'It sounds as if these boys missed an opportunity to get out of all this.'

Fenski smiled. 'Well, there's no doubt about their bravery and their patriotism. I'm not so sure it reflects well on his intelligence.'

The other officers dutifully laughed at this. Manfred looked at the group and felt appalled. Among those laughing were men who'd sanctioned the patrol. A patrol that took over twenty tanks out of the safety of the anti-tank gun screen, within range of the enemy guns. And for what? Manfred's face was set in stone. Anger uncorked a well of adrenaline through his body. The faces of Overath and Kastner swam into view. The men in the other tanks, all sacrificed needlessly.

Once more, Manfred felt a seed of doubt. Not about the justness of their cause. That much was clear to him. No, this was about leadership. Rommel was exceptional. The Afrika Korps was exceptional. Their training. Their equipment. All superior. However, Manfred was less sure that these fools were capable of delivering the victory that their many advantages warranted.

Basler, at least, seemed unamused. He motioned for them to follow him. On their way to the tanks Basler questioned them on the events of yesterday and their trek back to the camp. The questions were precise and pushed Manfred for more detail on the South Africans. Manfred was unable to say much.

'They didn't give me a guided tour,' replied Manfred. Basler stopped and shot Manfred a glance. Manfred realised what he'd said and his face reddened. 'Sorry, sir, what I meant was …'

Basler shook his head and began to walk forward again; the others struggled to keep up; the effect of their long march was now catching up with them. As they walked forward through the leaguer, they saw the other crews looking at them. It was clear what had happened to them. A few came over to say hello. Then Manfred saw his friend, Gerhardt. Had Manfred not felt so sore by this stage he'd have laughed when he saw his friend's mouth fall open.

Then Gerhardt jogged over to them. They shook hands warmly. Manfred was just as relieved, in fact, to see his friend was still alive.

'We thought you were goners,' admitted Gerhardt, a few minutes later as they trudged past their comrades sitting or lying on the ground eating in sullen silence.

Manfred shook his head. The events of the last twenty-four hours and his fatigue were beginning to tell on his emotions.

'We were lucky,' admitted Manfred. 'I was lucky. Had Fischer and Kohler not dragged me out of the tank, I'd be dead now. What did I miss, then?'

'When the other tanks returned, we went back along the valley towards the escarpment south of Sidi Rezegh. So, we were north-west of you. We got involved with the Tommies at the south of the airfield.'

'How did it go?' asked Manfred.

'We battered them, Manfred. You've no idea. They were sitting ducks. Their tanks can't take it. We must have destroyed all their tanks. There was a Tommy in a car. You wouldn't believe it. He was driving up and down leading them. We just kept firing at them all afternoon. The only reason we stopped was because we ran out of ammunition. So, we had to pull back. We were to withdraw east, ten kilometres south of Gambut that night. It was after midnight when I went to sleep. I've never slept so well, Manfred. Next morning, we travelled over the Trigh Capuzzo to the northern escarpment. We didn't do much to be honest. We made our repairs and waited for orders. Then we moved back to the southern escarpment because we still had to finish off the British armour.'

'Sounds like you've been on holiday,' said Manfred, grinning.

'Holiday's over, then. We're making ready to launch an attack tonight.'

Basler returned from organising a new home for the boys. It was likely they would be together in one of the Mark IIIs recovered from the battlefield that had not been too badly damaged. This was a nightly chore which, in the past, had often seen German soldiers in contact with their British counterparts recovering tanks. There was rarely any attempt to continue the battle. They had a job to do at that moment which did not involve killing.

'Come with me,' said Basler.

The lieutenant led them down the leaguer to a Mark III lit up brightly by spotlights. A maintenance crew was working on it. The noise being made must have carried for miles in the silence of the desert, thought Manfred. Sitting by the tank were a couple of men that Manfred had seen before but did not know well.

Lieutenants Peters and Thurow looked up as Basler arrived with the three boys. The two lieutenants acknowledged one another.

'Who are they?'

'Stragglers from yesterday.'

'God in heaven,' said Lieutenant Peters.

'Have you got room for them?'

'Yes,' replied Peters. 'A few of my boys have dysentery.'

'I'll leave them with you,' said Basler. 'I have to go now.'

Manfred joined Fischer in Peters' tank while Thurow took Kohler off to join another crew. Although neither said as much, both Manfred and Fischer were happy with the arrangement. Kohler was a morose presence. He didn't feel 'lucky'.

What Manfred knew of Peters was positive. He'd been over since the beginning; he'd know his way around. Fischer began inspecting the battered Mark III.

'Not very pretty, is it?' said Peters crouching down alongside Fischer who was running his finger in a particularly large dent at the rear. He stood up and introduced the other crew members. Corporal Werner was the gunner. He was in his thirties with shrewd eyes and deep lines on his forehead.

The driver was a small, bespectacled Austrian called Lang. He looked like a travelling salesman for Bosch. Manfred was amused to see Fischer bristling at the relative 'demotion' back to wireless operator. The introductions were quick because it was apparent, much to Manfred's horror, that they were preparing to pull out. A swift glance at Fischer and he saw the same thought was racing through the Bavarian's head.

'No rest for the wicked,' whispered Fischer when the others were out of earshot. A few minutes later the crew were inside the cabin and waiting for the order to march.

'I'm sorry about Overath and Kastner. They were good men,' said Peters when Fischer had finished. Then his attention turned to the tank. He pointed to the wireless and then the breech. 'I presume you can all do these jobs.'

Manfred and Fischer responded immediately: 'Yes, sir.'

Major Fenski's voice came over the radio.

'Close formation. This is not a time to get lost.'

It wasn't. It was after ten o'clock at night and visibility was from the lights from the tank directly in front. The atmosphere inside the cabin was the opposite of tense. The men were tired from days of continuous fighting and lack of sleep. Neither Manfred nor Fischer were alone in their exhaustion. A lumpy confusion reigned in the tank. The reasons for making a reconnaissance accepted without question by men too tired to sleep.

Manfred looked at the tired, dull eyes of the crew and hoped they would not encounter any enemy. The weariness would dull their reactions and endanger them. It made no sense to Manfred to take such a risk.

He was wrong. Youth gives you vigour and endurance, but experience brings insight and empathy. Manfred was about to learn that the enemy could feel as he did. Sleep-deprived tiredness left them detached from the very things that could ensure their survival. But men like Cramer, like Fenski, knew that victories were as likely to be forged in managing exhaustion as they were in equipment, supply lines and tactics.

It was by accident that Cramer ran into the Allied 4th Armoured Brigade's headquarters. A happy meeting between coincidence and opportunity. A white Very Light, sent up by the HQ to guide Brigadier Gatehouse on the road to attend a conference, revealed to Cramer the presence of a large number of Allied armoured vehicles only a matter of metres away. He ordered Fenski's battalion to attack.

Manfred heard the radio crackle as the extraordinary situation became clear. An electric current seemed to surge through the tank. There was no time to feel fear. The enemy had, quite literally, been caught sleeping.

'Kummel and Steifelmayer move to the left of the perimeter. Kertscher, Weinert to the right. Commence free fire on my orders'

Fenski's Panzer ran forward into the middle of the assembly area followed by one other tank. Lieutenant Bock began sending up Very lights. Within seconds the camp was lit up like a Christmas fair.

'Panzers, turn on your headlights,' ordered Fenski. 'Free fire.'

The Allied headquarters was now completely at their mercy. Manfred was shocked at the speed with which events were occurring. He heard some machine gun fire and he peered through his periscope at the chaos they were causing. Allied soldiers were being shot, running for cover, or surrendering. But not all. He and Peters saw it at the same moment.

'Some tanks are making a break,' shouted Manfred.

'Traverse left and load,' ordered Peters.

Moments later Werner confirmed he had them in his sights. Manfred opened the breech and loaded a cartridge.

'Fire,' ordered Peters.

'Yes,' shouted Werner triumphantly. Manfred watched the Honey tank explode. Another one, nearby, went up. Behind it, Manfred saw another couple get away. No one seemed in a mood to give chase. The big prize was in front of them. The British appeared to be surrendering. The wireless crackled once more.

'Cease fire. Panzer commanders' dismount. Take machine guns with you.'

Peters looked down into the turret.

'Werner and Brehme stay in the tank. Brehme take over on the machine gun. Lang, Fischer come with me.' Manfred poked his head out of the turret into the cold night air. The camp was lit up by the tank headlights; men were running around while machine guns chattered briefly then stopped.

'Everyone, get out peacefully.'

Fenski was calling on the British to surrender. Most were doing so but some had chosen to fight. Another set fire to one of their own tanks.

Manfred folded his finger around the trigger of the machine gun and trained it on a group of British soldiers standing dumbstruck at

267

what they were witnessing. There were hundreds of them. Manfred couldn't believe his eyes. He counted twenty-five tanks standing idle. All the fatigue he'd experienced earlier had evaporated. It had been so simple. He began to laugh.

A few minutes later, Fischer returned with a face lit by more than just the tank headlamps. He shouted up to Manfred, 'The lieutenant wants us to raid their provisions; tell Lang to take over on the machine gun. We'll grab everything we can before the others think of this.'

Manfred communicated this to Lang and then joyfully hopped down from the turret onto the ground. He felt a sting of pain in his foot. A reminder that his body had not recovered from their trek. But Manfred didn't care. His body could take any kind of punishment when he was feeling such ecstasy.

The joy of pilfering the enemy's food while they looked on in horror gave renewed energy to the two boys. That they had stolen a march on many of their comrades, as Fischer kept reminding Manfred, added to their delight. The night ended a few hours later with nearly two hundred prisoners including the Brigade second in command as well as dozens of armoured vehicles and tanks.

The tank leaguered at the assembly area near Sciaf Sciuf, fifteen miles east of Sidi Rezegh. A meal awaited Manfred and the rest of the crew although they had already begun feasting on the food claimed from the British. An air of celebration masked the fatigue they were feeling. And they still had to rearm, refuel, check and clean their weapons.

The weariness in Manfred's muscles had spread like a contagion to his bones. He succumbed to sleep within minutes, content, unafraid and almost happy. It was a feeling that would last only as long as the night. When light came, the fear would return but it would meet someone different. Manfred had aged years in two days. Although he would never admit as much, the death of his comrades had been shattering, but somewhere within the pain of loss and the ache of his body his mind and tissues were reconstituting themselves into something stronger.

Chapter Twenty-Nine

Nr. Sidi Rezegh Airfield, Libya, 22nd November 1941

'You off then?' asked Arthur.

'Looks like it,' said Danny crouching down and taking a sip from Arthur's tea.

'You're welcome,' said Arthur sourly. 'What's it all about anyway?'

Arthur was sitting by a small campfire. It was 0430. Danny had been up for the previous thirty minutes in anticipation of his column pulling out from the Brigade HQ. There was a hum of activity everywhere. Men were brewing tea over small fires. Engines were started up, some stalled, some died, and others ticked over. The air was crisp with cold. A hint of dampness clung to the clothes of the men.

'There's no tanks left so they've formed these flying columns. We're to harass Jerry wherever we can. You'll be here I suppose,' explained Danny.

'You suppose right. Actually, I'm glad you came over Danny-boy,' replied Arthur. All of his usual good humour had disappeared to be replaced by a fatigued fatalism of what the day held in store. From his breast pocket he extracted a letter and handed it to Danny. 'Don't ask, Danny. Just take it.'

The question, half-formed on Danny's lips, died immediately. He took the letter and nodded. Instead, he grinned and said, 'I'll give it back to you later.'

'Don't read it. I said some nasty things about you.'

'You mean I smell.'

'Something 'orrible. And all your rabbiting. Puts my head away it does.'

Both listed a few of Danny's other qualities which helped lighten the funeral-black mood that hung in the atmosphere. Finally, shouts coming from the edge of the HQ told Danny it was time to leave. The two men looked at one another and shook hands.

'See you in Tripoli,' said Arthur, grinning.

'Have the beers ready. We'll drink one for Phil.'

Danny rose to his feet and headed off in the direction of the noise. Arthur watched his friend jog away from him. His tall, lean frame silhouetted against the vehicle lights. He went to sip his tea and realised that Danny had drained it.

'Cheeky bugger,' laughed Arthur. 'I'll get you back for that.'

'Name,' asked the sergeant. He was in his thirties and clearly a 'lifer' in the army.

'Private Daniel Shaw, sarge, 6th RTR,' responded Danny.

'Tanks? Very well, go over there. You'll be with the artillery. You've fired two pounders before?'

'Yes, sarge.'

'Off you go.'

There were four 15-ton trucks with the two-pound guns mounted *en portee*. This method of transport meant the guns could be fired from the truck as well as the ground. A lieutenant stood by one of the trucks.

'Excuse me, sir,' said Danny. 'The sergeant sent me over.'

The lieutenant hardly seemed older than Danny. He was holding a clipboard. He asked for Danny's name and details.

'Fine,' said the lieutenant scribbling down what Danny told him. He looked up from the clipboard and pointed to an empty truck. Sit over there. Not in the driver's seat, though.

'Sir,' said Danny saluting before running over to the truck and sitting in the back, near the gun. It was like the two pounder he'd fired the previous day which gave him a boost. The prospect of doing something different had given him a few butterflies. Strange, he thought, that he should feel nervous after having been through the experience of yesterday. Being in the open air rather than encased in a tank was something he'd once thought made him more vulnerable. The reality had proven to be devastatingly different.

A couple of men joined Danny in the truck. They nodded to him as they climbed in.

'Hullo,' said the first. 'John Buller.' He was a corporal. John Buller? Danny realised he wasn't winding him up. Parents with a mean sense of humour, thought Danny.

The second man, a sergeant, made straight for the driver's seat. He was different from the sergeant Danny had spoken with earlier.

'Gray,' said the sergeant, starting the engine. 'Who are you?'

Danny introduced himself and explained where he'd come from. Buller's face registered surprise when he heard that Danny was from a tank regiment. He did not seem very pleased about having someone so inexperienced in their team.

'Have you handled this before?' His voice betrayed his concern.

Danny registered the tone of Buller's voice. It irritated him.

'I got some practice yesterday with Brigadier Campbell down at the airfield.'

That stopped Buller in his tracks and a slow smile spread over the corporal's face. Before he could say anything else, the lieutenant jumped into the passenger seat and turned around.

'You've introduced yourself, I take it, Shaw.'

'Yes, sir,' replied Danny.

Another soldier joined Buller and Danny in the rear of the truck. Buller introduced him to Danny.

'Fitz, this is Shaw. He's a tank man,' said Buller.

The new arrival was a little older than Danny. He grinned and said, 'I'm Gerry Fitzgerald. Fitz is fine though. Welcome to the team.'

He was Irish but clearly from the south, unlike Craig who was an Ulsterman. They were soon joined by a fourth man in the back, making it six in total on the truck. Buller nodded to the new arrival.

'Hullo, the sergeant told me to come here,' said the new man. 'I'm Evans.' He was Welsh.

'Bloody hell,' retorted Buller, 'we're only missing a jock and we'd have the whole of the British Isles represented, wouldn't we, Fitz.' He gave the Irishman a nudge in the ribs.

'You're a funny man, Bully.' Fitz didn't seem too put out. It was clear there was more than a degree of badinage among the group.

'Are you artillery or do we have another virgin?' asked Buller.

'I'm with the 60th,' replied Evans. The smile was artless, but his eyes had a hunted look. Perhaps they all did.

'That's a relief. So, it's just you, Shaw, that we have to train up.'

The lieutenant gave the order to drive, and the truck jerked forward. Pale streaks of dawn were visible in the sky. The column moved out from the brigade headquarters and into the desert. At this point none of the men in the back had any idea where they were headed. Danny was too tired to care. The truck bumped along the road as the sky grew lighter. As much as he wanted to close his eyes and sleep more, Danny felt he should use the time to find out more about his new companions.

Fitz seemed to be the friendliest. Twenty-seven years of age, he'd left Ireland to enlist.

'I was a journalist on my local newspaper in Galway City. Never liked it though. Hated my boss. He hated me.'

'Is that why he fired you?' asked Buller.

Fitz laughed good-naturedly.

'To be fair I did give him a reason. One day when he was off work sick, just for a laugh, I printed a copy of the paper with an article making all these libellous comments about the leading citizens in the town and their wives. Anyway, I sent the paper to his home. Wasn't he in the office ten minutes later rantin' and ravin'? Of course, when he realised that I'd set the type and printed only one copy he really went mad. Fired me on the spot. Ended up here.'

Danny and Evans erupted into laughter at the story. Buller, who'd probably heard the story a hundred times smiled, too. Evans spoke next. He, along with Danny, was the youngest in the truck.

'I'm like you, Fitz. I joined year before last. I was working in the mines. Glad to get out really. Didn't have any thoughts on where I should go. They sent me to join the artillery. I came here at the end of last year. Just in time to see the Eyeties off. I thought, this is easy. Then Rommel came. Different story that was.'

Gunner John Buller was older than both Danny and Fitz. He'd been in the army for four years. Buller had a hardness to his face that Danny guessed had been there long before he set foot in North Africa. He suspected it was not a topic for discussion. Buller didn't waste much time on his time on the army either even when prompted by Fitz to tell them of his escape from Dunkirk in a fishing boat.

'I swam,' said Buller in reply.

'Nobody wanted you in their boat, you big lug,' retorted Fitz immediately.

The big Liverpudlian grinned. It was clear that Fitz had earned the right to say what he wanted. Buller motioned with his head to the two men at the front.

'The lieutenant's new. His name is Blair. Don't know him. The sarge has been with me since France.'

Buller introduced the topic of his training. As there was nothing else to do except sit in the back, Buller decided to give a quick introduction to the art of artillery warfare. He pointed to the dozen containers that were loaded in the centre of the truck.

'These contain the shells. Eight in each. There's also a couple of reserve containers on the gun itself.'

Danny glanced over and saw the containers attached to the gun. He nodded to Buller to continue.

'First things first, you're sitting in my seat.'

Danny grinned and shrugged an apology.

'I'm the gunner so I always sit on the driver's side, rear. You say you were a loader?'

Danny nodded.

'Fine, I'm sure Fitz won't mind taking a break from that.'

Fitz held his hands up and nodded.

'You sit opposite. You and I offload the gun. The first thing we do is raise and lock the shield. Then we unlock the legs so that we can lift the gun up at each side. This allows the lieutenant to remove the wheels. I sit in the gunner position, and you load. Evans and Fitz bring the ammo over. The lieutenant stays behind me and gives me directions. Done right, we should be in place in thirty-five seconds. When we've a break, we'll take you through it.'

Fitz grinned at Danny. 'If Bully can do it, any idiot can.'

Buller made a great show of removing one of the two-pound shells and pretending to throw it at Fitz.

'Bugger would too,' said Fitz laughing.

As they drove away from the airfield, they heard the sound of gunfire and the crump of eighty-eights. The men in the truck looked at one another. A sense of guilt, perhaps? Danny thought about Arthur. He and the remaining tanks would be up against an overwhelming force if yesterday was anything to go by.

The firing was irregular as if both sides were repairing and resupplying themselves. This made Danny feel better.

'Doesn't seem so bad today,' said Evans. It was as if they all wanted to have validation for not being with the others.

This quietened the group again. A reminder that they were escaping from a cauldron. It seemed to haunt the truck like a bad conscience. Sensing the mood in the truck had become more despondent, the lieutenant turned around and spoke to the men.

'I know it seems we may be abandoning our comrades at Sidi Rezegh. This is certainly not the case. We can be of more use to them by making a nuisance of ourselves like this. We'll be able to carry the battle to the enemy and when they've woken up to what we're doing, move on. You can't hit what you can't see. And don't forget, the 7th Armoured are going to be supported by two other armoured brigades. Jerry won't have it all his own way, mark my words.'

The column slowly worked its way along the endless plateau. Mile after mile of nothingness stretched before them. They were bathed in a light drizzle of dust thrown up by the wheels of the trucks.

Conversation ceased, replaced by ennui. The glitter of the light sand immersed Danny in a hypnotic trance. For an hour he said nothing and simply sat staring at the unyielding barren wasteland which was enveloping them all.

Two hours later they stopped for a brew up and to give the vehicles a chance to cool down. Lieutenant Blair and Sergeant Gray joined the rest of the group as they drank some tea with a biscuit. The lieutenant filled them in on their mission.

'I'm Blair, good to have you along. I've been doing these columns for quite a few months now. I haven't been with this group before. That's our commanding officer over there, Captain Arnold.'

A few heads nodded in recognition.

'I see some of you know him. In simple terms, we need to divert Jerry's attention, and some of his strength, westwards, away from Tobruk. This will give our chaps a better chance of breaking out successfully. The more he thinks we've stolen a march on his flank the more likely he is to disperse his armour.'

Blair reminded Danny of Lieutenant Turner. Young, public school and seemingly capable. Captain Arnold came past to introduce himself.

'Don't get up,' were the first words he said to them. 'For those of you that don't know me, my name is Arnold. Hello, Gray. Bully, Fitz, glad to see you're still with us. Lieutenant Blair will fill the rest of you in on what we're doing. This is our chance to give the Axis something to think about in places where he's least expecting it. Make no mistake, it will be hard work. We've lost many men on these operations in the last year, but we've created a lot of disruption to the enemy.'

Arnold moved on to the next group, drinking tea. After he'd left, Buller signalled to Danny that he would give him a rapid overview of the two pounders. Gray joined them over at the gun.

'You fired one of these before?' asked Gray.

'Wait'll you hear this, sarge,' said Buller.

Danny explained that his introduction to the gun had come from Brigadier Campbell. Gray whistled and smiled.

'Well, he's an artillery man so he would know. I'll leave Bully to give you a quick tour now. You won't find much difference as a loader. Just get to grips with unloading and loading. Every second counts.'

'Yes, sarge,' grinned Danny. Sergeant Gray left the big Liverpudlian in charge of giving Danny a brief tour of the two-pounder gun. Any demonstration would have to wait until they'd stopped and, most probably, were in action.

The column headed off after a few more minutes towards the shimmering haze on the horizon. Vehicle after vehicle rolled over the rocks, the carpeted ridges, the sunburned sand and half-buried brush. Each mile took Danny away from the enemy and closer to his next fight.

He looked around at the men with him. They'd all killed and seen killing. He was now like them. At the very least he'd killed in yesterday's engagement. A vague thought the previous evening was now at the forefront of his mind.

He felt no remorse.

The death of Phil Lawrence had given birth only to one desire in his mind. To kill the enemy. The attack on the airfield while he manned the gun brought forth another overwhelming desire that had nothing to do with revenge.

Survival replaced all other thoughts now. Yesterday, he'd faced death time and time again. By rights he should have died like Reed, like Holmes, like Phil. Perhaps even Arthur, now. Yet here he sat, alive but wearied beyond imagining; sentient yet stripped of sorrow; impotent yet able to kill.

He removed from his pocket a letter. The paper had crinkled, and greased fingerprints decorated the edges like a black lipstick. The fragrance had long since evaporated. Twenty-four hours had passed since he'd last gazed at her writing. This was the longest he'd gone without reading it. Tears stung his eyes. For fear that the others would see him he turned his head towards the empty wasteland around him. He held onto the letter for a few minutes, then folded it up and put it back in his pocket.

The realisation of what it meant to him was all too clear. The letter not only connected him to her, but it also connected him to a part of his better self. A self that would not barter his soul to the brutality that he would encounter as well as inflict.

Whatever forfeit this war demanded from him he would not lose this.

Chapter Thirty

Sciaf Sciuf (Twenty-five kilometres south-east of Sidi Rezegh), Libya, 23rd November 1941

'You look good,' said Fischer, staring at the red-rimmed eyes of Manfred and, surprisingly, seemed concerned.

Manfred nodded absently too tired to notice the sarcastic tone of his comrade; perhaps he was past caring. It was five in the morning, and they'd managed a few hours of sleep following the capture of the British brigade headquarters. A thick layer of fog clung to the ground. It added a dreamlike quality to the atmosphere in the camp.

Manfred looked at Fischer and asked, 'Do you know what day it is?'

Fischer was as exhausted as Manfred and the mental arithmetic took a few moments. Finally, he offered an uncertain answer.

'Sunday?'

'Yes, Sunday. It's *Totensonntag* (Sunday of the Dead).'

This seemed to surprise Fischer. Manfred wasn't sure if this was because he was not religious or if it was for the more plausible reason that he'd completely lost track of time. The months of ennui, of waiting for something to happen, had been followed by ceaseless days of struggle against the twin enemies they faced: the Allies and the desert.

'I hadn't realised,' replied Fischer. 'Do you pray, Manfred?'

It was Manfred's turn to be surprised. The answer was 'no' and had been 'no' since his early teens. Even when he was walking away from the South Africans half expecting to be shot in the back, he hadn't prayed. Even when he'd heard of the death of his mother, it hadn't occurred to him to pray for her soul. Was this because he'd become so inured to death or simply because he no longer cared for his mother? The tears were stinging his eyes now.

'My mother died two months ago,' said Manfred absently. A moment later he felt Fischer's hand tap his elbow.

'I'm sorry.'

Manfred shook his head. He felt guilty now and wanted to give Fischer a reason not to think of this anymore.

'She wasn't well. It was a release,' he lied. Guilt and shame welled up within him. It felt as if he was disowning his mother. He wanted to say something else. Instead, he pointed behind Fischer. Major Fenski, accompanied by Captain Kummel, was walking along the ranks of the Panzer crews. They stopped every so often to chat to some men before continuing their inspection.

The smile on Fenski's face was contagious. And no wonder. He was fresh from the previous evening's triumph. Even Manfred felt a surge of confidence through his body waking up his dulled senses.

'Are you ready, boys?' asked Fenski as he arrived at Manfred's Mark III.

'Yes, sir,' grinned Lieutenant Peters, climbing down from the turret to greet their battalion commander.

'Good. We have a big day ahead of us,' said the major before swiftly moving on to the next crew.

Peters looked at his crew and said, 'Hurry.'

Manfred glanced up to the sky and offered a brief silent prayer to his mother. Then he and Fischer began rolling up their bedding to the sound of engines, then men, coughing into life. Someone cracked a joke. No one laughed.

The tank rumbled forward. Much to the evident annoyance of Fischer, Manfred was asked by Peters to sit at the top while he went down to the wireless. He wanted to listen and respond to the instructions issuing from Fenski. Although he and Fischer were clearly much closer now, it still gave him a lift to get one over the Bavarian. Peters stayed with Fischer for some minutes giving Manfred the opportunity to absorb what he was seeing. It was quite a sight.

Manfred's battalion was at the head of a fearsome phalanx of destructive intent. Around thirty heavy Panzers led while a column of tall lorries, protected on their flanks by light tanks and armoured cars, followed behind. They were heading in a south-west direction towards Bir el Gubi to link with the Italians.

After a few minutes Manfred reluctantly had to surrender his position in the cupola to Lieutenant Peters. Manfred returned to his position in the turret and glanced at Fischer. The Bavarian had a rueful grin on his face. Peters began to explain more of the plan on the radio.

'We're marching to retake the Sidi Rezegh airfield from the Allies. In this we will be helped by the Ariete and Trieste divisions of the Italian Motorised Corps. We will advance north with them.'

Peters broke off for a moment to demonstrate using his hands what would happen. Putting his left palm flat he clenched his right hand into a fist.

'We are the hammer. To the north of the airfield is the light infantry and Battlegroup Knabe. They are the anvil. In the middle are the Allies occupying Sidi Rezegh. We will strike and destroy them.'

Peters smacked his fist against his palm. It was abundantly clear that intense fighting lay ahead for all of them. At that moment, the prospect held no fear for Manfred. Instead, he felt emboldened by his time sitting outside the turret looking at one half of the force that would take on the Allies in the late afternoon.

Following his outline of the plan, Peters returned to his position in the cupola. Manfred felt a tap on his shoulder. It was Werner.

'What do you think?'

Manfred wasn't sure what the right answer was to the grizzled veteran. He felt the corporal's eyes boring into his mind. He answered truthfully, 'I don't know. I'll just keep loading until you tell me to stop.'

Werner laughed and clapped him on the back.

'You'll do.'

It was 0800 when the radio crackled. Manfred immediately put his eyes to the periscope. Directly ahead, in the lead tank, was the battalion commander Major Fenski. In front of Fenski, cresting the brow of a hill, were a couple of Axis light armoured reconnaissance vehicles driving at high speed towards the column. They drew up to Fenski's tank.

Fenski halted the column and jumped out to consult with the officer from the reconnaissance vehicles. The officer was pointing excitedly in the direction of the rise. Fenski jumped back up into his vehicle and called for the march to continue.

'Get ready,' said Werner to Manfred. Peters came on the radio with a similar instruction.

Manfred opened the breech and took a cartridge from the rack in readiness to load. All at once he felt a nervousness that had been

283

singularly missing all morning. They rolled forward, Manfred's eyes pinned to the periscope gazing straight ahead. Just at that moment three armoured scout cars appeared. The flags on the antennae were British. Werner spoke first. There was wry amusement in his voice.

'I wonder what they're thinking now?'

Manfred smiled. Imagine driving over the crest of a hill only to be confronted by the greatest fighting machine on the planet? He wondered what the conversation would be among the British when they saw what they saw.

Peters shouted into his microphone, 'Scout cars, twelve o'clock. One thousand yards, HE grenade. Free fire.'

Werner fired.

'Damn,' said the gunner. The round had overshot the target. Seconds later the scout cars disappeared over the hill all in one piece. 'You got the distance wrong, sir,' shouted Werner into his microphone.

'You missed, not me,' pointed out Peters. 'My pet poodle could have hit them from here.'

'Can we get him to mark the distances in future, then?' responded Werner before gleefully switching off his mic as a string of obscenities erupted good-humouredly from the turret.

Manfred laughed but he could feel them beginning to accelerate as Lang pressed his foot down on the accelerator. Already Major Fenski was racing ahead and over the crest of the hill. The engine whined as they trundled up the hill. Seconds later, they had reached the ridge and were now flying downhill. Manfred's mouth dropped open at what he saw.

Around two kilometres away was a camp consisting of dozens of light yellow soft-sided supply trucks. They were stationary like cows innocently grazing in a field.

Manfred was transfixed by the sight of the shocked expressions on the faces of the Tommies, caused by their arrival. He saw the kettles boiling on top of the campfires; he saw the cups in their hands; he saw the breakfast rolls fall to the ground as the full weight of comprehension dawned that they were drinking tea while the might of the Afrika Korps descended on them like a malevolent fog. Manfred could barely supress his laughter. It all seemed so easy.

Some of the Tommies had woken up at last. Fenski's tank was within half a kilometre of them when the echelon erupted into life. Vehicles began to tear off in different directions.

'Don't fire yet,' ordered Peters.

The air was already singing with gunfire. Dust fountains erupted in front of them, and a percussive rhythm of bullets echoed around the interior of the tank. An utterly futile gesture thought Manfred.

A nod from Werner and the breech block clanged as the first shell went in. The firing started. Manfred was aware of explosions happening all around him but by now he was too busy loading cartridges into the cannon. Werner was firing at the escaping vehicles counting off his hits and ignoring his misses.

A louder clang on their front armour suggested heavier weapons were now engaging them.

'What's that?' shouted Werner.

Peters responded, 'Tanks to our left. They're too far away to do us much damage.'

'Do you want me to get closer?' asked Lang.

'No,' ordered Peters, 'maintain course.'

The tank was now nearing the middle of what had once been the British artillery park. Manfred risked a swift glance through his periscope. Smoke obscured his view. Burning vehicles lay strung out everywhere that was visible.

'Lang, faster,' shouted Peters urgently. 'Cramer and Fenski are alone in the middle. We need to get near them to support.'

Manfred looked ahead and saw the two tanks fifty metres ahead. Behind them and the burning vehicles was the cloud of dust kicked up by the British vehicles disappearing into the distance. Manfred felt an overwhelming sense of elation. Something that transcended relief. Conviction. The feeling of vulnerability that had taken root after the loss of Overath and Kastner was dissolving rapidly in the face of a second triumph in the space of twelve hours. The sense of elation lasted barely a minute.

'Sir,' shouted Fischer, 'Major Fenski's been hit.'

All at once the atmosphere inside the tank changed to shock. Manfred felt like he'd received a blow to the stomach. How could this happen? It had been a rout. Like going on a hunt.

'Can you confirm this, Fischer?' said Peters. His face betrayed the concern he felt for a man he'd served under since their arrival in North Africa. Werner sat in mute disbelief. Silence fell on them as they waited for news of Fenski.

Fischer listened intently on the wireless. The shooting outside was dying down. The remnants of the British echelon had been scattered across the desert. Finally, Fischer turned towards everyone. Peters and Werner ducked their heads down into the hull.

Fischer nodded slowly.

'Yes, sir. It's confirmed. The major is dead. Lieutenant Foders also.'

Manfred looked at his watch. It was not yet nine o'clock. Totensonntag had begun. It had claimed its first lives.

Many more would fall that day.

Chapter Thirty-One

South-east of Sidi Rezegh Airfield, Libya, 23rd November 1941

It was midday when the regiment halted to rearm, refuel and reorganise following the death of the battalion commander, Major Fenski. Manfred could see the regiment commander, Hans Cramer, standing with the other senior officers and troop leaders in a conference.

'Who will take over?' asked Manfred to no one in particular.

'Kummel,' said Werner with complete certainty. 'He's good.'

Manfred nodded. Kummel was known as the 'Lion of Capuzzo' following his heroism during the summer. His tank had been decorated by the soldiers with a roaring lion. Manfred looked at the dark-haired captain with a Roman nose. He was moving towards them accompanied by his lieutenants. Work on the tanks stopped for a few moments when Kummel arrived.

'I've been asked by Lieutenant Colonel Cramer to take over from Major Fenski as commander of the First Battalion. I would like us all to pay our respects for a few moments to our fallen comrade.'

Silence fell on the First Battalion. Manfred glanced around him. Men were openly weeping. Was this really for the loss of Fenski or out of fear for what lay ahead? Somewhere in the distance the Second Battalion was working to re-equip their vehicles. Manfred wondered how Gerhardt was. Would he be feeling the same apprehension? In the distance Manfred could hear artillery fire. Then Kummel continued.

'Our orders from General Neumann-Silkov are clear. The enemy must be defeated decisively today. We believe the enemy lines will be quite deep. The attack will be on a wide front. The First Battalion will have the honour of leading this attack. The second line will be composed of the infantry regiments. Because of the likely depth of the enemy positions, they will stay in their vehicles until we have breached the front line.'

A sadness crept into the eyes of the captain, and he looked around at the men of his battalion. He knew many of them would die over the course of the day.

'Expect the enemy to be resolute. We must be stronger. Expect them to be brave. We shall be lions. They will fight to the last man. We shall make them. And remember, we do not go into battle alone. We will be accompanied by the spirits of our fallen comrades, by our fathers who were denied victory in the last war, and by the hopes of our Fatherland.'

At 1445 hours the advance of over one hundred Panzers began to the sound of artillery from both sides. Manfred glanced at Werner. His eyes were darting everywhere with every sound from the outside. This did little to quell the pounding of Manfred's heart. Fischer's body was tensed over the wireless like a cat about to pounce. Peters was quiet. There was nothing more to say. What happened now would owe as much to fate as fortitude.

The thunder of explosions grew louder. Manfred began to sense the ground was trembling for reasons not just to do with the motion of the tank. This was different from anything he'd experienced before. The intensity of the bombardment made the air crackle like a separate presence in the cabin.

Peters was now yelling into the mic. Manfred immediately snapped the breech open and loaded the first round. Werner shot Manfred a look and winked. This made Manfred grin. Fear evaporated at that moment. Manfred's mind, body and emotions coalesced into the act of performing a single task: loading shells.

Billowing black smoke rolled across the desert obscuring Manfred's occasional glances through the periscope. Momentarily, light reappeared to reveal they were now almost amongst the enemy. Debris fell like rain. Manfred saw a small flag waving to the side of them. It seemed familiar. Then it came to him. These were South Africans. Manfred remembered the men who had briefly taken them prisoner. Hard men. He cast aside any more thoughts and returned to loading.

Manfred glanced down at the driver, Lang. He was aware that the tank had been zigzagging for a while now. Lang was drenched in sweat and steering like a racing driver. Manfred felt a shock wave as one explosion rocked the side of the tank. Shards of metal sang against the armour like malevolent hailstones.

Werner laughed nervously.

'Bit close.'

The dull boom of field guns sides beat out a regular rhythm; the crack and whine of shot followed by explosions merged into one for Manfred. However, they were making progress. Manfred saw one Allied two-pound anti-tank gun after another destroyed.

'Hand me some grenades,' ordered Peters.

Manfred handed up two to the lieutenant. Moments later he popped his head through the cupola and threw one then another before diving back inside to cover.

Then the tank stopped.

'What's wrong?' shouted Peters.

'I don't know,' replied Lang. There was more than a hint of panic in his voice. The engine hadn't stalled. Something was blocking them on the ground.

Peters glanced down at Manfred.

'Go outside with Fischer and see what's wrong.'

After you, thought Manfred as the tank absorbed yet more gunfire.

'Yes, sir,' said Manfred. In a moment he grabbed a grenade and was ducking down into the hull to boot open the hatch. Fischer removed his headphones and followed Manfred whispering curses or prayers. Manfred couldn't decide which.

Outside the cabin the air was cooler than he'd imagined it would be. Cordite-filled smoke stung both their eyes. The noise of battle had a different quality in the open air. It felt fresh and real in a way that was different when experienced from the interior of the tank. Manfred's head was swimming with adrenaline and fear. He saw Fischer pointing to the front of the tank. They made their way along the ground inch by inch. Bullets threw up dust.

A quick inspection of the front revealed no blockage. It also revealed dozens of dead bodies of South Africans strewn like autumn leaves. German infantries were now mixed in with the South Africans but there was no time to view the fighting. Around at the other side of the tank they saw the problem. An unexploded shell had become wedged in the tracks. The two boys looked at one another.

'What the hell do we do now?' asked Manfred.

'Do you really want to know?'

'No,' replied Manfred moving towards the shell. They both examined it. It was wedged between the wheel and the track. 'If Lang were to reverse half a metre, then one of us could pull it out.'

Fischer nodded and looked at Manfred. The same question in both boys' eyes. Who would direct Lang and who would remove the unexploded bomb? Manfred grinned at the same moment as Fischer. It was madness.

'Quick, tell Lang to reverse,' said Manfred. Fischer nodded and disappeared around the back of the tank.

The ground seemed to pulse around Manfred as he waited for the tank to move. Oddly, despite the roar of battle, he could hear Fischer yelling into the tank. Seconds later the tank wheels began to crank. Bit by bit they rolled backwards. Bone-melting fear gripped Manfred as he reached forward in anticipation of the moment the shell was loosened.

All of a sudden the tank backed up a quarter of a metre. Manfred reached into the tracks, hauled out the shell and threw it over his shoulder. He watched it fall ten feet away. It was only then he realised he was still holding his breath.

Fischer appeared at this moment. Manfred nodded to him. Then he saw Fischer's face contort in agony. He fell forward onto the ground. Manfred ducked down and grabbed the grenade he'd taken with him. Thirty yards behind Fischer he saw a number of South African infantry. The grenade was launched directly at them. As it exploded, Manfred was on his feet immediately and running to Fischer. He rolled Fischer over and saw that he was alive but in agony from a shoulder wound.

'Sorry, my friend,' said Manfred positioning himself behind Fischer. He cupped his arms underneath Fischer's armpits and began to drag him to the hatch. Fischer's face was ashen with pain. At the hatch, Manfred felt a couple of arms reach out to help him pull his stricken comrade back into the cabin.

Just then Manfred felt a stinging pain in his calf as hot metal shards ripped through his trousers and brushed against his leg. He kept moving and within seconds he was inside, and Lang was pulling the hatch door closed.

'I'm fine,' said Fischer who looked anything but. Manfred nodded and resumed his position near Werner.

'Move,' shouted Peters.

The tank crunched forward again. Peters nodded down to Manfred and then turned back towards the battle.

'When you're ready,' said Werner.

Manfred reached towards the stack of shells; his moment of heroism forgotten. Survival was now the only thing on his mind. On all their minds.

'Allied tanks to the left,' shouted Peters. He glanced down at Fischer who was slowly rising to resume his position on the wireless. Manfred glanced through the periscope and counted twenty Crusaders on their flank. By now Fischer had his earphones back on.

'Tell artillery to get those tanks; otherwise Zintel's infantry will get wiped out,' shouted Peters.

Manfred stared ahead at the South African supply trucks scattering. They were now in the middle of the South African box and squeezing the Allies as the original plan had set out. But at what cost? Manfred's brief exposure to the battle outside had revealed dozens of dead Germans and destroyed Panzers.

'Traverse left,' ordered Peters.

Soon the Crusaders were in their sights. So were some South African infantry. They were running directly for the tank. Manfred glanced down at Fischer. His left arm was hanging limply to one side.

Manfred jumped over to Fischer's position. He grabbed the machine gun chattering deadly bursts to discourage any ideas of attacking them directly. Werner had taken to loading and firing the gun himself. More

South African infantry emerged from the smoke. Manfred took aim, finger tightening on the trigger.

Nothing.

'It's jammed,' exclaimed Manfred, looking at Fischer in bewilderment. Without thinking, Manfred cleared the chamber and tried firing again. A burst of rounds tore up dust around the advancing soldiers, sending them scattering.

The radio crackled and Fischer put the palm of his hand over the earphone.

'Enemy tanks are fleeing,' said Fischer, grimacing as he spoke.

Werner confirmed this with a few choice words of farewell to the Crusaders that raised a laugh inside the cabin.

The men were still chuckling just as an explosion rocked the front of the tank. All at once the tank stopped dead in its tracks and smoke began to fill the inside. There was no need to give an order. Manfred was already kicking the hatch open. He and Lang helped Fischer out from the hatch. Above them, Manfred sensed Peters and Werner escaping from the turret.

Each taking an arm, Manfred and Lang carried and dragged Fischer towards a crater. Manfred ducked just as the tank exploded. Black smoke wafted around the blackened metal. The popping of shells and bullets suggested another explosion was imminent. He had no idea where Peters and Werner were.

Fischer grimaced a smile in Manfred's direction.

'I suppose we're even now.'

'No, my friend, this is the second time I've rescued you.'

Earth spat up in front of them. Machine gun fire shredded the air. Manfred and Lang kept their heads down.

'We can't stay here,' said Lang jerking his head down as an explosion rocked the remnants of their tank. Manfred resisted the urge to thank him for pointing out the obvious. He popped his head up over the dugout and looked around. Then something caught his eye.

'What the hell is that?' said Manfred, staring ahead at an extraordinary sight. The German infantry was surrounding a South African Dressing Station like a halo. Wounded men were being treated by doctors in the middle of the mayhem. Lang glanced at Manfred and shrugged.

'We should take Fischer there,' said Manfred. Lang looked askance at Manfred. It would require them to carry Fischer at least forty yards across the pandemonium they were witnessing.

'Where?' said Fischer, groggily aware something was afoot. There was no answer from his crew mates. Instead, the two men hoisted him up to the sound of his groans and marched him across ground pitted by craters, destroyed guns, debris and dead bodies.

A strange dance took place as they navigated their way through the hellish scene around them. At one point a South African soldier raced past them, then another. Neither took any notice of the three Germans. Manfred glanced to his right and saw a Panzer moving forward. It stopped firing for a moment. Manfred was vaguely aware that the South Africans were benefitting from the cover they were providing.

As they neared the Dressing Station it became noticeable that the devastation was less marked than just a few yards outside the perimeter of the Station. A German infantry soldier nodded to Manfred as he and Lang carried Fischer through the line of soldiers into the medical zone.

Fischer was now dimly aware of where they had taken him. All he could think to say was, 'Is this a dream?'

Manfred and Lang gently lowered Fischer to the ground alongside a South African soldier. As they did so a doctor was passing them. A South African doctor.

'Doctor,' called out Manfred. The doctor stopped and looked at him. Manfred pointed down to Fischer. 'My friend. His shoulder.' He was speaking in English to the doctor.

The doctor crouched down and quickly scanned Fischer.

'Any other wounds?'

Fischer shook his head and grimaced.

'No, doctor.'

The doctor rose. He was in his forties. Sadness and fatigue haunted his features. It had been a long day for him, and it was only just beginning. He addressed Manfred in English.

'He's not critical. Get him some bandages. You'll have to bandage him. See that man over there.'

Manfred looked towards a man standing beside a supply tent. A German soldier was standing with him. Manfred glanced at the doctor and nodded and said, 'Thanks'. Then he jogged over to the tent.

'Bandages. Please.'

The South African handed Manfred a small roll.

'Thank you,' said Manfred. With a nod to the soldier Manfred turned to run back to Fischer and Lang. He stopped momentarily to allow a South African soldier and a German soldier past. They were carrying a bloodied South African with an arm that looked like it would not survive the hour.

Manfred looked at them pass and saw the South African doctor run towards the new arrival. He tried to take in the extraordinary scene before his eyes. Dozens of wounded men lay on the ground. Around them were a handful of doctors and a stream of soldiers carrying other injured comrades. Outside the perimeter of the Dressing Station the devastation generating these horrifying injuries continued unabated.

Seconds later Manfred crouched down and, with Lang's help, gently removed Fischer's shirt and cleaned the wound as best they could.

Lang examined the injury front and back. There was an exit through his shoulder blade. He gave Fischer some good news.

'I think the bullet passed through.'

'Oh, good I can re-join the fight then?' said Fischer, grimacing as Lang tightened the bandage, before adding drily, 'Thanks.'

'You're welcome,' replied Lang with a chuckle. His light-hearted tone sounded strange amongst the groans, the gunfire and the gut-wrenching explosions happening less than fifty yards away from this extraordinary zone of safety.

'We can't stay here,' said Manfred. The former accountant, Lang, was thinking exactly the opposite. His eyes posed a question to Manfred.

Fischer answered for him. 'You need to help the others.' Manfred looked down at Fischer. He was about to speak when Fischer smiled and said, 'Go. I'll be all right here.'

The two men rose and bid a brief farewell to Fischer. They started back towards the area through which they'd arrived. More soldiers were streaming in from both sides. Manfred marvelled at the sight of two German stretcher bearers carrying a South African. It was madness. Manfred spun around as he walked trying to take in what he was witnessing.

They arrived at the inner edge of the Dressing Station. A couple of German Infantrymen stood aside to let them pass. In front of them they saw the battle raging. The German army had now occupied the South African position. Dead bodies lay everywhere. Twisted metal that once had been anti-tank guns dotted the area like grotesque sculptures. Amongst all of this, noticed Manfred, were dozens of destroyed Panzers. If this was victory, then it had come at a terrible cost.

If it was victory.

The battle had not finished. Artillery fire was still landing all around the Dressing Station. The two men glanced backwards at the haven they were leaving. Then Lang looked up nervously at Manfred and raised one eyebrow.

'After you, then.'

About the Authors

Jack Murray

Jack Murray lives just outside London with his family. Born in Ireland he has spent most of his adult life in England. Jack has written a series of books set in the post WWI period involving a fictional detective Lord Kit Aston. Several characters from this series appear in this book.

J Murray

Jack Murray is the nephew of the author. Jack is currently at Portsmouth University studying Software Engineering. He is also an avid student of World War II and tanks, in particular. Jack has provided research and contributed ideas to the development of this story.

CPSIA information can be obtained
at www.ICGtesting.com
Printed in the USA
LVHW092214281022
731835LV00018B/805

9 781839 014437